# A Shadow in Silk

Copyright – Sarah Jenkins

All rights reerved. No part of this publication may be reproduced, stored in a retravel system or transmitted, in any form or by means, electronic, mechanical, photoopting, recording or otherwise without the prior written permission of the author.

Published by KR Publication 2025

# Chapter 1: The Proposal

## "A Suitor in the Parlor"

*London, 1870*

They say a woman ought to know her mind by the time a man proposes marriage. I knew mine—clear as winter frost on a windowpane—and still, when Edward Harroway took my hand in his, the words I had rehearsed a thousand times in the mirror dissolved like sugar in rain.

The parlor felt smaller than usual that evening, as if the very walls had conspired to press us together in this moment of reckoning. Edward stood before me with the bearing of a man accustomed to having his desires met, his tall frame casting a shadow that seemed to swallow half the room. The fire in the grate had burned low, reduced to glowing embers that threw dancing shadows across the faded floral wallpaper—roses that had once been pink but now appeared the color of dried blood in the dim light. Everything in our crumbling townhouse smelled of the past: dust motes that had settled into the very bones of the furniture, the ghost of rosewater that my mother still dabbed behind her ears each morning out of habit rather than hope, and beneath it all, the musty scent of genteel poverty that no amount of scrubbing could quite erase.

My mother had lit one of her last precious beeswax candles for the occasion—a silent benediction, an unspoken acknowledgment that she knew what was coming. The flame flickered bravely in its brass holder, casting a warm glow that made Edward's features appear almost handsome. Almost. She had suspected this moment would arrive, of course. Mothers always do. The entire neighborhood had been whispering about it for weeks, their voices carrying on the autumn wind like leaves rustling with secrets. The butcher's wife had given me knowing looks when I passed. Mrs. Pemberton from next door had taken to lingering by her front window whenever Edward's carriage appeared on our street. Even the scullery maid had begun to curtsy with unusual deference, as if I were already transformed into something grander than Miss Eleanor Ashcombe of the declining Ashcombes.

Edward looked every inch the part of a suitable husband—tall and composed, dressed in mourning grey that spoke of respectability and restraint. His waistcoat was perfectly pressed, his cravat tied with mathematical precision, and his dark hair was pomaded into submission. There was a glint of ambition behind his civility, sharp as the edge of a well-honed blade, though he kept it carefully sheathed beneath layers of proper breeding. His dark eyes were not cruel, exactly, but they held the practiced quality of a man who had learned early that charm was a tool to be wielded with the same precision as his father's business ledgers. They were polished eyes, like the gold cufflinks he wore—both gleaming with his father's crest, a reminder of the weight of expectation that rested on his shoulders and, by extension, would soon rest on mine.

I had once imagined him kissing me with those perfectly sculpted lips, had allowed myself the dangerous luxury of wondering what it might feel like to be desired by a man like Edward Harroway. In the safety of my bedroom, with moonlight streaming through the threadbare curtains, I had conjured fantasies of passion and romance, of being swept away by love so powerful it would transform the very air around us. Now, standing before him in the flesh, I found myself fearing not the absence of such passion, but what might follow in its wake—the slow suffocation of becoming exactly what he expected me to be.

"Eleanor," he said, and my name fell from his lips like a verdict handed down from on high, weighted with finality and expectation. "You are of singular character. I admire you. I respect you. And I would see you cared for, always."

The words hung in the air between us, and I waited—breath held, heart hammering against my ribs like a caged bird—for the declaration that would make this moment complete. But it did not come. He did not say he loved me. The omission stretched between us like a chasm, and I felt something inside my chest grow cold and still.

His proposal followed in measured tones, each word carefully chosen and delivered with the precision of a man conducting a business transaction. He spoke of compatibility and mutual benefit, of the wisdom of uniting our families' interests. The union made perfect sense, he explained, his voice never wavering from its practiced cadence: my family's name, ancient and respected despite our reduced circumstances, paired with his family's wealth, newly minted but undeniably substantial. I was to bring dignity to the match, the patina of old blood and older traditions. He was to bring salvation—financial security, social advancement, and the promise of a future that stretched beyond the crumbling walls of our townhouse.

I smiled then, or attempted to, though the expression felt foreign on my face, like a mask that didn't quite fit. My throat tightened with the weight of a thousand unshed truths, words that pressed against my teeth like prisoners begging for release. I had rehearsed this moment countless times—some nights in giddy hope, spinning dreams of romance and devotion, others in creeping dread, imagining exactly this scenario where duty and desire stood at odds. But I had not expected the feeling that now overwhelmed me: suffocation, as if the very room conspired to press me down into a mold not of my own making, to reshape me into something smaller and more manageable than the woman I had fought so hard to become.

Edward mistook my silence for maidenly modesty, that becoming reticence that society demanded of unmarried women when faced with such momentous decisions. His smile grew more confident, and he pressed on with renewed enthusiasm, painting a picture of our future together with broad, confident strokes.

"You would want for nothing," he continued, his voice warming with the pleasure of a man describing his most prized possessions. "My home is yours to shape as you see fit. I'll provide you with a carriage—a proper one, not some hired hack—and a full staff to attend to your every need. You'll have security, Eleanor, the kind of security your family once knew. We could travel in the summers—Italy, perhaps, or the Swiss Alps. I've heard the air there works wonders for delicate constitutions. And children, if God allows it. Two, maybe three. A son to carry on the family name, and daughters to grace our drawing room."

He recited these promises like a merchant listing his wares, ticking off each benefit with the satisfaction of a man who believed he was offering the world on a silver platter. But as I listened, I felt myself growing smaller with each word, as if his vision of our future was a box designed to contain me, complete with air holes for breathing but no room for growth.

"And what of companionship?" I asked finally, finding my voice though it trembled like a leaf in an autumn gale. "Of affection? Of... love?"

The word hung between us, naked and vulnerable, and I watched Edward's face carefully for his reaction. He blinked, his composure faltering for just a moment, as if I had asked him to recite poetry in ancient Greek or explain the mysteries of the stars. His recovery was swift, but not swift enough to hide the flash of something—surprise? annoyance?—that crossed his features.

"I believe we would suit admirably," he said, his tone carefully neutral. "Love can grow, Eleanor. It often does, in marriages built on mutual respect and shared purpose. The poets may sing of grand passion, but I've observed that such feelings rarely survive the trials of daily life. What we would have is something far more valuable—partnership, stability, affection born of familiarity and shared experience."

I heard the unspoken truth beneath his carefully chosen words: Love is not necessary. Love is not expected. Love might even be inconvenient. I was to be a manageable wife, not a woman with thoughts too loud or wants too wild. I was to be grateful for his offer, to accept it with the proper mixture of humility and joy, and to spend the rest of my days proving myself worthy of his generosity.

Outside, the sounds of London evening life continued their familiar symphony. Horses clattered by on wet cobblestones, their hooves striking a rhythm that spoke of freedom and movement. I found myself imagining one of them breaking free from its traces, galloping wildly through Hyde Park with its mane streaming behind it like a banner—untethered, magnificent, answerable to no master but its own wild heart. I imagined myself astride such a creature, my hair loose and my skirts flying, racing toward a horizon that held infinite possibilities.

The fantasy was so vivid, so intoxicating, that for a moment I forgot where I was. Then Edward cleared his throat, and I was pulled back to the parlor, to the dying fire and the weight of expectation that pressed down on me like a physical thing.

I stood slowly, my gloved hands clenched at my sides so tightly that I could feel my nails digging into my palms even through the kid leather. The movement seemed to surprise Edward, who had perhaps expected me to remain seated in demure acceptance while he outlined the terms of our future together.

"Edward," I began, and was surprised by the steadiness of my own voice. "I am grateful for your regard. Truly, I am. But I must decline your generous offer."

The words fell into the silence like stones dropped into still water, creating ripples that seemed to spread through the very air around us. Edward's mouth did not fall open—he was too well-bred for such obvious displays of shock—but his eyes narrowed, and I saw something cold and calculating flicker in their depths. He had not prepared for refusal. Men like Edward Harroway never had to. They moved through the world with the confidence of those who had never been denied anything they truly wanted, who had learned to expect compliance as their natural due.

"Forgive me, Eleanor," he said, his voice carefully controlled but with an edge that had not been there before. "I don't understand. Perhaps you need time to consider—"

"I believe you do understand," I interrupted, giving him a smile that I hoped was gentle but could feel the steel behind it, sharp and unyielding. "And I have considered. My answer is no."

For a long moment, we stared at each other across the small space of the parlor, and I felt as if I were seeing him clearly for the first time. The handsome features were still there, the expensive clothes and careful grooming, but beneath it all I glimpsed something harder, less appealing. His disappointment was transforming into something sharper, more dangerous.

"You would rather remain in this decaying house," he said, his voice dropping to a whisper that somehow carried more venom than a shout, "with your fading name and your dying father, than accept a respectable life? You would choose genteel poverty over security, obscurity over prominence?"

The cruelty of his words hit me like a physical blow, but I forced myself to stand straighter, to meet his gaze without flinching. "Yes," I said simply. "I would."

He laughed then—a single, cold note that held no humor whatsoever—and executed a stiff bow that was more insult than courtesy. "You'll regret this, Miss Ashcombe. Independence is a romantic notion until it is priced in hunger. Beauty fades, and so does the luxury of choice. You may find that suitors are not so plentiful when your circumstances become even more... reduced."

The threat was delicately delivered but unmistakable, wrapped in the language of concern but sharp with malice. He straightened his cuffs with deliberate precision, gathered his hat and gloves from the side table where he had placed them with such confidence only an hour before, and moved toward the door with the measured pace of a man who refused to appear hurried despite his obvious desire to escape.

He paused at the threshold, his hand on the brass doorknob that had grown tarnished with age and neglect. For a moment, I thought he might say something else, might make one final attempt to change my mind or deliver one last cutting remark. Instead, he simply inclined his head in a gesture that might have been mistaken for politeness by anyone who had not witnessed what had just transpired.

"Good evening, Miss Ashcombe," he said, and then he was gone, leaving only the click of the door closing behind him and the faint scent of his cologne lingering in the air like an unwelcome ghost.

The moment the latch caught, I collapsed into the worn velvet armchair that had been my father's favorite before his illness confined him to his bedroom upstairs. My breath came in shallow bursts, as if I had been running for miles instead of simply standing in my own parlor. My hands shook as I pressed them to my face, feeling the heat of my own skin through the thin kid leather of my gloves.

My mother did not come in, though I knew she had been listening from the hallway. I had heard the soft whisper of her skirts against the floorboards, the careful way she had positioned herself just out of sight but well within earshot. She would not speak to me until morning, would not offer comfort or condemnation until she had time to process what had just occurred and decide how best to respond. It was her way—measured, careful, always thinking three moves ahead like a chess master planning her strategy.

And I—I wept. The tears came suddenly and without warning, great heaving sobs that shook my entire body and left me gasping for air. But these were not tears of regret or loss, not the weeping of a woman mourning a future that might have been. Instead, I cried from the terrible knowledge that what I had just done had set something in motion, had pulled a thread that would unravel the careful fabric of our lives in ways I could not yet imagine.

I wept for the look of cold fury in Edward's eyes as he left, for the promise of retribution that had lurked beneath his polite farewell. I wept for my mother, who had pinned so many hopes on this match, who had seen in Edward Harroway the answer to prayers she had been too proud to voice aloud. I wept for my father, wasting away upstairs, who would never know that his daughter had chosen honor over security, principle over pragmatism.

But beneath the tears, beneath the fear and uncertainty, I felt something else stirring—a fierce, bright flame of satisfaction that no amount of worry could extinguish. I would not marry a man who saw me as an ornament to be displayed in his drawing room, a prize to be won and then forgotten. I would not trade my soul for security, my dreams for respectability, my very self for the promise of comfort.

Let them say I was proud. Let them whisper that Eleanor Ashcombe had grown too particular, too demanding, too unwilling to accept the natural order of things. Let them call it foolish, this choice to remain true to myself rather than bend to the expectations of a world that would reshape me into something smaller and more convenient.

At least the choice had been mine. At least, in this one moment, I had been the author of my own fate rather than a character in someone else's story. Whatever came next—poverty, spinsterhood, social exile—I would face it as myself, unbowed and unbroken.

The fire in the grate gave one final flicker and died, plunging the parlor into darkness. But I remained in the chair, my tears slowly subsiding, my breathing gradually returning to normal. Outside, London continued its eternal dance, indifferent to the small drama that had just played out in our shabby parlor. Somewhere in the distance, a church bell tolled the hour, marking the passage of time and the beginning of whatever came next.

I had made my choice. Now I would live with the consequences, whatever they might be.

# Chapter 2: Social Suicide

## "The Price of Refusal"

The invitations stopped arriving by the end of the week, but their absence filled our house like a presence—heavy, suffocating, impossible to ignore.

It was not a dramatic severing, nothing so honest as slamming doors or public denouncement. Society is far more sophisticated in its cruelties. I was erased with surgical precision, as if someone had taken a pearl-handled letter opener to my very existence and cut me out of London's consciousness one careful slice at a time.

The first cut came Tuesday morning. The Witherspoons' spring musicale invitation arrived addressed only to my mother, though I had attended their gatherings for the past five years. Mama held the cream-colored card with trembling fingers, reading my absence in the elegant script as clearly as if it had been written in blood. Her face went very still, very white, and she set the invitation on the mantelpiece without a word. But I saw her hands shake as she turned away.

By Thursday, the garden party at the Lyntons' was "regrettably full"—though Lady Lynton had personally assured me only a month prior that she was counting on my attendance. The note of apology was brief, impersonal, devoid of the warm familiarity that had characterized our correspondence for years. I read it three times before the words truly penetrated, each reading like a small death.

Friday brought the cruelest blow. I overheard Mrs. Penwhistle in Madame Rousseau's shop, her voice pitched just loud enough to ensure I would hear every poisonous word as I stood behind a display of silk gloves, frozen like a rabbit sensing the hunter's approach.

"Some women," she declared to her simpering daughter, "are simply unsuited for polite company. They lack the proper... feminine instincts. Poor breeding will tell, eventually.

Mark my words, Clarissa—a woman who refuses a good man's honest proposal has something fundamentally wrong with her constitution."

Her daughter's giggle was like broken glass. "Oh, Mama, surely not—"

"I've seen it before," Mrs. Penwhistle continued with relish, warming to her subject. "There was a girl in Yorkshire when I was young—refused three perfectly acceptable suitors. Died alone and mad, they say. Fed cats from silver spoons and talked to herself in mirrors."

I stood there, paralyzed, clutching a pair of kid gloves I had no money to purchase, listening to them dissect my future like physicians examining a particularly interesting corpse. When I finally found the courage to emerge from behind the display, Mrs. Penwhistle's eyes met mine with a smile so cold it might have frozen wine.

"Miss Ashcombe," she said, her voice dripping false sympathy. "How... unfortunate to see you here."

I had made myself unspeakable. Untouchable. A cautionary tale whispered in drawing rooms across Mayfair.

At first, I tried to pretend it didn't matter. I took longer walks through Hyde Park, my chin lifted defiantly as I passed groups of ladies who fell silent at my approach. I visited Mudie's lending library twice daily, checking out novels I had no heart to read, simply to feel the weight of books in my hands—proof that there were other worlds beyond this suffocating cage of social expectation.

I even tried to write—a short story about a woman who climbed mountains, who explored uncharted territories, who lived free as the wind. But the words felt hollow on the page, mocking echoes of dreams that seemed more impossible with each passing day.

It was no use. The air itself changed when I entered a room now. Conversations didn't just pause—they died, withering like flowers touched by frost. Smiles became surgical instruments, precise and cutting. I was a fallen woman without having fallen, a scandal without having sinned. My only crime was refusing to be grateful for a cage, however gilded.

The worst part was not the strangers who whispered and pointed. It was watching my mother wither before my eyes, watching her shoulders bow under the weight of my choice as if I had placed stones upon her back, one by one, until she could barely stand upright.

At dinner—our meals growing simpler each day as our funds dwindled—she spoke only in fragments, her voice like autumn leaves crumbling underfoot. She pushed boiled potatoes around her plate with mechanical precision, creating small, neat patterns that she would then destroy and rebuild, over and over, as if trying to impose order on chaos through the arrangement of root vegetables.

"He was willing to overlook everything," she said finally, not looking at me, her words barely above a whisper. "Your age—twenty-six, Eleanor, twenty-six and unmarried. Our debts, our reduced circumstances, the way your father's illness has... diminished us. The scandal when Papa lost the shipping investments. The way we've had to let servants go, one by one, until only Mrs. Hartwell remains, and she stays more from pity than wages."

She paused, still not meeting my eyes, her fork suspended over her plate like a conductor's baton frozen mid-symphony.

"Edward Harroway was willing to overlook all of it. To take you as you are, damaged goods and all. And you—" Her voice cracked like ice breaking. "You threw it back in his face as if his offer were an insult rather than salvation."

I bit the inside of my cheek until I tasted copper, the pain sharp and grounding. "I did not throw anything. I declined, respectfully and with gratitude for his consideration."

The words sounded weak even to my own ears, a child's protest against an adult world that had already rendered its judgment.

My mother finally looked at me then, and what I saw in her eyes was worse than anger—it was defeat, complete and devastating. Her face seemed to have aged years in the past week, new lines carved around her mouth and eyes, her skin taking on the papery quality of pressed flowers.

"It was your last chance, Eleanor." Her voice was steady now, but it carried the finality of a death knell. "Do you understand that? Your last chance at any kind of life worth living. You are not young—not anymore. You are not rich—we have nothing left to offer but our name, and even that is tarnishing with each passed-over invitation, each whispered conversation, each day that you remain unmarried and... and strange."

She set down her fork with deliberate care, her movements precise and controlled, as if she were performing a ritual of enormous importance.

"You are not beautiful in the way that forgives all other failings. You are clever, yes, but cleverness in a woman is like salt in tea—a little might be interesting, but too much ruins everything. You are..." She struggled for the word, her hands fluttering like trapped birds. "You are difficult, my dear. Difficult and stubborn and so terribly, terribly proud."

Each word fell like a stone into still water, creating ripples that spread through my chest and settled somewhere deep in my bones. I wanted to argue, to defend myself, to explain that I was not proud so much as desperate—desperate to remain myself in a world determined to reshape me into something smaller, more manageable, more convenient.

But looking at my mother's face, seeing the genuine anguish there, the fear of a woman watching her only child choose poverty over pragmatism, loneliness over security, I swallowed my protests. The truth was, I was difficult. I was difficult because I would not pretend contentment with a life that felt like slow burial. I was difficult because I believed I deserved more than to be some man's well-dressed possession, more than a decorative object to be admired and ignored in equal measure.

But her words carved themselves into me, anyway, finding all the tender places where my own doubts lived and pressing until I bled inside.

In the days that followed, our house took on the quality of a mausoleum. We received only one caller—Mrs. Grimsby, the seamstress, arriving with bills clutched in her red, chapped hands and determination written in the set of her jaw. She had sewn the gowns I wore to the parties that no longer invited me, had created the dresses I thought would help me catch a husband I ultimately refused to marry.

The irony was not lost on me.

My mother took to her bed after Mrs. Grimsby's visit, claiming headaches that lasted from dawn to dusk. But the walls of our narrow townhouse were thin, and I could hear her crying at night—deep, wrenching sobs that seemed to come from the very centre of her being. She wept as if she were mourning not just my prospects, but her own hopes, her own future, her own security that had been tied so completely to my marriage that my refusal felt like abandonment.

I sat by my window those long evenings, watching the endless parade of carriages roll past our door—carriages that no longer stopped, that no longer brought invitations or social calls or any acknowledgment that we existed at all. The sound of hooves on cobblestones became a lullaby of exclusion, a rhythmic reminder of all the lives continuing without us, all the parties proceeding in our absence, all the conversations happening as if we had never been part of them at all.

When desperation finally drove me to Bond Street to purchase ink with coins scraped from the bottom of my jewellery box—determined to write letters, to somehow repair the damage I had done—I heard them. Two girls, probably seventeen or eighteen, their voices carrying the casual cruelty that comes so naturally to the young and secure.

"That's her," one whispered, though her whisper was loud enough to stop conversations three shops away. Her eyes were wide with the mock sympathy of someone delighting in another's downfall. "Eleanor Ashcombe. The one who turned down Edward Harrowby. Can you imagine? All that money, all that respectability, and she said no like she was declining a second helping of pudding."

"But why?" her companion asked, her voice breathy with fascination. "Surely she must have had a reason. Was he... was there something wrong with him?"

"Wrong with him?" The first girl laughed, a sound like silver bells celebrating someone else's funeral. "Nothing wrong except that he wasn't good enough for Miss High-and-Mighty

Ashcombe. They say she did it because she's... peculiar."

"Peculiar how?" The question was hungry, eager for gossip to devour and redistribute.

"You know," the first girl said, dropping her voice to what she clearly thought was a dramatic whisper. "Peculiar like... unnatural. Like she has strange ideas about her place in the world. Like she thinks she's too good for marriage itself."

"Oh my," the second girl breathed. "How scandalous. How very... unwomanly."

I walked past them with my spine straight and my head high, though inside I felt as if I were crumbling like week-old bread. Their words followed me down the street, echoing off the buildings, bouncing back from shop windows, filling the air with poison.

Unnatural. Unwomanly. Strange ideas about my place in the world.

That word—unnatural—lodged itself in my chest like a splinter, working deeper with each breath. What was unnatural about wanting to choose my own life? What was unwomanly about refusing to be grateful for the privilege of becoming someone's beautiful, silent ornament? What was strange about believing I deserved to be loved for who I was rather than purchased for what I represented?

But their voices haunted me. In the empty hours that stretched like desert plains through our increasingly quiet house, I found myself questioning everything. Perhaps they were right. Perhaps there was something fundamentally wrong with me, some essential feminine quality I lacked, some instinct for submission and gratitude that had been left out of my nature like an ingredient forgotten in a recipe.

Perhaps a normal woman would have seen Edward's proposal as the gift it was meant to be—security, respectability, a place in the world that was defined and protected. Perhaps a normal woman would have smiled and accepted and spent her wedding night thanking God for delivering her from the uncertainty of independence.

Perhaps. But I was not normal, it seemed. I was difficult and strange and unnatural, and there were no answers to be found in the whispered cruelties of Bond Street, only the rot of reputation decay, spreading through our lives like Mold through bread.

The smell of it was everywhere now—in the silence of our drawing room where no callers came, in the pile of unpaid bills growing like accusations on my father's desk, in the way my mother's face had taken on the grey pallor of defeat. London had rendered its verdict: I was no longer a woman to be received, to be included, to be considered worthy of civilized company.

I had chosen independence, had grasped it like a rope thrown to a drowning woman.

Now, as I sat alone in our crumbling house, listening to my mother weep and watching the world continue without us, I was learning the true weight of that rope—and wondering if it would save me or drag me down into depths from which there might be no return.

The cost of freedom, I was discovering, was higher than I had ever imagined. But the bill had already come due, and there was nothing left to do but pay it, coin by bitter coin.

# Chapter 3: The Death of Options

## "Ashes at the Hearth"

I didn't weep when my father died.

Not at first.

He went quietly in the end, as if afraid to cause us any more trouble than he already had. Death came to him like a hesitant visitor, tiptoeing through the door while we weren't looking, settling into the chair beside his bed with infinite patience. I had been reading to him—*The Rime of the Ancient Mariner*, his favourite—my voice growing hoarse as I struggled through Coleridge's haunting verses about souls lost at sea.

"Water, water, everywhere, nor any drop to drink," I had whispered, and Papa's eyes had flickered with what might have been amusement or might have been recognition of how perfectly those words captured our own situation.

One moment his fingers were wrapped around mine, paper-thin skin still warm, still fighting. His breathing had been laboured for days, each exhale a small victory, each inhale an increasingly difficult battle. I had memorized the rhythm of it, the way his chest rose and fell like waves against a distant shore, growing weaker with each tide.

Then, between one breath and the next, he simply... stopped.

His hand didn't release mine so much as it seemed to melt away, like snow touched by sunlight. His lips parted as if he had one last thing to tell me—perhaps an apology, perhaps a blessing, perhaps just my name spoken with the love that had sustained us both through these dark months. But no sound came. The silence that followed was so complete, so absolute, that for a moment I thought the entire world had stopped breathing with him.

My mother's wail came then—a sound I had never heard from her before and pray I never hear again. It tore from her throat like something wild and wounded, the sound of a soul being ripped in half by grief. She threw herself across his still chest, her carefully arranged hair coming undone, her dignity dissolving into raw, animal anguish that seemed to shake the very foundations of our crumbling house.

I just sat there, still holding his cooling hand, staring at the cup of tea that steamed gently on the bedside table—tea he would never drink, warmth he would never feel, comfort he would never need again. The afternoon light slanted through the thin curtains, illuminating dust motes that danced in the air like tiny spirits, indifferent to our devastation.

He had been the last warm thing in our house, the final ember of love and laughter and hope. Now even that was gone, snuffed out like a candle in the wind, leaving us in darkness so complete I wondered if we would ever find our way back to light.

The days that followed blurred together like watercolours in rain. Black crepe draped every surface, making our already dim rooms feel like a tomb. The house filled with the smell of dying flowers—cheap ones, the only kind we could afford, wilting brown at the edges and dropping petals like tears onto the worn carpet.

No one came to pay their respects. The silence was deafening, more pointed than any insult. In the old days, before our fall from grace, our parlour would have overflowed with mourners. Ladies in elegant black would have filled every chair, their husbands standing in solemn clusters, children sitting wide-eyed and well-behaved on the stairs. There would have been casseroles and condolences, flowers from every garden in Mayfair, a steady stream of visitors offering comfort and support.

Instead, we had only the rector—a nervous young man who kept checking his pocket watch as if he had somewhere more important to be—and Mrs. Hartwell from next door, who attended more from a sense of Christian duty than any genuine affection. She sat stiffly in our best remaining chair, her lips pursed in disapproval, as if Papa's death were somehow another mark against our family's already tarnished reputation.

The funeral itself was a sparse affair. Six pallbearers hired from the undertaker's establishment carried Papa's simple pine coffin—we couldn't afford mahogany, couldn't afford brass handles or silk lining or any of the dignified trappings of a proper goodbye. The cemetery was grey and cold, the ground hard with winter frost. We stood beside the rectangular wound in the earth while the rector mumbled through prayers that felt hollow as wind through empty rooms.

When it was over, when the first shovelful of dirt hit the wooden lid with that final, terrible sound, I realized that we had buried more than my father. We had buried our last connection to respectability, our final claim to a place in the world that had already forgotten our names.

That evening, I stood in our drawing room and took inventory of what remained of our life. The sofa, worn thin at the arms where Papa used to rest his elbows while reading his newspapers. The cracked porcelain vase that my mother still called "antique" though we all knew it was simply old and broken. A bookshelf half-empty—most of the volumes already sold to cover mounting debts, leaving behind only the books too damaged or too worthless to interest any buyer.

Everything was covered in dust, as if grief itself had settled over our possessions like a shroud. The air tasted of endings, of dreams deferred so long they had withered and died.

I opened the desk drawer where Papa had once kept his meticulous account books, where he had tracked our family's financial decline with the precision of a scientist documenting the progress of a fatal disease. I thumbed through the pages, watching the numbers dwindle month by month, watching hope transform into desperation in neat columns of figures. Red ink bloomed across the final entries like blood seeping through bandages—a haemorrhage of debt that no amount of careful management could stanch.

There was no money. Not for coal to heat the house. Not for bread to fill our stomachs. Not even for the proper mourning gloves that would mark us as respectable women in grief rather than paupers who had simply lost another mouth to feed.

I found my mother in her bedroom, lying atop the coverlet still wearing her funeral dress—the same black gown she had worn to every social occasion for the past two years, carefully mended and re-mended until the fabric was more darning thread than original cloth. Her eyes were open but unfocused, staring at the water stain on the ceiling that had grown larger with each passing storm, a brown splotch that spread like the ruin consuming our lives.

"Mother," I said gently, settling on the edge of the bed. "We need to discuss arrangements. We'll have to let Mrs. Davies go."

She didn't respond, didn't even blink.

"The cook has already left," I continued, my voice carefully neutral. "She said she couldn't wait any longer for her wages."

Still nothing. My mother's face might have been carved from marble, beautiful and cold and utterly remote.

"We'll need to sell the pianoforte," I whispered, though the words felt like blasphemy. That piano had been her pride, her last connection to the accomplished young woman she had been before marriage and motherhood and poverty had worn her down to this hollow shell.

Only when I gathered my courage and said the words, we both knew were coming—"We'll have to vacate the house"—did she finally turn her head to look at me. The movement was slow, deliberate, like someone underwater fighting against the current.

"Find someone to take you in," she said, her voice hoarse and barely recognizable. "Go to

Edward. Apologize. Beg, if you have to. He might still—"

"No." The word escaped before I could stop it, sharp and decisive as a blade.

She studied my face for a long moment, and I saw something die in her eyes—the last flicker of maternal hope, extinguished as surely as if I had blown out a candle.

"Then we are both lost," she whispered, and turned her face away.

I knew then that I would receive no help from her, no comfort, no shared strength to face what was coming. She had folded in on herself like a love letter never sent, all the words of affection and support locked away where they could never reach me. I was more alone than I had ever been, even in a house that still technically sheltered us both.

I did what I could. I sold the remaining silver piece by piece, watching our family's history disappear into the pawnbroker's hands—the tea service that had been my grandmother's wedding gift, the candlesticks that had graced our table for forty years, the serving tray where Papa used to arrange his morning correspondence. Each sale felt like a small death, another connection to our past severed and sold for coins that disappeared almost as quickly as I earned them.

Then went the curtains—heavy velvet drapes that had once made our windows look grand but now simply blocked out the light we could no longer afford to supplement with candles. The mirrors followed, including the great gilt-framed looking glass in the front hall where I had practiced my curtsy as a child, where I had arranged my hair for parties I would never attend again, where I had seen myself transform from hopeful young woman to whatever I was becoming now.

I wrote to Uncle Charles in Devon, crafting careful sentences that tried to explain our situation without sounding like begging. The letter came back unopened, marked "Return to Sender" in handwriting I didn't recognize.

Perhaps he had moved. Perhaps he had died. Perhaps he simply wanted nothing to do with the shame that clung to our family name like smoke.

I considered writing to Edward—my fingers actually picked up the pen several times, hovering over blank paper while I tried to find words that wouldn't taste like ashes in my mouth. But each time I imagined his face when he read my plea, imagined the satisfied smile that would curve his lips as he realized how completely I had fallen, how thoroughly life had punished me for my pride. The thought of his pity, his smug benevolence, his careful calculation of exactly how much my desperation was worth made my stomach turn with such violence that I had to rush to the washbasin.

I would sooner starve. And I nearly did.

The walks began out of necessity—creditors had learned our address, and the house no longer felt safe during daylight hours. I took to wandering the streets with my skirts pinned up to hide their frayed hems, my eyes downcast to avoid the stares that followed me wherever I went. Men passed too close now, close enough that I could smell gin on their breath and feel the heat of their bodies through my thin shawl. They seemed to sense something different about me, something that marked me as vulnerable, available, fallen.

Women looked away when they saw me coming, crossing to the other side of the street with elaborate casualness, as if my misfortune might be contagious. I visited places I had once entered freely—bookshops where I had browsed for hours, tea rooms where I had met friends for afternoon gossip—and felt the air shift when I stepped inside. Conversations paused. Eyes tracked my movement. People know when someone is drowning, can smell desperation like blood in the water.

I ate sparingly—a crust of bread here, a bruised apple there, whatever I could afford with the few coins in my reticule. Hunger became a constant companion, a gnawing ache that followed me through my days and kept me awake at night. I learned to ignore the way my clothes hung loose on my shrinking frame, the way my cheekbones grew sharp and prominent, the way my mother's eyes filled with tears when she looked at me.

The jewellery went next—my grandmother's pearl earrings, my confirmation ring, even the gold locket that held a curl of Papa's hair from when he was young and handsome and full of dreams. That was the hardest thing, watching the pawnbroker examine it with cold, calculating eyes before offering me a sum that couldn't have bought a decent meal. It was the last sentimental thing I owned, the final link to happier times, and I watched him pocket it with the same indifference he might show for a broken pocket watch.

By the end of the month, the house stood empty of everything that had once made it home. The rooms echoed with our footsteps, bare walls showing pale rectangles where pictures had once hung, windows naked and stark without their curtains. We were like ghosts haunting our own former life, wandering through spaces that no longer recognized us.

That's when I found the note on the mantelpiece—my mother's careful handwriting on paper so thin I could see through it to the words beneath.

*Eleanor,*

*Mrs. Whitmore has agreed to take me in, though she says she hasn't room for two. I cannot bear to watch you destroy yourself for the sake of pride. Go to Edward. Go to anyone who will have you. But I cannot stay to witness this slow suicide you have chosen.*

*Forgive me, if you can.*

*Mother*

I read it three times before the words made sense, before I understood that she was truly gone, that I was now completely and utterly alone. The woman who had given birth to me, who had raised me and worried over me and loved me despite everything, had chosen her own survival over mine.

I couldn't blame her. Not really. But the pain of her abandonment hit me like a physical blow, doubling me over until I had to grip the mantelpiece to keep from falling. The tears came then—finally, violently, all the grief I had been holding back pouring out of me like water through a broken dam.

I wept for Papa, for the gentle man who had tried so hard to protect us and failed. I wept for my mother, driven to such desperation that she had to choose between her daughter and her own survival. I wept for the girl I had been, the woman I had hoped to become, the life that had slipped through my fingers like sand.

But underneath the tears, underneath the grief and fear and crushing loneliness, burned a different kind of pain—the bitter irony of what had brought us to this point.

I hadn't done anything wrong. Not really.

I had said no to a man who would have caged me, who would have bought me like a piece of property and expected me to be grateful for the transaction. I had refused to trade my soul for security, my dreams for respectability, my very self for the promise of comfort.

That was all. One word—*no*—spoken with quiet dignity in a parlour that smelled of dying roses and broken dreams.

And somehow that single act of defiance, that moment of choosing myself over society's expectations, had turned my entire life to ash.

Now I stood alone in an empty house, with nothing left but my pride and the terrible knowledge that pride, as it turned out, was not enough to keep a person warm when winter came calling.

# Chapter 4: Hunger and Cobblestone

## "Whitechapel Shadows"

There is a peculiar kind of silence to starvation.

Not the dramatic collapse of fainting novels or the theatrical swoon of Gothic heroines. True hunger is quieter than that—more insidious. It creeps into your bones like morning frost, numbing you from the inside out until you forget what warmth felt like. Your body begins to betray you in small ways: your hands shake when you try to smooth your hair, your vision blurs at the edges like watercolours bleeding into gray, and your thoughts become thick as porridge, stirring slowly around a single, constant ache.

Food. The word becomes a prayer, a curse, a phantom that haunts every waking moment. All other concerns—pride, dignity, the careful construction of who you once believed yourself to be—crumble like day-old bread in the rain.

By the time I arrived in Whitechapel, I had shed more than weight. I had shed my name, my polish, the careful pronunciation that marked me as educated, the straight spine that spoke of drawing room deportment. Layer by layer, like a snake moulting its skin, I had left pieces of Eleanor Ashcombe scattered across London's streets until what remained was something harder, sharper, more desperate than the woman who had once refused Edward Harrowby's proposal.

But I had not yet shed everything. Deep inside, buried beneath layers of grime and hunger and shame, some stubborn kernel of my former self remained—a girl who had once believed she deserved better than to be bought and sold like cattle at market. That kernel would prove to be both my salvation and my torment in the months to come.

I remember the first night with the clarity that comes only from extremes of suffering—each detail etched into memory like acid on copper. It was raining but calling it rain seems inadequate. This was London unleashing its fury, sending down needles of ice-cold water that cut through my threadbare shawl as if it were gossamer. The drops struck the cobblestones with tiny explosions, filling the air with the sound of a thousand small violences.

I had tried to find shelter beneath a wooden awning behind Henley's butcher shop, but the stench drove me away—old blood and rotting offal, the sweet-sick smell of meat gone bad that seemed to coat my throat and cling to my clothes. The irony was not lost on me: I was starving yet surrounded by the smell of food too foul to eat, too precious to waste.

I wandered the twisting streets until my boots—my last good pair, now soaked through and splitting at the seams—squelched with every step. My fingers had gone past cold into something worse: a burning numbness that made me fumble with the buttons of my coat, made me drop the few coins I had clutched so desperately.

Eventually, when exhaustion outweighed discomfort, I found a spot against a chimney wall behind a row of tenements. The bricks still held some trace of warmth from the fires within—families gathered around their hearths, eating supper, telling stories, existing in a world of light and safety that seemed as distant as the moon. I pressed my back against that wall and tried to absorb whatever heat I could, pulling my knees tight beneath my skirts in a futile attempt to create warmth where none existed.

I did not sleep. Sleep was a luxury I could no longer afford, not when every shadow might hide danger, not when the cold bit so deep it felt like dying. Instead, I watched the fog roll through the narrow streets like grey fingers searching for something to grasp. I listened to rats scurrying beneath wooden crates, their tiny claws scratching against stone with sounds that might have been Morse code if I had been educated in such things. I counted the church bells marking the hours—one, two, three—then started again when I lost track, the numbers dissolving in my weary mind like sugar in rain.

Morning did not arrive so much as reveal itself reluctantly, the darkness bleeding away by degrees until the world took on the colour of old pewter. The rain had stopped, but everything dripped with a rhythm that sounded almost musical if you were desperate enough to find beauty in such places. I was.

That first day was the worst, though I did not know then how much worse things could become. I still carried the foolish hope that someone would see me—truly see me—and recognize that I did not belong in this place. I believed that a constable might stop and ask if I needed assistance, that a kind woman might press a coin into my palm, that some stranger might look at me and think, "This one is different. This one has fallen from somewhere higher."

But no one did. The few people who ventured into these narrow streets moved with purpose, their eyes fixed straight ahead, their faces set in expressions of grim determination. They had learned the first rule of survival in places like this: do not see what you cannot help. Do not acknowledge what you cannot change. Do not waste sympathy on those who have already fallen.

Those who did notice me looked with the particular disgust reserved for the genteel poor—the ones who had once been above such circumstances, who served as uncomfortable reminders that fortune was more fragile than most cared to admit. I was a cautionary tale walking among them, living proof that the comfortable assumptions about class and breeding and inherent worth were nothing more than pretty lies we told ourselves to sleep better at night.

I had fallen through a crack in the world, tumbled into that shadowy place where London hides its failures, its mistakes, its inconvenient truths. The city had opened like a mouth and swallowed me whole, then sealed itself behind me as if I had never existed at all.

Hunger does terrible things to pride. By the third day, when the gnawing in my stomach had become a constant companion, I found myself standing outside Brennan's bakery, breathing in the yeast-scented air like a drowning woman gasping for breath. The smell was torture and salvation combined—close enough to touch, impossible to afford.

I watched through the window as the baker's boy arranged loaves in the display, each one golden and perfect, still warm from the ovens. My mouth watered so fiercely I had to swallow repeatedly to keep from embarrassing myself further. When he emerged to sweep the front step, I gathered what remained of my courage and approached him.

"Please," I said, and was shocked by the sound of my own voice—hoarse, cracked, barely recognizable. "Might you have any bread that's gone stale? Anything you might otherwise throw away?"

The boy—he could not have been more than twelve—looked me up and down with the calculating eyes of someone who had grown up hard. He saw my torn gloves, my muddy hem, the way I swayed slightly on my feet from hunger and exhaustion. And then he laughed—not with cruelty, exactly, but with the careless brutality that children learn when tenderness is a luxury they cannot afford.

"Go home, madwoman!" he shouted, scooping up a handful of flour from his pan and flinging it at me. The white powder exploded across my dark coat like snow, settling in my hair, dusting my eyelashes. "We don't give handouts to beggars!"

I stood there, covered in flour, feeling the weight of his words settle into my bones. Madwoman. Beggar. Was that what I had become? The girl who had once recited Shelley from memory, who had played Chopin nocturnes on the pianoforte, who had dreamed of traveling to Italy to see the works of the great masters—was she truly lost beneath this creature of rags and desperation?

The boy had already turned away, whistling tunelessly as he swept. I was forgotten as quickly as I had been dismissed, another piece of human debris cluttering the streets of his world.

Days blurred together after that, each one a repetition of the last with small variations of misery. I sold the last of my gloves to a rag-woman for threepence, then the pewter buttons from my coat for another penny. I tore the lace trim from my undergarments—lace that had once been my grandmother's, that had adorned christening gowns and wedding dresses, that carried the weight of family history—and traded it for half a tin of stale biscuits that tasted of sawdust and despair.

When even those were gone, I tried to sleep the hunger away, curling up in doorways and under bridges, telling myself that unconsciousness was better than awareness. But hunger is a jealous companion; it follows you even into dreams, transforming peaceful sleep into fever visions of banquets just out of reach.

Illness came next, creeping through my weakened body like water through cracked stone. It began with a cough—dry, hacking sounds that seemed to echo off the narrow walls of whatever shelter I had found for the night. Then came the fever, burning through me with such intensity that I shivered even while my skin felt on fire. My head pounded with a rhythm that matched my heartbeat, and a constant ringing filled my ears, as if someone were striking tiny bells inside my skull.

The hallucinations started on the fourth day of fever. I saw my mother, young and beautiful as she had been in the portrait that hung in our parlour, brushing my hair with long, gentle strokes while humming a lullaby I half-remembered from childhood. I felt the phantom weight of her hands, smelled her rose water perfume, heard her voice whispering words of comfort and love.

"There, my darling," she said, her voice like honey and sunlight. "Rest now. Everything will be all right."

I reached for her, desperate to make the vision real, to hold onto this moment of peace in the midst of so much suffering. But my fingers closed on empty air, and when I opened my eyes, I found myself alone beneath a sheet of yesterday's newspaper, the ink smudged and running in the damp.

The loneliness was almost worse than the hunger. In my former life, even in our reduced circumstances, I had been part of something—a family, a social circle, a community of sorts. Now I existed in a liminal space, neither fully alive nor completely dead, invisible to those who might have helped and ignored by those who shared my circumstances.

I began to recognize others like me—women who drifted through the streets like ghosts, hollow-eyed and limping, carrying their entire lives in patched bags or simply in their memories. Some had fallen as I had, victims of circumstance and cruel fortune. Others had been born to this life, knowing no other world than the one of constant want and struggle.

We did not form friendships, exactly. Hunger leaves little room for the luxury of human connection, and competition for resources—a dry doorway, a charitable coin, a crust of bread—could turn potential allies into enemies in the space of a heartbeat. But we developed a kind of understanding, a shared recognition of suffering that created its own fragile bonds.

Some of the women had found ways to survive that I was not yet desperate enough to consider. I saw them in the alleyways after dark, lifting their skirts for men who pressed coins into their palms before disappearing back into the night. Others drowned their circumstances in gin, trading tomorrow's suffering for tonight's oblivion. A few simply vanished—there one day, gone the next, leaving no trace except empty spaces where they used to sleep.

Still, there were moments of unexpected kindness that kept some small flame of hope alive in my chest. An old woman named Dora, her face carved with lines of hardship but her eyes still kind, would sometimes let me share the warmth of her spot near the baker's ovens. She had lost most of her teeth to poor nutrition and time, but when she smiled, her whole face transformed into something beautiful.

"You'll get used to it, pet," she told me one particularly cold night, pulling a threadbare blanket over both our legs. Her voice carried the wisdom of someone who had survived more than most people could imagine. "The trick is to stop remembering who you were before. That girl—she's gone now. Grieve her if you must, but don't spend your strength trying to bring her back."

But I could not take her advice, however well-meant. I did not want to forget Eleanor Ashcombe—the girl who had read poetry by candlelight, who had played piano sonatas until her fingers ached, who had believed fiercely that she deserved to be loved rather than purchased. That girl felt like the last sacred thing I possessed, the final treasure that poverty had not yet managed to steal.

I clung to her memory like a talisman, even as my nails grew black with grime and my cheeks hollowed into sharp angles that made me look like a medieval saint in a painting—beautiful in an otherworldly way, but clearly more spirit than flesh.

One morning, perhaps a month after my arrival in Whitechapel, I caught my reflection in the window of a milliner's shop. I stopped so suddenly that a cart nearly ran me down, the driver shouting curses that I barely heard. The woman looking back at me from the glass was a stranger—or perhaps she was someone I had always been, finally revealed by the stripping away of everything false and comfortable.

My hair, once my vanity, had turned into matted ropes that hung around my face like a curtain of shame. My eyes, which had once been called lovely, now appeared bruised, set too deep in a face that had lost all its softness. I stood hunched forward like a crone, my shoulders curved inward as if trying to protect what little remained of my heart.

A well-dressed woman passing behind me caught sight of my reflection and followed it to my actual form. Her expression moved through several stages—curiosity, recognition of my genteel origins, disgust at my current state, and finally, fear. Fear that what had happened to me might somehow be contagious, that proximity to my failure might contaminate her own carefully ordered life.

She hurried away, pulling her shawl tighter around her shoulders as if warding off evil.

I wanted to scream after her: I was someone once! I had a name, a family, hopes and dreams and a future that stretched bright with possibility! I read books that would challenge your small mind! I played music that would make you weep! I loved and was loved, and I chose principle over convenience even when it cost me everything!

But the words remained trapped in my throat, too large and too desperate to escape. Instead, I simply turned away from the window, the soles of my ruined shoes flapping with every step like the wings of some broken bird and let the city swallow me again into its grey, indifferent belly.

The woman I had been was dying by degrees, but something else was being born in her place—something harder, more resilient, tempered by suffering into a different kind of strength. I did not know it then, but this transformation would prove essential for what lay ahead.

For now, I simply survived, one day at a time, learning the bitter lessons that London's streets had to teach.

# Chapter 5: The Woman Who Disappeared

## "Ghost in the Gaslight"

I do not remember the moment I stopped being Eleanor Ashcombe.

There was no ceremony to mark the death of that carefully constructed self, no funeral bell tolling for the girl who had once worn silk gloves and discussed Wordsworth over tea. The transformation was as gradual and inexorable as winter becoming spring—you notice one day that the world has changed around you, but you cannot pinpoint the precise moment when bare branches gave way to green buds.

One morning I simply woke up and realized that the name Eleanor Ashcombe had become meaningless as smoke—something that once existed, once had weight and substance, but had since dissipated into nothing. The syllables felt foreign in my mouth when I tried to form them, like a language I had once spoken fluently but could no longer remember.

That name, which I had once written with such careful penmanship in dancing masters' books and lending library registers, now lived nowhere. Not on a lease—I had no permanent address. Not on a letter—I had no one left to write to, and no one who would write to me. Not even in speech—the handful of people who acknowledged my existence at all had never bothered to learn what I was called.

Instead, I collected other names like a beggar collects scraps. "That one," said with a dismissive wave when someone wanted me moved along. "Her," spoken with the particular disgust reserved for women who had fallen too far to be considered properly female anymore. "The rag-witch by the bridge," whispered by children who dared each other to throw stones in my direction.

Once, a constable found me sleeping in the doorway of a closed haberdashery and shoved me awake with the toe of his boot. As I stumbled to my feet, clutching the tattered remains of what had once been a respectable coat, he spat a single word that followed me down the street like a curse: "Filth."

But never Eleanor. Never Miss Ashcombe. Never the name that my father had spoken with such pride when introducing me to his business associates, or that my mother had embroidered on handkerchiefs with threads of gold and silver.

At first, in those early months when the wounds of my fall were still fresh and raw, I tried desperately to maintain some connection to who I had been. I created small rituals to keep time from becoming a meaningless blur; to preserve some sense of the person I was underneath the rags and grime.

I had saved one thing from my former life—a narrow ribbon of blue silk that had once trimmed a Sunday dress, hidden now in the deepest fold of my skirts where searching hands could not find it. Each morning, if I could manage it, I would work my fingers through the matted tangles of my hair and tie it back with that ribbon, whispering to myself that this was Eleanor Ashcombe preparing for the day ahead, just as she always had.

In the evenings, when I had found some corner or doorway that might shelter me through the night, I would whisper poetry into my cupped palms—fragments of Keats and Shelley and Byron that I could still remember, words that had once seemed to contain all the beauty and meaning in the world. I would breathe those verses into my hands as if they were prayers, as if the mere act of remembering might keep some essential part of myself alive.

But those rituals became harder to maintain as the months stretched on. The ribbon grew dingy and frayed, its blue fading to the grey of everything else in my new world. The verses became fragmented, words dropping away until I could only remember pieces—"bright star" and "she walks in beauty" and "season of mists"—phrases that floated in my mind like debris from a shipwreck.

Eventually, even these last desperate attempts at preservation fell away. The ribbon finally dissolved into threads that disappeared on the wind. The poetry became silence. And with them went the last conscious connection to Eleanor Ashcombe, leaving behind only the hollow shell that continued to breathe and move and survive.

I forgot which month it was first—was it October? November? The distinctions seemed meaningless when every day was the same struggle for food and warmth and safety. Then I lost track of the year itself. 1871? 1872? Time had become elastic, measured not in calendar pages but in the rhythm of seasons, the patterns of survival, the slow accumulation of small defeats and smaller victories.

What remained when everything else had been stripped away was pure instinct—the animal knowledge of how to stay alive when civilization has written you off as expendable. I learned the hidden geography of London's waste and charity, mapping a city invisible to those who lived in the world of clean streets and lit windows.

I knew that Mulligan's bakery on Dorset Street threw their day-old bread into the alley at dusk, but only on days when the wind was from the south—otherwise, the rats got there first. I learned that Thursday nights brought coal wagons to the shipyard, and if I moved quickly enough, I could steal a handful of warm ash that would keep my hands from freezing for precious hours. I discovered which church steps offered the most shelter, which constables were likely to move you along with words rather than blows, which shopkeepers might be convinced to part with spoiled produce if you approached at precisely the right moment.

These became the coordinates of my existence—not street names or house numbers, but a careful calculus of survival that had nothing to do with the woman who had once navigated London's drawing rooms with equal precision.

I spoke little in those years. Most of us who lived in the city's shadow didn't. Words were a luxury when every calorie had to be hoarded, every breath preserved for the essential work of staying alive. Conversation required energy that could be better spent searching for food or shelter, and besides, no one wanted to hear your story—especially not the kind that began with "I used to be."

Those three words carried too much weight, too much accusation. They suggested that the fall was not inevitable, that different choices might have led to different outcomes, that we who lived in the margins might once have been people worth knowing. It was easier for everyone—the fallen and the still-standing alike—to pretend that we had always been this way, that our circumstances were the natural order rather than the result of forces beyond our control.

But though I spoke little, I watched everything.

Invisibility, I discovered, was a peculiar kind of power. When people cannot see you—really see you, as a human being worthy of consideration—you become privy to truths they would never reveal to someone they considered their equal. I watched the way gentlemen turned their faces away when passing beggars, but also how their hands moved unconsciously to their purses, counting the weight of coins they would not share. I watched housemaids slip love letters to footmen in shadowed corners, their faces bright with the kind of hope I had almost forgotten existed. I watched the city itself breathe and shift like some enormous organism—the morning rush of soot and commerce, the languid afternoons when heat rose from cobblestones in shimmering waves, the hungry nights when danger prowled the narrow streets looking for prey.

I saw lovers meet in secret gardens, their whispered promises carrying on night air that also carried the sound of bodies being pulled from the Thames at dawn—the ones who had loved unwisely or not at all, who had gambled everything on hope and lost.

There was strange power in this watching, in being witness to the countless small dramas that played out around me. Even invisible things cast shadows, and I had become London's shadow—present but unacknowledged, observing but unobserved, collecting secrets that would die with me in whatever unmarked grave awaited those who disappeared from the world's memory.

Sometimes, when the loneliness became too heavy to bear, I would follow strangers through the streets just to feel the illusion of belonging to something larger than my own small circle of survival. I trailed a young governess with a neat brown bun and squeaky boots, imagining the children she taught, the parlour where she sat reading aloud from improving books, the bed she slept in that had clean sheets and a window that let in morning light.

I followed a limping messenger boy through his rounds, watching him navigate the city with the confidence of someone who had a purpose, a destination, people waiting for the words he carried. I shadowed a laundress with a distinctive mole beneath her left ear, following her to the river where she beat clothes clean against stones worn smooth by generations of women doing the same necessary work.

These small journeys gave me the temporary gift of motion with meaning, of movement that was more than just the endless search for food and shelter. For a few hours, I could pretend I was going somewhere, that my steps had purpose beyond mere survival.

But one evening—one unforgettable, devastating evening—I followed a woman who wore a ribbon of pale lilac in her dark hair and moved through the gaslit streets with the particular grace that comes from never having doubted your place in the world. She was perhaps my age, or what my age had been when such things mattered, and she carried herself with the unconscious elegance of someone who had never learned to make herself small.

As she passed beneath a street lamp, the wind caught her skirts and brought with it a scent that stopped me in my tracks—French lavender soap, the kind my mother had once ordered from a shop on Bond Street, the same soap that had scented the water in our hip bath on Saturday evenings when the world was still whole and I was still someone worth being clean for.

I followed her through streets that grew progressively more familiar, past shops where I had once been welcomed, through squares where I had once walked with my head held high. She moved with the confidence of someone who belonged in these spaces, who had never been made to feel unwelcome or unwanted, who had never learned the particular shame of being looked through rather than at.

It was only when she turned onto Grosvenor Street—my old street, the street where I had lived when I still had a name and a family and a future—that I realized I was crying. The tears came silently, without warning, streaming down my face as I stood in the shadows watching this stranger approach the life that might have been mine if I had been willing to pay its price.

The house she entered was not the one I had lived in—that had been sold long ago to pay debts I could no longer even remember—but it could have been. The warm light spilling from its windows, the sound of piano music drifting through glass, the simple assumption of safety and belonging that emanated from every brick and beam. This was the world I had refused, the cage I had been too proud to enter, the life I had chosen to sacrifice on the altar of my own stubborn principles.

Standing there in the darkness, watching lamplight play across windows that would never welcome me, I wept not just for what I had lost, but for what I had never really understood I was losing. I had thought I was choosing freedom, but what I had really chosen was this—to be a ghost haunting the edges of other people's contentment, forever looking in from the outside at lives I would never be permitted to share.

In the months and years that followed, I dreamed strange dreams that came to me in the fitful sleep of doorways and bridge shadows. Dreams of tables groaning under the weight of food I could not name—roasted fowl and cream sauces and crystallized fruits that dissolved on the tongue like sweet snow. Dreams of rooms where fires burned in marble hearths and people spoke my name with warmth and recognition, where I existed not as a shadow or a problem to be moved along, but as someone worthy of love and consideration.

But the cruellest dreams of all were the ones that brought me back to that parlour where Edward Harroway had made his careful, calculated proposal. In these dreams, I saw myself as if from above—the girl in the ivory dress with her spine straight and her hands folded, listening to him outline the terms of her future with the precision of a business contract. And in these dreams, when he reached the end of his speech and waited for her answer, she smiled and nodded and said the words that would have saved her from everything that followed:

"Yes, Edward. I would be honoured to be your wife."

I would wake from these dreams with my face wet with tears, mourning not just the life I had lost, but the woman I had been—the one who had believed she deserved better than to be purchased, who had trusted that integrity was worth more than security, who had been naive enough to think that choosing love over convenience was a luxury she could afford.

What frightened me most in those long, empty years was not the hunger that gnawed at my bones, or the sickness that came with sleeping rough, or the filth that had become so much a part of me that I no longer noticed its smell. What terrified me was the growing realization that I did not miss Eleanor Ashcombe as much as I should have.

I should have mourned her—the girl who had played Chopin nocturnes with such feeling that listeners wept, who had read poetry aloud with perfect diction, who had believed with fierce certainty that she was worth more than any man's money could buy. I should have grieved for her lost potential, her silenced voice, her dreams that had died unborn in London's unforgiving streets.

But I didn't. Or couldn't. The energy required for mourning was energy I needed for survival, and there was something almost merciful about the gradual numbing that allowed me to let her go without tearing myself apart in the process.

Eleanor Ashcombe became a story I told myself on the worst nights, like a fairy tale from childhood that grows less real with each telling. Once upon a time, there was a girl who believed in her own voice, who thought she could choose love over security, who trusted that being true to herself was worth any sacrifice. She lived in a house with books and piano music and people who spoke her name with pride. She wore gloves of soft kid leather and dresses that rustled when she walked, and she believed—oh, how fervently she believed—that she deserved to be loved for who she was rather than what she could provide.

But that girl had been a luxury that life could not afford. She had vanished as completely as if she had never existed, leaving behind only this shadow-creature who knew how to find food in gutters and warmth in the breath of sleeping horses, who had learned to make herself so small and quiet that she could disappear entirely from the world's attention.

They all vanish, eventually—these bright, stubborn girls who think they can rewrite the rules of a world that has no patience for their dreams. They disappear into marriages that cage them, or poverty that erases them, or madness that swallows them whole. One way or another, they all learn that wanting more than your offered is the most dangerous luxury of all.

And so, Eleanor Ashcombe joined their ranks—another cautionary tale, another dream deferred until it withered into nothing, another voice silenced by the terrible arithmetic of survival.

But something else was growing in the space she had left behind, something harder and sharper and infinitely more dangerous than the girl who had once believed that love was worth any sacrifice. I did not know it yet, but the woman who would emerge from these ashes would be worth ten of the creature Edward Harrowby had wanted to buy and display in his drawing room.

For now, though, there was only the watching and the waiting, the slow accumulation of bitter wisdom, the patient endurance of one who has learned that sometimes you must lose everything—including yourself—before you can discover what you're truly made of.

# Chapter 6: A Glimpse of Silk

## "A Family Under Umbrellas"

It was raining again—that peculiar London rain that falls not in honest drops but in a fine, relentless mist that seems to rise from the very stones of the street. The kind of weather that makes the city feel like it's dissolving at the edges, where chimney smoke bleeds into grey sky and cobblestones weep black tears that run in rivulets toward gutters already choked with debris.

I had taken shelter beneath the narrow overhang of a boarded apothecary on Hanover Street, my knees drawn up to my chest in a futile attempt to make myself smaller, more compact, less visible to the world that had long since stopped seeing me. My skirts were soaked through and had gone stiff with cold, the fabric clinging to my legs like a second skin of misery. The wooden boards above my head leaked steadily, each drop finding its way to some new part of my body with the persistence of Chinese water torture.

I was not looking for anything in particular. I had long since stopped looking—stopped scanning faces for recognition, stopped searching shop windows for glimpses of the life I had once known, stopped hoping that around the next corner I might find some door that would open to me, some warm hearth that would welcome the ghost I had become.

Existence had narrowed to the immediate and the essential: where to find food, where to sleep, how to survive the next hour and then the one after that. Hope was a luxury I could no longer afford, and expectation was a cruelty I had learned to avoid.

And then I saw them.

A flash of silk first—ivory pale, moving through the grey morning like captured light flowing across dark water. The colour was so clean, so impossibly bright against the soot-stained backdrop of the street, that it seemed to glow with its own inner radiance. Then came the rustle of fine fabric, the soft whisper of quality cloth that had never known the touch of harsh soap or desperate mending, followed by the low murmur of a voice that reached across the years and struck me like a physical blow.

I turned my head, and time seemed to stutter, to hiccup like a broken timepiece, throwing me backward through the years to drawing rooms and garden parties and a world where I had once belonged.

Edward.

Even through the veil of rain and the blur of years, he was unmistakable. Older, certainly—the sharp angles of youth had softened into the more comfortable lines of middle age. He was broader around the waist, his frame settled into the prosperous solidity of a man who had never known want, never gone to bed with hunger gnawing at his bones. Silver was just beginning to creep into his temples, adding distinction to features that had always been more commanding than handsome.

But the essence of him remained unchanged. He still moved through the world with that particular confidence that comes from never having been denied anything truly important, never having been told that his desires were unreasonable or his expectations too grand. The rain parted around him as if it wouldn't dare to inconvenience someone of his standing, and his footsteps rang against the wet cobblestones with the authority of a man who had never doubted that the world would arrange itself for his comfort.

His gloved hand—leather so fine it seemed to glow in the dim light—held a large black umbrella with a carved ivory handle. And beneath that umbrella, sheltered from the rain that soaked through my rags and chilled me to the bone, she stood.

Clara.

Clara Harrington—no, Clara Harrowby now. Clara of the lilac ribbon and the effortless laugh that had once made every other woman in the room feel like she was trying too hard to be noticed. Clara who had married Edward Harrowby eighteen months after I had refused him, who had stepped so seamlessly into the life I had rejected that it was as if she had been waiting in the wings all along, perfectly prepared to claim what I had been too proud to accept.

The years had been kinder to her than they had been to me—but then, the years are always kinder to those who make the choices that society approves of, who bend when they are expected to bend, who smile and nod and accept what they are offered with appropriate gratitude. She had grown into her role as Edward's wife with the same easy grace with which she had once navigated the ballrooms of our youth, her small hands resting lightly on his arm with the unconscious ownership that comes only from absolute security.

And between them, like living proof of everything I had lost, walked two children.

The boy—he could not have been more than six—ran ahead despite the efforts of a starched and flustered nursemaid to keep him properly within the shelter of the umbrella. He splashed through puddles with the careless joy of someone who had never been told that getting wet might mean going without clean clothes, or warmth, or any of the hundred small comforts that children like him took as their natural due. His laughter rang out clear and bright above the sound of the rain, and when he turned to call something back to his parents, I could see Edward's nose, Clara's chin, the particular blend of features that marked him unmistakably as their child.

The girl was younger—perhaps four—and clung to Clara's silk skirts with the trusting devotion that only children can give. She hummed something under her breath, a tuneless little melody that spoke of security so complete she had never learned to fear the world around her. When she stumbled slightly on the uneven stones, Clara's hand was there immediately to steady her, the gesture so automatic, so perfectly maternal, that it might have been choreographed.

They looked like they had stepped from the pages of an illustrated storybook—the perfect family portrait, complete and harmonious and utterly, devastatingly real. Everything about them spoke of prosperity and contentment, from the quality of Edward's wool coat to the careful way Clara held her skirts to keep them from trailing in the puddles, to the obvious health and happiness of the children who danced around them like satellites orbiting a warm and steady sun.

I pressed myself further back into the shadows of the boarded doorway, my breath caught somewhere between my ribs and my throat, trapped like a bird in a cage too small to contain it. The rain continued to fall, but I no longer felt it. The cold that had been seeping into my bones for hours suddenly seemed distant, unimportant, overwhelmed by something far more powerful and far more painful.

I tried to tell myself I didn't know what I was feeling that the emotions churning in my chest were too complex to name or understand. But that would have been a lie, and I had grown tired of lying to myself about the things that mattered.

I knew exactly what it was.

Envy.

Pure, crystalline, perfect envy that cut through me like a blade made of winter light. So sharp and clean and devastating that for a moment it felt almost like joy—the terrible joy of finally seeing the thing you have lost, of understanding with perfect clarity the true weight of the choices you have made.

This was what I had refused. This was what my pride had cost me. This warm circle of belonging, this safe harbour in a world that showed no mercy to those who fell outside its carefully drawn boundaries. This was the life that had been waiting for me if I had only been willing to swallow my dreams and accept what was offered instead of demanding what I thought I deserved.

Clara was not especially beautiful—I could see that even through the haze of rain and regret. Her eyes were rather small, and her mouth had a tendency to droop slightly when she wasn't consciously smiling. Her figure had thickened somewhat since the birth of her children, and her complexion lacked the porcelain perfection that the society papers so admired.

But there was something about her that transcended mere physical beauty—something that suggested she belonged not just to Edward, but to the world itself. She moved through the morning rain with the unconscious grace of someone who had never been made to feel unwelcome, never been looked at with disgust or pity, never been forced to question her right to exist in whatever space she chose to occupy.

That should have been me.

The thought came unbidden, bold and dangerous and absolutely undeniable. It blazed through my mind with the force of revelation, burning away years of careful rationalization and hard-won acceptance.

I should have been the one beneath that umbrella, sheltered from the rain that now soaked through my rags and chilled me to the marrow. I should have been holding that little girl's hand, feeling the trust and love that radiated from her like warmth from a fire. I should have been the wife who could draw Edward's attention with nothing more than a gentle touch to his shoulder, who could speak his name and see his face soften with affection and possession.

Those should have been my children running ahead through the puddles, carrying my features blended with his, my blood mixed with his money to create something new and precious and infinitely valuable. That should have been my drawing room they would return to, my servants who would dry their clothes and prepare their dinner, my life that would continue in smooth and predictable comfort until old age carried me to a respectable grave marked with a proper headstone bearing the name of Harrowby.

They turned down Brook Street, walking with the unhurried pace of people who knew exactly where they belonged in the world and had never been given reason to doubt it. The umbrella bobbed gently above them like a black flower blooming against the grey sky, and I could hear the soft murmur of conversation punctuated by the children's laughter and Clara's gentle corrections.

They were unaware of the woman clinging to a crumbling doorway just yards away, watching with eyes that had been hollowed by hunger and hardship and years of learning that the world had no use for stubborn principles or inconvenient dreams. To them, I was part of the landscape—no more worth noticing than the puddles they stepped around or the soot-stained buildings that lined their path.

I should have let them go. Should have turned away and lost myself again in the grey maze of London's streets, carrying this glimpse of what I had lost like a fresh wound that would eventually heal into another scar.

But I couldn't.

Instead, I found myself pulling my tattered shawl over my head and following them, keeping to the shadows and the blind spots, moving with the practiced stealth of someone who had learned to observe without being observed. I told myself I was merely curious—that I simply wanted to see where they lived, what their world looked like from the outside. I would only go as far as their front gate, I promised myself. Just far enough to see the house that should have been mine, and then I would leave them to their happiness and return to my own grey half-life.

But when they stopped to admire something in a shop window—toys, perhaps, or sweets for the children—I found myself ducking behind a red post box, my heart hammering against my ribs as I watched Clara rest her head against Edward's shoulder with the casual intimacy of long marriage. The gesture was so natural, so unconsciously affectionate, that it spoke of countless such moments, countless small intimacies shared and taken for granted.

The little girl tugged at her mother's skirts and whispered something, her face turned up with the complete trust that only children can give. I could not hear the words, but I saw Clara's smile, saw her bend down to answer whatever question had been asked, saw Edward's hand move to rest protectively on his daughter's head.

"Mama, look," the child said, and though the words were soft, they carried clearly across the rain-soaked street.

That single word—Mama—pierced me like a blade between the ribs, sharp and clean and devastating. It carried with it the weight of everything I would never be, every connection I would never make, every love I would never know. In that one syllable was contained all the warmth and belonging and purpose that I had traded away for the cold comfort of my own uncompromising principles.

I turned away then, unable to watch any longer, my heart thudding so hard I was certain it would burst. The rain continued to fall, and I let it wash over me as I stumbled blindly back toward the maze of narrow streets and forgotten corners where creatures like me belonged.

That night, sleep would not come. I lay beneath a narrow staircase behind the Lyceum Theatre, listening to the scratch and scurry of rats making their nests in the debris that accumulated in such forgotten places. The stones beneath my body were cold and damp, and the wind that whistled through the gaps in the boards above carried the sound of civilized people going about their civilized lives—carriages rolling past, voices calling goodnight, the distant sound of music from some warm and well-lit parlour.

I closed my eyes and tried to summon every detail of what I had seen: the exact shade of Clara's silk dress, the texture of her fine leather gloves, the way her hair had been arranged beneath her modest bonnet. I memorized the sound of her laughter, the gentle authority in her voice when she spoke to the children, the perfect confidence with which she had moved through the world that had once been mine.

What had she done to deserve it all? What great sacrifice had she made, what terrible price had she paid for the privilege of walking beneath Edward's umbrella, of being called Mama by those bright-faced children, of belonging so completely to the world of light and warmth and safety?

She had not fought. She had not bled. She had not spent years learning the bitter lessons of London's streets or discovered how many different ways a human being could be made to feel less than human.

She had simply married.

That was all. That was enough.

She had said yes when I had said no, had smiled when I had frowned, had bent when I had remained rigid with pride and principle. She had understood what I had been too stubborn to accept—that sometimes survival requires compromise, that sometimes the cage is preferable to the wilderness, that sometimes the price of freedom is higher than any reasonable person should be expected to pay.

And I—who had once been her equal, perhaps even her superior in wit and education and all the qualities that society claimed to value—I was here, half-mad with hunger and exposure, stinking of gutters and desperation, invisible to everyone but the rats who shared my shadowy kingdom.

But now I had seen her. Now I had been forced to confront the full weight of what my choices had cost me, the true magnitude of what I had lost when I chose principle over pragmatism, dignity over security, the uncertain promise of love over the solid guarantee of comfort.

A thread had been pulled, and somewhere deep inside me—in places that had been numb for so long I had forgotten they existed—something began to stitch itself together again. Not as it had been before, not as the naive girl who had believed that wanting something badly enough would make it possible, but as something new and strange and infinitely more dangerous.

Not Eleanor Ashcombe, who had died by inches in London's gutters.

Not the nameless beggar in rags who haunted the city's forgotten corners.

Something else entirely. Something that had learned the true value of the things it had lost, something that understood exactly what it would take to reclaim them, something that had been tempered by suffering into a form both harder and more flexible than what had come before.

I did not yet know what that something would become, or what it might be capable of. But as I lay there in the darkness, listening to the rats and the rain and the distant sounds of other people's happiness, I felt it stirring to life inside me like a seed that had waited years for the right conditions to finally sprout.

The woman who would emerge from this chrysalis of rage and loss and bitter wisdom would be someone entirely new. Someone who understood that the world did not reward virtue or punish vice with any consistency, someone who had learned that survival sometimes required becoming the very thing you had once sworn never to be.

And perhaps—just perhaps—someone who was finally ready to take back what should have been hers all along.

# Chapter 7: The Spark of Madness

## "The Idea That Took Root"

It began with the ribbon—though perhaps it would be more accurate to say it began with what the ribbon represented, with the sudden, devastating recognition that some lives continue in silk and comfort while others dissolve into shadow and ash.

I found it near the tram stop on Piccadilly; a narrow strip of deep plum silk caught in the iron railing like a butterfly pinned to a collector's board. The wind had been playing with it, making it flutter and dance in a way that caught the weak afternoon light and transformed it into something almost alive. No other woman in that part of the city wore silk—certainly none of the hollow-eyed creatures who haunted the spaces between respectability and ruin. Only Clara moved through these streets wearing fabric that cost more than most of us saw in a month.

I stared at it for a long time before daring to touch it, my fingers trembling as I reached toward this fragment of a world I had lost. The silk was impossibly soft, finer than anything I had felt in years, and when I held it up to the Gray light, I could see the individual threads woven together with a precision that spoke of skilled hands and patient craft. It was warm from the sun, or perhaps from having recently rested against Clara's throat, and it carried with it the faintest ghost of her perfume—French lavender mixed with something else, something expensive and complex that I could not name.

I told myself it meant nothing as I folded it carefully into my palm, just a scrap of fabric that would serve no practical purpose, that could not keep me warm or fed or safe. But even as I lied to myself, I was already tucking it deep into the breast pocket of my tattered coat, right over my heart where it would rest like a secret, like a promise, like a small piece of the life that should have been mine.

That night, curled beneath the arches of Waterloo Bridge with the Thames lapping at the stones below, I dreamt of Clara's life with a vividness that felt more real than waking. But for the first time, I was not watching from the outside, not pressed against windows or hiding behind post boxes, hungry and cold and separate. Instead, I was her.

I stood in a sunlit nursery painted in soft yellows and greens, surrounded by toys that gleamed with newness—wooden horses with real hair manes, dolls with porcelain faces and silk dresses, picture books with gilt edges that caught the light like treasure. A fire glowed warmly in the marble grate, casting dancing shadows on walls hung with watercolour paintings of meadows and streams. The carpet beneath my feet was thick and soft, patterned with roses that had never known mud or tears.

A child—my child, in this dream—clutched at my skirts with small, clean hands, looking up at me with Edward's dark eyes and my own stubborn chin. The weight of that small body against my legs felt like an anchor, like belonging, like the kind of love that transforms you from the inside out and makes you more than you ever thought you could be.

Edward sat in a leather armchair by the window, reading aloud from a children's book, his voice warm with affection and patience. When he looked up and caught my eye, he smiled—not the calculated smile he had worn during his proposal all those years ago, but something genuine and tender, the smile of a man looking at the woman he loved, the mother of his children, the centre of his carefully ordered world.

In the dream, I wore a dressing gown of deep blue velvet, tied with a sash that emphasized the curves that hunger had long since stolen from my body. My hair was clean and pinned in a style that was both fashionable and flattering, and when I moved, the fabric whispered against my skin with the particular sound of quality that I had almost forgotten existed.

This was how it should have been. This was the life that my pride and principles had cost me—not just the comfort and security, but the love, the belonging, the sense of being essential to someone else's happiness. This was what I had traded for the cold satisfaction of refusing to be bought, and as I stood there in that perfect, impossible room, I felt the weight of that choice like a stone in my chest.

When I woke, gasping and disoriented in the grey dawn light that filtered through the bridge's arches, the ache in my chest was so sharp and sudden that I thought for a moment I might be dying. The dream clung to me like perfume, so vivid that I could still feel the velvet against my skin, still hear the child's laughter echoing in my ears, still see Edward's smile warming me like sunlight.

The return to reality was brutal—the cold stones beneath my body, the smell of the river and human waste, the gnawing emptiness in my stomach that had become as familiar as breathing. But worse than the physical discomfort was the emotional devastation, the terrible knowledge that what I had just experienced was not a glimpse of what might be, but a cruel mockery of what would never be, not for me, not anymore.

After that, I followed them daily.

It was easier than I had expected, this transformation from accidental observer to dedicated stalker. They were creatures of habit, moving through their privileged world with the predictable rhythm of people who had never learned to fear the unexpected. Morning walks through Green Park, where Edward would point out interesting birds to the children while Clara gathered wildflowers for the drawing room vases. Visits to Mrs. Pemberton's flower stall every Thursday, where Clara would spend long minutes selecting just the right blooms, her face serious with concentration as if the fate of empires hung in the balance of choosing between roses and lilies.

Sunday mornings brought them to St. George's on Hanover Square, where they sat in the same pew each week—third row from the front, on the right side—Clara's gloved hands folded neatly in her lap, Edward's attention divided between the sermon and his restless son, the little girl leaning against her mother's shoulder with the absolute trust that only children can give.

I stayed far enough behind to avoid detection, just another shadow in the city's vast population of the forgotten and ignored. But I watched with the intensity of a scholar studying ancient texts, memorizing every detail, cataloguing every gesture, building a comprehensive understanding of the life that moved just beyond my reach.

I learned her gait—light and efficient, as if she were always exactly two steps away from some important purpose that only she could fulfil. I studied the way she tilted her head when Edward spoke to her, the slight angle that suggested both attention and affection, the unconscious intimacy of two people who had learned each other's languages over years of shared mornings and quiet evenings.

I watched how she rested her hand on his shoulder for exactly three seconds when she wanted his attention—long enough to be noticed, not so long as to be possessive or demanding. I observed the way she kissed the children on the crowns of their heads, her lips barely brushing their hair so as not to disturb her carefully applied rouge, but the gesture so tender and automatic that it spoke of countless such moments, an endless accumulation of small loves that built a life worth living.

It wasn't just admiration anymore—though it had begun that way, with the kind of wistful envy that any poor woman might feel when watching the rich move through their charmed lives. This was something deeper, more systematic, more dangerous. This was study.

I began whispering her words under my breath as I followed her through the streets, memorizing not just what she said but how she said it. "Darling, don't forget your gloves"—

spoken with just enough authority to be obeyed, but softened with endearment so as not to wound. "Henry, let your sister have the ribbon"—firm but fair, the voice of a mother who understood that justice was more important than peace, but who could deliver correction without cruelty.

I practiced the cadence of her speech until I could reproduce it perfectly, the particular rhythm of someone who had never doubted that her words would be heard, valued, obeyed. I found broken mirrors in alleyways and abandoned buildings and stood before them practicing her smile—not the broad, desperate grin of someone trying too hard to please, but the subtle curve of lips that spoke of contentment, of secrets worth keeping, of a woman who knew her own worth and expected others to recognize it as well.

I didn't know exactly what I was becoming during those long weeks of observation and imitation, but I could feel the transformation happening inside me like a chrysalis forming around a caterpillar. Something was dying in those shadows between buildings, in those hours spent watching other people's happiness from the outside. And something else was being born, something harder and more focused and infinitely more dangerous than the woman who had begun this strange pilgrimage of obsession.

One morning in late October, when the air carried the first real bite of winter and the trees in the parks had begun to shed their leaves like golden tears, I followed them farther than usual. Instead of their normal route through the familiar streets of Mayfair, they walked south toward Kensington, their pace unhurried, their conversation punctuated by the children's laughter and excited observations about everything they passed.

They stopped before a small café with lace curtains in the windows and flower boxes beneath the sills, the kind of place that catered to respectable families with money enough to spend on such luxuries as meals eaten for pleasure rather than mere survival. Edward held the door for Clara with the automatic courtesy of a gentleman, and she swept inside with the unconscious grace of someone who had never doubted her welcome anywhere.

I dared to move closer than I usually allowed myself, pressing against the window glass like a moth drawn to flame, my heart hammering so hard against my ribs that I was certain it must be audible even through the barriers of glass and wood and carefully maintained social distance. Inside, they settled at a table near the window, Clara arranging her skirts with the particular care of someone wearing fabric too fine to be treated carelessly, Edward helping the children into their chairs with the patient attention of a father who had time for such small rituals.

The scene was so perfectly domestic, so utterly normal and content, that it might have been painted by one of those artists who specialized in capturing the quiet happiness of the middle classes. The warm light streaming through the café windows turned Clara's hair to gold and softened Edward's features until he looked almost handsome. The children chattered and pointed at things on the menu, their faces bright with the anticipation of treats to come.

And then Edward said something—I could not hear the words through the glass, but I could see his expression, the slight smile that suggested he was teasing her about something—and Clara laughed. Not the polite, controlled laugh of a lady in company, but a real laugh, open-mouthed and bright, the kind of spontaneous joy that transforms a face from merely pretty to genuinely beautiful.

He looked at her with such softness then, such obvious affection and pride, that it was like watching someone unwrap a precious gift. This was not the dutiful attention of a husband performing his social obligations, or the calculated regard of a man pleased with a particularly successful acquisition. This was love—messy and complicated and deeply felt, the kind of love that grows over years of shared mornings and whispered conversations and small kindnesses offered without expectation of reward.

I had never received such a look from him. Not even in the beginning, when he had been courting me with his careful compliments and calculated courtesies. I had been a prize to be won, a trophy to be displayed, a means to an end that had nothing to do with love and everything to do with social advancement and the merging of respectable names with useful money.

But Clara—Clara was beloved. Clara was cherished. Clara was the centre of a world that revolved around her happiness, and she wore that privilege like a second skin, so naturally that she probably never even thought to be grateful for it.

My reflection caught in the glass beside them—hollow eyes sunken deep in a face that had forgotten how to be soft, skin the colour of old parchment stretched too tight over bones that jutted like the framework of some abandoned building. My hair hung in matted ropes around shoulders that curved inward as if trying to protect a heart that had been broken too many times to ever heal properly. I looked like what I was—a ghost, a shadow, a woman who had died by inches and was too stubborn to lie down.

The contrast was so stark, so devastating, that something inside me simply... broke.

Not loudly, not like the dramatic shattering of glass in Gothic novels or the operatic collapse of heroines overwhelmed by their circumstances. No, this was quieter than that, more final—like a teacup dropped on carpet, making barely a sound but leaving fragments too small and numerous to ever be repaired.

The breaking was soft, internal, irreversible. And with it came a question that rose from some dark place in my soul where reason had long since given way to something far more primitive and dangerous.

Why her?

The words formed themselves in my mind with perfect clarity, each syllable weighted with years of suffering and loss and bitter understanding of how arbitrary the world's distributions of happiness really were.

Why not me?

She had not earned this life through any particular virtue or sacrifice. She had not fought for it, had not bled for it, had not spent years learning the harsh lessons that London's streets taught to those unfortunates enough to need their instruction. She had simply been there when Edward decided he needed a wife, had smiled at the right moment and said yes when saying no might have meant something, had bent when I had remained rigid with pride and principles that had proven to be worth less than nothing in the cold arithmetic of survival.

She had stolen the life that should have been mine.

The thought came from nowhere—or perhaps it had been growing quietly all along, putting down roots in the dark places where resentment lived, fed by every cold night I had spent shivering in doorways, every meal I had missed, every kindness I had been denied, every moment I had been forced to confront the magnitude of what my choices had cost me.

It didn't matter whether it was true or fair or reasonable. Truth was a luxury I could no longer afford, and fairness was a concept that belonged to people who had never been forced to choose between dignity and survival.

What mattered was that it felt true. What mattered was that it gave shape to the formless rage that had been building inside me for months, gave direction to the desperate hunger that had nothing to do with food and everything to do with the human need to matter, to belong, to be essential to someone else's happiness.

From that moment on, I stopped being content to observe from the margins, to collect scraps of their life like a beggar gathering crumbs. I needed to know more—not just the public performance of their happiness, but the private details, the intimate moments, the small vulnerabilities that would help me understand exactly what I was dealing with, exactly what I would need to become if I was going to take back what was rightfully mine.

I followed Clara to her seamstress on Bond Street, lingering outside while she was fitted for new gowns, catching glimpses through the window of her reflection in the shop's mirrors as yards of silk were draped around her like Armor made of beauty. I pressed my ear to the keyhole of the confessional at St. George's after she had entered, straining to hear what sins someone like her might have to confess, what small guilts troubled the sleep of someone who had never known real want or genuine desperation.

When she dropped a handkerchief at the flower market—fine linen edged with lace and embroidered with her initials in silk thread the colour of spring leaves—I snatched it up like a relic and tucked it beneath the thin pillow I had fashioned from rags and newspapers. At night, when sleep would not come and the cold seemed to seep into my very bones, I would press that scrap of fabric to my cheek and breathe in the faint traces of her lavender soap, her French perfume, the indefinable scent of someone whose skin had never known the touch of harsh winter air or cheaper soap.

I told myself it was research, this careful cataloguing of her habits and preferences, this systematic study of how she moved through the world. I was simply gathering information, learning everything I could about the life I intended to reclaim, preparing myself for the moment when opportunity would present itself and I would need to be ready to seize it.

But if I were honest—and in the dark hours before dawn, when the barriers between conscious thought and deeper truth grew thin, I sometimes was—I would have had to call it something else entirely.

Devotion.

Obsession.

Love and hatred twisted together into something that was both holy and hideous, pure and corrupt, sacred and profane all at once.

The ribbon over my heart seemed to tighten with each passing day, binding me to her with threads that grew stronger rather than weaker the more I pulled against them. I could feel myself changing, feel the woman I had been dissolving like sugar in rain while something new and strange and infinitely more dangerous took shape in the hollow spaces she left behind.

The first threads of the plan began to stitch themselves into place during those long nights of watching and waiting and wanting—not a conscious design, not yet, but a gradual recognition of possibilities, a slow understanding of how the world might be rearranged to serve justice rather than accident, how the arbitrary distributions of fortune might be corrected by someone willing to take the necessary risks.

I would not remain a ghost haunting the margins of other people's happiness. I would not spend whatever years remained to me watching through windows at lives I would never be permitted to share. I would not die in some anonymous gutter, forgotten and mourned by no one, my name erased from the world as completely as if I had never existed at all.

She had stolen my place in the world—perhaps not deliberately, perhaps not with any conscious malice, but stolen it, nonetheless, claimed what should have been mine through nothing more than the accident of being in the right place at the right time with the right willingness to accept what was offered instead of demanding what was deserved.

And I meant to take it back.

Every bit of it. The house, the husband, the children, the safety, the belonging, the love that should have been mine from the beginning if the world had any justice, any logic, any recognition of the fact that some people earn their happiness while others simply stumble into it through no virtue of their own.

I would become Clara Harrowby. Not through imitation or impersonation, but through replacement, through the simple and elegant solution of taking the life that was rightfully mine and wearing it as naturally as she wore her silk dresses and lavender soap.

The plan was still forming, still gathering shape and substance in the dark corners of my mind where reason had given way to something far more primitive and powerful. But I could feel it growing, feel it putting down roots and sending out tendrils, feel it becoming something that might actually be possible if I was willing to pay whatever price such transformation would require.

And I was willing. God help me, I was more than willing.

I was eager.

# Part II: The Doppelgänger's Game

*How to become someone else: lie, layer, repeat.*

# Chapter 8: Threads of the Past

## "Needle and Knowledge"

Becoming someone else takes time—far more time than the poets would have you believe with their tales of instant transformation and miraculous rebirth. This is not the stuff of fairy tales where a wave of a magic wand can turn rags to silk and despair to joy. This is archaeology in reverse—not the careful excavation of what was buried, but the deliberate construction of something that never existed, layer by painstaking layer.

True transformation requires the complete erasure of the self you came from. You must take who you were and sand it down to its very bones, scraping away every familiar curve and comfortable angle until what remains is raw material that can be reshaped into something unrecognizable. You must bury the woman you once were so deep that even you begin to forget she ever drew breath, and then you must speak the proper words over her grave—not mourning, but condemnation, not grief, but good riddance.

I began with books, because books had always been my refuge, my escape, my way of becoming larger than the small cage of my circumstances. But now I stole them with purpose rather than desperation, selecting each volume with the careful calculation of an architect choosing materials for a building that must stand against storms.

At first, I took only small ones that I could tuck beneath my tattered coat without creating suspicious bulges—a pocket grammar guide printed on thin paper, a slim volume of improving sermons bound in cracked leather, an etiquette manual written specifically for the daughters of minor gentry who aspired to move in better circles than those of their birth. I haunted the bookshops of Charing Cross Road like a ghost, slipping through their narrow aisles when the proprietors were distracted by paying customers, my fingers quick and desperate as I selected the tools that would help me rebuild myself from the ground up.

I read with the fevered intensity of someone whose life depended on each word, each rule, each subtle distinction between what was acceptable and what marked one as irredeemably common. The knowledge carved tunnels through my mind, displacing the gnawing hunger that had been my constant companion, silencing the voice that still whispered my real name in the dark hours when sleep would not come. Page by page, lesson by lesson, I began to construct the framework of someone who had never known desperation, never learned the bitter taste of charity, never been forced to choose between dignity and survival.

Mrs. Westmore.

That was the name I chose for this new creature I was building from books and observation and sheer force of will. I tested dozens of combinations on my tongue during those long nights when I sat by a candle stub in whatever corner or doorway I had claimed for shelter, whispering possibilities into the darkness like incantations. Mrs. Richardson. Mrs. Bellingham. Mrs. Fairfax. Each name carried its own history, its own implications, its own suggestion of the life that might have produced such a woman.

But Mrs. Westmore felt right in a way that the others did not. It sounded gentle without being weak, slightly tragic without being pitiable, respectably ordinary without being forgettable. It suggested a woman who had known comfort but also loss, who had been educated but not spoiled, who carried herself with the quiet dignity of someone who had learned that breeding was more important than wealth, that character mattered more than circumstances.

I practiced writing it again and again in a ledger I had stolen from a counting house, my hand moving across the pages with the careful precision of someone learning a new language. Mrs. Adelaide Westmore. The Adelaide had come to me in a dream—or perhaps a memory of someone I had known long ago, before the world had taught me that kindness was a luxury and trust was a form of suicide.

I wrote it in different scripts, with different levels of confidence, until the signature became as natural as breathing. I created a history for Mrs. Westmore—born in Devonshire, educated at a respectable ladies' seminary, married young to a cavalry officer who had died heroically in some distant colonial war. Widowed, childless, genteel but not wealthy, the sort of woman who might be found on the margins of good society, serving as a companion to elderly ladies or teaching the daughters of merchants who aspired to better things.

The more I wrote the name, the more real she became, until even I began to forget that she was a fabrication, a careful lie built from necessity and nurtured by desperation. She lived in my mind with increasing clarity—her preferences, her memories, her small sorrows and quiet hopes. She was becoming more real to me than Eleanor Ashcombe had ever been, more substantial than the hollow-eyed creature who had haunted London's alleys for so many months.

I found a room to rent—a narrow attic space in a boarding house near Camden where the landlady asked no questions as long as the rent was paid promptly and her tenants caused no trouble. It was barely large enough for a bed and a washstand, with a single window that looked out onto a courtyard where cats fought over scraps and laundry hung like prayer flags between the buildings. But it was mine, the first space I had been able to call my own since leaving my father's house, and I treated it like a sacred temple where the transformation could be completed in privacy.

I paid for it with coins saved from the cleaning work I had managed to find in the early morning hours when respectable people were still asleep—scrubbing steps and washing windows for housekeepers who were grateful to find someone willing to work for almost nothing and ask no questions. Some of the money came from the few successful begging expeditions I had undertaken when desperation overcame pride, each coin extracted from reluctant hands with a combination of manipulation and genuine need that left me feeling both grateful and ashamed.

The rest came from the sale of my mother's bracelet—the last relic I had preserved from my former life, a simple circlet of gold set with garnets that had been her mother's before her. I had hidden it in my boot for months, telling myself I was saving it for some ultimate emergency, some crisis that would make its sacrifice worthwhile. But as I stood in the pawnbroker's shop, watching him examine it with the dispassionate eye of someone who dealt in the remnants of other people's tragedies, I understood that this was that emergency, that the emergency was not some future catastrophe but the ongoing disaster of my existence, the daily battle to become something more than what circumstances had made me.

The money from the bracelet was enough to secure the room for three months and purchase the basic necessities I would need to continue my transformation. I spent it carefully, strategically, investing in the tools that would allow me to build Mrs. Westmore from raw materials and stubborn determination.

I scavenged clothing from sources that would have horrified the woman I had once been—forgotten trunks in boarding house basements, bundles of discarded garments in alley bins behind the homes of the wealthy, cast-off items from church charity boxes that I approached with the stealth of a professional thief. Most of what I found was damaged in some way—stained, torn, sized for women whose bodies had been shaped by different lives than mine—but I had learned to see potential where others saw only waste.

I taught myself to mend lace with thread pulled carefully from mattress seams, to dye fabric with tea and coffee grounds, to reshape bodices and take in waists with the patient precision of someone who understood that perfection lay in the details. I learned to bleach yellowed cotton with mixtures of lemon juice and salt, to remove stains with concoctions of vinegar and soap, to press wrinkles from silk using heated irons borrowed from other tenants when they were away.

I made blouses from bedsheets, carefully hemming and pleating the fabric to create the suggestion of quality where none had existed before. I stitched gloves from the salvageable portions of ruined petticoats, learning to create seams so fine they were nearly invisible, to shape fingers with the precision of a sculptor working in cloth instead of stone. Each garment was a small miracle of transformation, proof that with enough patience and determination, anything could be made to appear other than what it truly was.

The first time I caught my full reflection in the cracked mirror that hung on my attic wall, I startled so violently that I nearly knocked over the candle that provided my only light. The woman looking back at me was neither the girl I had been nor the hollow-eyed creature I had become during my months in the streets. She was someone entirely new pale but not sickly, poised but not rigid, watchful but not hunted.

She could pass. Perhaps not among the highest levels of society, where every detail would be scrutinized by experts in the detection of pretence, but near enough to their edges to serve my purposes. She could be a governess seeking new employment, a lady's companion between positions, a genteel widow managing on a small pension and the kindness of distant relatives. She had the look of someone who had known better days but faced reduced circumstances with dignity, who carried herself with the particular grace of the educated poor.

I spent my evenings in systematic practice, turning my tiny attic into a laboratory where I could experiment with the elements of Mrs. Westmore's persona until they became as natural as breathing. I worked on speech first, reading aloud from books until I could eliminate every trace of the regional accent I had acquired during my months among London's underclass, until my vowels were properly rounded and my consonants crisp with the particular precision that marked someone as educated, refined, worthy of respect.

I practiced stillness—learning to sit without folding into myself, without the protective hunching that came from years of trying to make myself as small and unnoticeable as possible. I studied how to smile with restraint rather than desperation, how to meet eyes without either defiance or pleading, how to occupy space with the quiet confidence of someone who had never been made to feel unwelcome anywhere.

Most challenging of all, I taught myself to walk again—not the quick, furtive scurrying of someone always ready to flee or hide, but Clara's walk, the one I had studied and memorized during those long months of observation. Her heels barely touched the ground, as if the earth itself were merely an inconvenience beneath her feet, something to be acknowledged but not dwelt upon. She moved through space as if she owned it, as if the world existed for no other purpose than to provide a stage for her graceful passage through it.

I began the systematic gathering of intelligence about Clara's past, approaching the task with the methodical thoroughness of a military strategist planning a campaign. Every detail mattered, every fact was a weapon that might prove useful when the time came to put my plan into action.

From Mrs. Jenkins, a laundress on Bruton Street who had worked for the Wycliffe family before Clara's marriage, I learned that she had been born Clara Wycliffe of Ashford Manor in Wiltshire, daughter of a family with distant connections to nobility but limited means. Her father had died when she was sixteen, leaving behind debts that had forced the sale of the family estate. Her mother, always delicate and prone to nervous complaints, had survived only two years as a widow before succumbing to what the doctor had diplomatically termed "a decline."

Clara had come to London at eighteen with little more than her breeding and her beauty to recommend her, dependent on the charity of better-situated relatives who had provided her with a modest season and the opportunity to find a husband before her youth and looks faded. She had married Edward at twenty, in what the society papers had described as "a union of mutual affection and practical advantage"—which I interpreted to mean that she had provided respectability while he had provided security.

They had two children—Henry, now seven, and Margaret, five. Clara took afternoon tea at Lady Hemsley's house every other Thursday, part of a rotating circle of ladies who gathered to discuss charity work and exchange gossip under the guise of moral improvement. She had a particular fondness for lavender—in her soap, her sachets, even the small bouquets she arranged for the breakfast table. She played Chopin with competent if not inspired technique, preferring the nocturnes to the more demanding études.

I recorded it all in the margins of books and on scraps of paper that I kept hidden beneath the loose floorboard under my bed. Dates, names, preferences, the small habits and larger patterns that made up the architecture of a life. I collected these fragments like a scholar gathering evidence for some crucial thesis, like a priest memorizing scripture, like a lover treasuring every detail of the beloved's existence.

Clara Harrowby was not merely a woman—she was a structure, a carefully constructed edifice built from years of habit and expectation, from the accumulation of small choices and the gradual settling into patterns that defined her as surely as the walls of her house defined the spaces where she lived and moved and had her being. And if she could be built through the patient layering of experience and decision, then surely, she could be copied by someone with sufficient dedication and skill.

The more I studied her, the more clearly, I saw her weaknesses—not moral failings, exactly, but the particular vulnerabilities that came from a life lived without ever having to question the fundamental assumptions upon which it was built. She was well-bred, certainly, educated and accomplished within the narrow confines deemed appropriate for women of her class. But she was also sheltered, protected by wealth and position from the harsh truths that might have taught her to be suspicious, might have sharpened her instincts for danger.

She was soft in the way that people become when they have never been forced to develop hard edges for protection. She trusted easily because she had never been given reason to suspect that trust might be misplaced. She smiled often because her experience had taught her that the world was generally inclined to smile back. She walked through life as if it belonged to her, as if she had some natural right to safety and comfort and the assumption that others would treat her with courtesy and respect.

That kind of woman—no matter how intelligent, no matter how fundamentally decent—never sees the wolves until they are close enough to bite. That kind of woman never imagines that someone might study her with the patient intensity of a predator learning the habits of its prey, might catalogue her vulnerabilities like a general planning a siege, might invest months or even years in the careful preparation necessary to destroy her world and claim it as their own.

And I—well, I was no longer Eleanor Ashcombe, the naive girl who had believed that virtue would be rewarded and that the world was fundamentally just. Eleanor Ashcombe had been ground down by London's streets until nothing remained but bone and bitter wisdom. She had died by degrees in gutters and doorways, mourned by no one, remembered by none.

Mrs. Westmore was something entirely different—harder, more focused, infinitely more dangerous. Mrs. Westmore had been forged in fires that would have consumed Clara Harrowby, tempered by experiences that would have shattered her delicate nerves and sent her fleeing back to whatever sanctuary money and breeding could provide. Mrs. Westmore understood that the world was not kind to those who could not protect themselves, that survival sometimes required becoming the very thing you had once feared.

Eleanor Ashcombe would have knocked on the door and waited politely to be admitted, would have accepted whatever scraps of courtesy might be offered and been grateful for any acknowledgment at all.

Mrs. Westmore would walk in as if she belonged there, as if the house and everything in it were already hers by right, as if the only question was when the current occupants would realize their mistake and step aside to make room for the rightful owner.

The transformation was almost complete. Soon, very soon, it would be time to put it to the test.

# Chapter 9: The Widow's Veil

## "The Invention of Mrs. Westmore"

Grief is the perfect disguise—better than powder or paint, more effective than the finest costume ever crafted by human hands. It wraps around you like armour made of shadow, protecting you from scrutiny while simultaneously making you invisible to those who might otherwise look too closely, ask too many questions, probe too deeply into the careful construction of who you claim to be.

No one questions a veiled woman with a soft voice and downturned eyes, a woman who moves through the world with the particular careful grace of someone who has learned that loud footsteps and sudden movements can shatter the fragile peace that holds her together. They do not ask where she came from, what roads led her to this place, why she walks alone through streets that should be dangerous for an unaccompanied woman. They assume a dead husband—young, handsome, taken too soon by war or disease or the thousand small cruelties that steal away the good while leaving the wicked to prosper. They imagine a tragic backstory, a love story cut short, a loss too profound and sacred to be spoken of in casual conversation.

And then—blessed mercy—they look away. Politely, respectfully, gratefully relieved that this particular sorrow is not theirs to bear, that they can return to their own small troubles without being forced to contemplate the larger tragedies that lurk at the edges of every comfortable life.

Mrs. Westmore became real on a Thursday morning, just before dawn, when the London sky was still grey with possibility and the streets were empty except for the earliest workers beginning their journeys toward respectability.

I stood before the cracked mirror in my attic room and took the name I had practiced so carefully, the identity I had built letter by letter like a seamstress stitching together a garment of impossible complexity. I dressed myself in it as deliberately as if I were putting on ceremonial robes, as if this transformation were a religious ritual that required perfect attention to every detail, every gesture, every breath.

I pinned up my hair—not in the casual, haphazard style of someone who had forgotten how to care about appearances, but with the precise attention to detail that marked a woman who understood that presentation mattered, that the world judged you first by what it could see and only later, if ever, by what lay beneath the surface. Each hairpin was placed with surgical precision, each strand smoothed and arranged until the effect was one of modest elegance, the kind of understated beauty that suggested good breeding tempered by genuine sorrow.

The black veil came next—a small square of fine netting that I tied beneath my chin with ribbons

I had salvaged from a discarded bonnet and dyed with ink until they matched the sombre fabric. It was not expensive lace, would not have passed close inspection by an expert in such things, but it served its purpose: to soften my features, to suggest mystery while providing a legitimate reason to avoid too much direct eye contact, to mark me as a woman set apart by loss and therefore entitled to the particular courtesies that society reserved for the grieving.

The mourning dress had been my masterpiece, the culmination of weeks of careful scavenging and patient sewing, of nights spent by candlelight learning to create the illusion of quality from materials that had been destined for rubbish heaps and charity boxes. It was constructed from three different garments—a bodice from one, a skirt from another, sleeves from a third—all dyed the same deep black and altered so carefully that the seams were invisible unless you knew exactly where to look for them.

The fit was not perfect—it could never be perfect, cobbled together as it was from pieces never meant to work in harmony—but with the right posture, with the right manner of carrying myself, those imperfections would be invisible to casual observation. The dress spoke the language that society understood respectability tempered by reduced circumstances, gentility that had learned to make do with less, a woman who had known better days but faced her current situation with dignity rather than bitterness.

I stood before the mirror and practiced the story I had refined through countless repetitions, each telling slightly different until I had found the version that felt most natural on my tongue:

My late husband, Jonathan Westmore, had been a surveyor—a profession respectable enough to explain modest means while obscure enough to make verification difficult. He had been quiet, devoted, one of those good men who make the world a better place simply by existing in it, the kind of husband that every woman hopes to find but few are fortunate enough to claim. Consumption had taken him—

that gentle killer that struck down the virtuous along with the wicked, that could explain a lingering illness without raising questions about character or habits.

We had been married five years but blessed with no children—a sorrow I could suggest with a downward glance, a slight tightening around the eyes, the kind of grief that needed no elaboration because every woman understood the particular ache of dreams unfulfilled. I had been left with modest means and no family to speak of, dependent on my own efforts to secure a respectable future, seeking employment that would allow me to maintain some semblance of the life I had known while acknowledging the reality of my reduced circumstances.

It was vague enough to resist casual investigation while providing enough detail to seem authentic, tragic enough to discourage too many questions while practical enough to explain why a woman of my apparent breeding might be seeking work as a governess or companion.

The first test came at a grocer's stall in Marylebone, where I had chosen to purchase the few supplies I would need for my initial foray into Mrs. Westmore's world. My heart hammered against my ribs as I approached the counter, certain that the shopkeeper would see through my carefully constructed disguise, would recognize me as the hollow-eyed creature who had once haunted these same streets in search of scraps and charity.

But he greeted me with the automatic courtesy reserved for respectable customers, his tone warm without being familiar, professional without being cold. "Good morning, madam," he said, and that single word—madam—struck me like a physical blow. It had been so long since anyone had addressed me with such simple respect, had seen me as worthy of the basic courtesies that marked the boundary between civilization and its absence.

"Good morning," I replied, proud of how steady my voice sounded, how perfectly it matched the character I had created. "I should like some tea, please. Something suitable for a small household."

He showed me several varieties, explaining the virtues of each with the patient attention of a merchant who understood that repeat customers were the foundation of any successful business. I selected a modest blend—not the cheapest, which might have suggested poverty, but not the most expensive either, which could have invited unwanted questions about my circumstances.

As I counted out the coins—real money, earned through the small jobs I had managed to secure over the past weeks—my hands trembled slightly. The shopkeeper interpreted this as the delicate nerves of a lady unused to handling her own affairs, and he packaged my purchase with extra care, even going so far as to suggest that I might find his establishment convenient for my future needs.

I walked away from that simple transaction feeling as if I had accomplished something miraculous, as if I had crossed an invisible bridge that separated the world of the lost and forgotten from the realm where people mattered, where they were seen and acknowledged and treated as if their existence had value.

Later that day, fortified by this small success, I approached the domestic staff agency on Great Russell Street—a narrow building squeezed between a milliner's shop and a seller of used books, its windows dusty but its reputation solid among the kind of women who needed to work for their living but wished to do so with as much dignity as circumstances allowed.

I remember every detail of that visit with the crystal clarity that comes from moments when your entire future hangs in the balance of a single conversation. The smell of ink and furniture polish filled the front office, mixing with the fainter scents of lavender water and the particular mustiness that seemed to cling to buildings where important papers were stored and sorted and filed away. A large clock ticked steadily on the wall above the desk where the clerk sat, its rhythm like a heartbeat counting down the seconds until my new life would either begin or end before it had properly started.

My heart pounded so hard I was certain it must be visible through the fabric of my dress as I approached the desk and handed over the reference letters I had spent so many nights perfecting—documents painstakingly written in two separate hands, each word carefully crafted to suggest exactly the right combination of competence and humility, experience and availability.

The clerk was a tired-looking woman in wire-rimmed spectacles, her hair pulled back in a style that suggested efficiency rather than vanity, her dress neat but worn in the particular way that marked someone who understood the necessity of making good things last. She skimmed my letters with the practiced eye of someone who had seen hundreds of such documents, her expression revealing nothing of what she thought about their contents or the woman who had presented them.

"You have governess experience, Mrs. Westmore?" she asked, her tone professional but not unkind.

"Yes," I replied, grateful that my voice remained steady despite the chaos of emotions churning in my chest. "I was employed by the Ashford family in Suffolk for three years. Two daughters, aged eight and ten when I began with them."

This was the most dangerous part of my fabrication—specific enough to seem real, but referencing a family I had invented entirely, in a county I had never visited, describing children who existed only in my imagination. But I had chosen Suffolk precisely because it was far enough from London to make casual verification unlikely, rural enough that the gentry there would be unknown to most people in the city.

"And you are seeking a new position now?" she continued, making notes on a sheet of paper with handwriting so small and precise it looked like embroidery.

"Yes," I said, allowing a slight tremor to enter my voice, as if the explanation were still difficult for me to speak aloud. "My circumstances have changed since my husband's death. London holds memories for me—we lived here briefly after our marriage—but I find I need... purpose. Employment. The opportunity to be useful again."

She nodded with the understanding of someone who had heard similar stories many times before, who knew that the ranks of governesses and companions were filled with women whose lives had been disrupted by death or misfortune, who needed to work not just for money but for the sense of belonging that came from being needed, from having a place in some family's daily routine.

"There may be a position opening with the Harrowby's," she said, tapping her pencil against the desk as she consulted what appeared to be a ledger of available situations.

I froze, every muscle in my body going rigid as if I had been struck by lightning. The name hit me like a physical blow, even though I had been preparing for this moment, hoping for it, working toward it with every fibre of my being. To hear it spoken so casually, to have my months of planning and preparation suddenly converge into this single, impossible opportunity—it was almost too much to process.

"The Harrowby's?" I managed to ask, proud of myself for keeping my voice level despite the earthquake happening inside my chest. I was certain she would notice my reaction, would see something in my face that would mark me as suspicious, but she seemed completely absorbed in her papers, shuffling through them with the mechanical efficiency of routine.

"A family in Belgrave Square," she continued without looking up. "Mr. Edward Harrowby is in trade—imports, I believe, though quite successful at it. Two children, a boy and a girl. The position would be primarily for the children's education and general supervision, though Mrs. Harrowby's health is somewhat delicate, so there might be additional duties involving her care."

She paused, consulting another document.

"I should warn you; they do go through staff rather quickly. Nothing scandalous, you understand, but Mrs. Harrowby can be... particular about her requirements. The salary is generous, however, which compensates for the challenges."

A thrill passed through me so sharp and sudden it felt almost like pain, as if someone had driven a needle straight through my heart. My hand clenched around the handle of my handbag so tightly that I could feel the cheap metal cutting into my palm through my gloves, but I welcomed the sensation—it helped ground me, helped keep me from floating away on the wave of triumph and terror that threatened to overwhelm my carefully constructed composure.

This was it. This was the moment I had been working toward through all those months of watching and planning and transformation. Clara's delicate health, her particular requirements, her tendency to go through staff quickly—it all suggested a woman who was demanding, difficult, perhaps even neurotic in the way that women of her class sometimes became when they had too much time and too little real purpose.

Such a woman would be vulnerable to the right kind of influence, susceptible to someone who understood her needs and could meet them with exactly the right combination of competence and deference. Such a woman might grow dependent on a governess who proved herself indispensable, who became not just an employee but a confidante, a friend, someone whose presence made her life easier and more pleasant.

"Would you like your name submitted for consideration, Mrs. Westmore?" the clerk asked, her pen poised over what I assumed was a list of candidates.

I nodded, slowly and carefully, as if I were weighing the decision rather than barely containing my excitement. "Yes, thank you. I believe I could be of service to such a family."

Inside, I wanted to laugh—wanted to scream with the pure, overwhelming joy of seeing my impossible plan beginning to take shape. Yes, submit my name. Let it pass across Edward's desk, let Clara read it on a list of potential employees. Let them invite me into their house, their lives, their carefully ordered world. Let me begin the work I had been preparing for all these months.

I walked the length of Regent Street afterward, my mind reeling with the implications of what had just occurred, the veil fluttering against my cheek like a small, dark flag of victory. The city seemed to open before me like a gate that had been locked for years but had finally recognized the correct key. Every step felt like a small miracle, every breath like the first breath of a new life.

People stepped aside for me as I passed—not with the instinctive avoidance they had shown when I was one of London's invisible poor, but with the automatic courtesy reserved for respectable women who deserved consideration. A gentleman in a well-tailored coat actually tipped his hat as I passed, his smile courteous and brief but unmistakably real. A carriage slowed as I crossed the street, the driver waiting patiently for me to reach the safety of the pavement before continuing on his way.

The world no longer saw a beggar, a ghost, a piece of human debris to be ignored or avoided. They saw a woman—respectable, worthy of basic courtesies, entitled to exist in the same spaces they occupied. And all it had taken was a name, a dress, and a lie told with sufficient conviction to make it indistinguishable from truth.

I returned to my attic room as evening was falling, the gas lamps beginning to flicker to life in the windows of houses where families were gathering for dinner, where children were being put to bed with stories and songs, where the comfortable rituals of domestic life were playing out as they had for generations. I climbed the narrow stairs to my small sanctuary, closed the door behind me, and stood for a long moment in the gathering darkness.

Then, with trembling fingers, I removed the veil that had served as both disguise and Armor, untying the ribbons with the same careful attention I had used to fasten them that morning. I held the small square of fabric in my lap, smoothing it flat against my skirt, feeling its texture beneath my palms like a talisman that had carried me safely through the most important day of my new life.

Mrs. Westmore had been born today, had taken her first tentative steps into a world that had been closed to Eleanor Ashcombe, had proven that she could exist not just in my imagination but in the real world of hiring agencies and respectable employment. She had passed her first test, had convinced at least one person that she was exactly what she claimed to be.

Soon—very soon, if luck and determination could achieve what months of planning had prepared—she would be invited in. She would cross the threshold of the Harrowby house not as a beggar seeking charity or a criminal planning theft, but as a welcome guest, a valued employee, someone whose presence would be seen as a blessing rather than a threat.

And once she was inside, once she had established herself as indispensable to Clara's comfort and essential to the children's education, then the real work could begin. The slow, patient work of replacement that would gradually and imperceptibly shift the balance of power in that house until the question was no longer whether Mrs. Westmore belonged there, but whether anyone else did.

I folded the veil carefully and placed it in the drawer with my other precious possessions—the ribbon from Clara's dress, the handkerchief she had dropped, the carefully forged documents that had given Mrs. Westmore a history and a future. Tomorrow, I would put it on again, would continue building the reality of this new identity one small interaction at a time.

But tonight, I allowed myself a moment of quiet triumph, a recognition of how far I had come from the broken woman who had haunted London's gutters not so long ago. I had created something from nothing, had built a person from imagination and will and desperate need.

Mrs. Westmore was real now. And soon, she would be home.

# Chapter 10: The Governess Position

## "Welcomed into the Nursery"

I arrived at Belgrave Square just before eleven o'clock on a Tuesday morning that felt like the first day of creation, dressed in the dark grey serge dress that had taken me weeks to perfect—sombre but not shabby, professional but not severe, the uniform of a woman who understood her place in the world but wore that understanding with dignity rather than resentment. My veil was lifted to show my face clearly, my gloves mended so carefully that only someone looking for signs of repair would notice where the original seams had given way to my patient needlework.

The house loomed above me like a cathedral built to worship prosperity rather than God—four stories of honey-coloured stone and gleaming glass, with brass fittings on the door that caught the weak sunlight and threw it back in small, perfect bursts. It possessed the particular kind of quiet elegance that speaks not of ostentation but of absolute confidence, the aesthetic choice of people who had transcended the need to prove their worth through display. They simply were, and the world arranged itself accordingly.

I stood there for a full minute on the pristine pavement, my heart hammering against my ribs like a caged bird desperate for freedom, before I could summon the courage to reach for the polished brass bell pull. This was the moment everything had been building toward—months of watching and planning and careful transformation distilled into a single interaction that would either open the door to everything I had dreamed of or expose me as the fraud I had become.

The butler who answered was older than I had expected—stooped and silver-haired, with rheumy eyes that suggested years of faithful service and a stiff gait that spoke of joints worn down by decades of climbing stairs and carrying trays. He peered at me without warmth but also without hostility, his expression that of a man who had learned to reserve judgment until he had more information than appearances could provide.

"Mrs. Westmore?" His voice carried the particular accent of someone who had spent his life in service to the wealthy but had never allowed that service to diminish his inherent dignity.

"Yes," I replied, smoothing my skirt with hands that I hoped appeared steadier than they felt. "I have an appointment with Mrs. Harrowby regarding the governess position."

He nodded and stepped aside to admit me, leading me down a hallway that seemed to stretch for miles, its polished wood floors gleaming like dark water under gas fixtures that threw warm, honey-coloured light across walls lined with paintings of pastoral scenes and portraits of stern-faced ancestors. The air was heavy with the scents of beeswax and lemon oil, the particular fragrance of a house where every surface was maintained to perfection by an army of servants whose work was invisible but essential.

Every step I took seemed to echo through the space, and I found myself walking more carefully, trying to make my footfalls as quiet as possible, as if afraid that too much noise might shatter whatever spell had allowed me to penetrate this far into the world I had been shut out from for so long.

The sound of laughter echoed from somewhere deeper in the house—high-pitched and wild and utterly unselfconscious, the particular music that only children make when they are completely absorbed in their own joy. A child's voice, probably one of Clara's children, and the sound struck me like a physical blow. I nearly stumbled, caught off guard by the sudden wave of emotion that washed over me—not just the old familiar ache of what I had lost, but something newer and more complex, a recognition that I was about to become part of their lives in ways they could never imagine.

Clara waited for me in the drawing room, and she rose as I entered with the automatic grace of someone who had been trained from birth in the precise choreography of social interaction. She was exactly as I remembered from my months of observation—poised and slim, draped in soft lavender silk that caught the light and made her seem to glow from within, her dark hair arranged in a style that was both fashionable and flattering, her bearing that of a woman who had never doubted her place in the world.

But up close, seeing her without the protective distance of street corners and shop windows, I noticed details that had been invisible from afar. There was tension at the corners of her mouth, fine lines that spoke of smiles held too long, and conversations navigated with more care than they deserved. The shadows beneath her eyes were faint but unmistakable, the kind that came not from a single sleepless night but from the accumulation of small anxieties, the constant low-level stress of maintaining a performance whose demands never ceased.

She was tired—not with the exhaustion that comes from physical hardship or genuine suffering, but with the particular weariness of someone who had been playing a role for so long that she had forgotten what her natural expression might look like when no one was watching.

Her eyes swept over me with the practiced assessment of someone accustomed to evaluating servants, taking in the quality of my dress, the state of my gloves, the way I carried myself, the thousand small details that would tell her whether I was suitable for the position she needed to fill.

"You were recommended by the Mayfair agency?" she asked, her voice carrying the pleasant but neutral tone that marked her as someone who understood that kindness to servants was a virtue, but familiarity was a mistake.

"Yes, ma'am," I replied, lowering my eyes just enough to suggest appropriate deference without appearing servile. "I have been caring for children since I was sixteen, and I believe I have the experience necessary to meet your family's needs."

"I read your references," she continued, moving to seat herself in a chair upholstered in pale blue silk, gesturing for me to take the smaller chair positioned at precisely the right distance to suggest that this was a conversation between employer and employee rather than equals. "You were with a family in Suffolk?"

The moment I had been preparing for, the lie that would either pass scrutiny or destroy everything I had worked toward. "The Ashford family, yes. They moved to France last spring when Mrs. Ashford's health began to decline. The climate there was recommended for her constitution."

Clara nodded with the understanding of someone who moved in circles where delicate health was common and expensive remedies were readily available. "That seems to be going around these days. So many ladies of my acquaintance seem to suffer from nervous complaints."

There was something in her tone, a slight tightness that suggested this was not merely idle conversation but a reference to her own struggles, her own delicate constitution that the agency clerk had mentioned as one of the challenges of working in the Harrowby household.

The air between us seemed to still, heavy with unspoken meanings and careful assessments. I kept my expression pleasant but modest, my hands folded neatly in my lap, my voice carefully measured. I did not rush to fill the silence, did not volunteer information that had not been requested, did not make the mistake of appearing too eager or too desperate. I let her lead the conversation, let her feel that she was controlling the interaction, that any decision made would be hers rather than something she had been maneuverer into.

"I have two children," she said finally, her voice warming slightly as it always did when she spoke of Henry and Margaret. "Henry is nine, and Margaret is six. They are... spirited, both of them. Intelligent, but strong-willed. They require someone with both firmness and patience, someone who understands that their education involves not just lessons but the cultivation of proper character."

She paused, studying my face for any signs of doubt or hesitation.

"My husband is often occupied with his business affairs, and I find that I need someone who can take full responsibility for the children's daily supervision. Someone discreet, who understands the particular requirements of managing an upper-class household, who can maintain appropriate standards without constant oversight."

"I understand completely," I said, allowing a note of quiet confidence to enter my voice. "In my previous position, I was responsible not only for the children's formal education but for their moral development, their social preparation, and their general welfare. I believe that children thrive when they have consistent expectations and genuine care, but also when they understand that there are boundaries that must be respected."

She leaned forward slightly, and for one terrible moment that seemed to stretch for hours, she looked at me more closely than she had before. Her eyes narrowed just a fraction, and I felt my heart stop beating as I waited for the flash of recognition that would destroy everything, the sudden understanding that would send me back to the streets where I belonged.

But it didn't come. Instead, her expression softened, and when she spoke again, her voice carried genuine concern rather than suspicion.

"You are quite pale," she said. "Are you well? I hope you haven't been affected by the influenza that's been making its rounds."

Relief flooded through me so powerfully that I almost gasped aloud. "My health is steady, thank you for asking. I have simply... endured a long season of loss. My constitution is sound, but grief leaves its own marks."

Her eyes flickered with immediate sympathy, and I saw in them the recognition of someone who understood that particular kind of suffering. "Yes," she said softly. "I know exactly what that is like. Time helps, but the shadows linger."

We sat in silence for several heartbeats, two women who had both learned that loss could reshape you in ways that remained invisible to casual observation but marked you forever for those who knew how to look for the signs.

She offered me the position that afternoon, after what she described as a brief consultation with her husband—though I suspected the consultation had been more courtesy than necessity, that Edward trusted her judgment in matters related to the children's care and would not overrule her choice unless there were obvious reasons for concern.

I was shown to my quarters by the elderly butler, who introduced himself as Mr. Pemberton and explained that I would take my meals with the upper servants unless specifically invited to dine with the family, that my duties would begin each morning at seven and continue until the children were settled for the evening, and that I would have Thursday afternoons and alternate Sundays free for my own pursuits.

The room was small but perfectly appointed—a narrow bed with clean white linens, a writing desk positioned beneath a window that looked out onto the back gardens where I could see carefully tended flower beds and a small fountain that caught the afternoon light, a wardrobe that would easily accommodate my modest collection of clothing, and a washstand with a pitcher and basin decorated with tiny painted roses.

When the door closed behind me, leaving me alone in what was now my sanctuary within the house that should have been mine from the beginning, I sank onto the mattress and pressed both hands to my mouth to stifle whatever sound might try to escape—laughter or sobbing or the kind of wordless cry that comes from the deepest places of the soul when something long hoped for finally comes to pass.

I did not laugh. I did not cry. I simply sat there, trembling with a strange, exquisite calm that felt like standing at the centre of a storm where the wind could not reach me, where everything was suddenly, impossibly still.

I was inside. After months of watching from street corners and doorways, after endless nights of planning and preparing and transforming myself into someone worthy of admission to this world, I had crossed the threshold not as a beggar or a thief but as a welcome guest, someone whose presence would be seen as a blessing rather than a threat.

I stood and walked the perimeter of my small domain, touching the walls that were now my walls, pacing across floors that would support my steps for however long it took to complete the work I had come here to do. I opened each drawer of the writing desk, imagining how I would arrange my few possessions, how I would make this space into a base of operations for the careful campaign I was about to undertake.

In the small mirror that hung above the washstand, I saw a stranger smiling back at me—Mrs. Westmore, the respectable widow, the qualified governess, the woman who belonged in places like this because she had earned her position through competence and character rather than accident of birth or marriage. She looked content, settled, as if she had finally found the place where she was meant to be.

That evening, as twilight was painting the windows purple and gold, I was summoned to meet the children. Henry stood beside his mother with the sceptical expression that nine-year-old boys reserve for adults who have not yet proven themselves worthy of respect or trust. He was tall for his age, with Edward's dark hair and Clara's fine features, already showing signs of the confidence that would mark him as someone born to command rather than obey.

Margaret—six years old and utterly enchanting—clung to her nursemaid's skirts with the shy intensity of a child who had learned that new people sometimes disappeared as quickly as they arrived, that attachment was a risk that required careful consideration. Her hair was lighter than her brother's, catching the lamplight like spun gold, and her eyes held the particular brightness that comes from intelligence allied with imagination.

I knelt to her level, bringing myself down to her height so that we could meet as equals rather than as adult and child, and offered her a small wooden horse that I had carved from scrap wood during the long evening hours in my attic room. It was not a sophisticated toy—my skills with a knife were limited, and the wood had been rough to begin with—but I had spent hours smoothing it, painting it with pigments mixed from whatever materials I could find, until it resembled something that might have stepped from a fairy tale.

Margaret looked at the horse, then at me, then at her mother, seeking permission for this small act of acceptance. When Clara nodded, the child reached out with careful fingers and took the gift, turning it over in her small hands as if it were made of precious metal rather than salvaged timber.

"What's his name?" she asked, her voice soft but clear.

"That's for you to decide," I replied. "He's been waiting for someone to give him a proper name, someone who would understand what kind of horse he wants to be."

She smiled then—a real smile, unguarded and bright, the kind that transforms a pretty child into something luminous. "I think... I think his name is Thunder."

"Thunder is a perfect name for a horse like that," I agreed. "He looks like he could run faster than the wind."

Clara watched this entire exchange with her arms crossed, her expression unreadable, taking note of how I interacted with her daughter, how I balanced friendliness with appropriate distance, how I managed to engage the child without overstepping the boundaries that separated servants from family.

Edward was not home that evening—away on business, Clara explained, though she did not elaborate on what business might keep him away from his family during the dinner hour. I did not ask, of course. Such questions would have been inappropriate, presumptuous, the kind of curiosity that marked someone as unsuitable for positions requiring discretion.

But later that night, as I lay in my narrow bed surrounded by sheets that smelled of lavender and expensive starch, I heard the sound of a carriage returning to the house, the clip-clop of hooves on cobblestones and the creak of wheels that spoke of quality construction and careful maintenance. I rose and peeked through the curtain that covered my window, careful to remain hidden in the shadows, and saw him step down from the carriage with the assistance of a footman.

He was older than when I had last seen him, certainly—silver threading through his dark hair, his frame settled into the comfortable prosperity of middle age—but he remained essentially unchanged in the way that men of wealth often do, protected from the ravages of time by money and comfort and the assumption that the world would continue to arrange itself for their convenience. He moved with the same confident stride I remembered, the same sense of ownership over whatever space he occupied.

I did not speak to him that night. It was too soon, too dangerous, too likely to shatter the careful facade I had constructed before I had time to make it stronger. But I watched him enter the house that should have been mine, listened to his footsteps on the stairs that I should have climbed as his wife rather than his employee, and felt the old familiar mixture of rage and longing twist in my chest like a knife seeking its target.

Soon, I told myself. Soon I would speak to him, would remind him of what he had lost when he settled for Clara instead of waiting for me to come to my senses. Soon I would show him what he could have had if he had been patient, if he had understood that some prizes are worth whatever price they demand.

But not yet. First, I needed to establish myself as indispensable to his children, essential to his wife's comfort, woven so deeply into the fabric of their daily lives that removing me would be unthinkable. First, I needed to become not just Mrs. Westmore the governess, but Mrs. Westmore the friend, the confidante, the woman Clara turned to when her delicate nerves required soothing, the one Edward trusted to manage the domestic sphere so that he could focus on the important business of making money.

I lay back against my pillow and pulled the clean, sweet-smelling sheets up to my chin, feeling the soft linen against my skin like a benediction, like the promise of all the comforts I had been denied for so long. Through the walls, I could hear the quiet sounds of a household settling into sleep—footsteps on the stairs, doors closing softly, the distant murmur of voices as husband and wife exchanged the small intimacies of married life.

I closed my eyes and whispered to the ceiling, so softly that even I could barely hear the words:

"I'm home."

And for the first time in years, it felt like the truth.

# Chapter 11: Mirror Lessons

## "The Imitation of a Woman"

There is an art to vanishing—the delicate skill of making yourself so small, so unobtrusive, that you slip through the cracks of other people's attention like smoke through a keyhole. But there is an even greater art to becoming, to constructing yourself piece by careful piece until the woman who emerges from that patient work bears no resemblance to the one who began it, until even you begin to forget which version is real and which is performance.

In the early mornings, before the children woke and the household stirred to life, I would sit in the pale pre-dawn light of my governess quarters and study my face in the small mirror that hung above my washstand. The glass was old and flawed, rippled with age until my reflection seemed to swim like something glimpsed beneath dark water. But still, when I tilted my head just so and let the weak light catch my features at the right angle, I could see her there—not Clara, not yet, but the possibility of her, the ghost of what I might become with enough time and determination and careful attention to detail.

I began with her voice, because voice is the most intimate betrayal—it carries with it not just words but the entire history of who you are, where you came from, what lessons life has carved into your bones. Clara spoke as if the world would stop to hear her, with that particular tone of assured softness that marked women who had never doubted their right to be listened to, to be taken seriously, to have their opinions matter in the small kingdoms of their domestic lives.

Every syllable was deliberate, clipped in that precise way that women of her class were trained to speak from childhood—not rushed or breathless like the poor who felt compelled to squeeze their thoughts into whatever brief moments of attention they could capture, but measured and controlled, shaped by years of elocution lessons and the quiet confidence that came from knowing that people would wait for you to finish whatever you had to say.

I listened to her at dinner, when she discussed the day's events with Edward or corrected the children's table manners with gentle but firm authority. I memorized her cadence during afternoon tea, when she entertained visiting ladies with carefully modulated conversation about charitable works and social events. I catalogued her inflections during the quiet moments when she read aloud to Margaret before bed, her voice taking on a storytelling quality that transformed even the most mundane children's tales into something magical.

Later, behind the safety of my closed door, I echoed her words like a priest practicing liturgy.

"Margaret, please fetch your shawl, darling."

"Henry, I won't ask you again about your posture."

"Edward, you're being quite absurd about this."

I practiced these phrases and hundreds of others until my throat ached with the effort of reshaping sounds that had been worn into different patterns by years of different experiences. My own voice—roughened by months on London's streets, coarsened by desperation and the kind of conversations that happen in gutters and doorways—gradually wore thin under this constant attention, like a stone polished smooth by patient water until it took on an entirely new shape.

The physical transformation was even more challenging than the vocal one. Clara moved through space with the unconscious grace of someone who had been taught from birth that her body was an instrument of communication, that every gesture carried meaning, that elegance was not an accident but a skill that required constant practice and attention.

Her hands never fluttered with nervousness or uncertainty—they floated through the air like pale birds performing an elaborate dance, whether she was arranging flowers in a vase or gesturing to emphasize a point in conversation. She didn't rush across rooms the way I had learned to do, always ready to dodge or flee or make myself scarce when trouble appeared. Instead, she glided with the serene confidence of someone who had never been made to feel unwelcome anywhere, who moved through her world like a queen touring her own palace.

Even in anger—and I had witnessed her anger, though it was always carefully controlled, never allowed to flare into anything that might be considered unseemly—her restraint was like a mask that never slipped, never revealed the raw emotions that surely existed beneath the surface. I learned that mask, studied it in mirrors and doorways and the reflection of darkened windows until I could wear it as naturally as my own skin. My muscles ached from the constant effort of maintaining such rigid control, from holding my shoulders at exactly the right angle, keeping my spine straight but not stiff, moving my hands with deliberate grace instead of the quick, furtive gestures that had become second nature during my time among London's forgotten.

Every night, after the household had settled into the quiet rhythms of respectable sleep, I would slip from my room like a ghost and make my way through the darkened corridors to the unused drawing rooms and morning rooms where I could practice without fear of discovery. I stood by the marble fireplace the way Clara did during social gatherings, with one hand resting lightly on the mantelpiece, my chin lifted just enough to suggest confidence without arrogance, my expression pleasant but composed.

I practiced sitting on the silk-upholstered settee with my ankles crossed and my back perfectly straight, never allowing myself to slouch or curl into the protective postures that had become habitual during my months of hiding and surviving. I rehearsed the art of entering a room—not scurrying or creeping but walking with the measured pace of someone who belonged wherever she chose to go.

And then there was her scent—that subtle but unmistakable fragrance that clung to her clothes and lingered in rooms after she had passed through them. Lavender, certainly, but layered with something fainter and sharper, like crushed lemon verbena mixed with the ghost of expensive French soap. It was the olfactory signature of someone who had never been forced to make do with harsh lye or the kind of soap that stripped skin raw in the name of cleanliness.

I became a thief of the most intimate kind, stealing a lavender sachet from the basket of linens waiting to be pressed, keeping it beneath my pillow where its scent would transfer to my hair during sleep. I pressed it against my clothes, rubbed it into my skin until that delicate fragrance clung to me like a memory of better days, until I carried with me the olfactory evidence of a life I had never lived but was determined to claim.

The children became both subjects of study and unwitting allies in my careful campaign of replacement. I watched them with Clara—how they responded to her different moods, how she held them when they were hurt or frightened, the particular way she corrected their behaviour without crushing their spirits, the rhythm of affection and authority that kept them secure but not spoiled.

I began to replicate that rhythm with mathematical precision: never too harsh, which would have made them fear me, but never too indulgent, which would have earned Clara's disapproval and marked me as someone who didn't understand proper child-rearing. I learned to anticipate their needs before they voiced them, to provide comfort without being asked, to become the kind of presence that children gravitate toward because it offers both safety and understanding.

Slowly, imperceptibly, they began to turn to me first when small crises arose. Margaret would run to me when she fell in the garden and scraped her knee, seeking comfort from my arms before remembering that her mother was the proper source of such consolation. Henry, initially stiff and aloof in the way that children often are with new servants, began bringing me his drawings and compositions, his young face lighting up with pleasure when I praised his efforts and offered gentle suggestions for improvement.

I told him his sketches were brilliant, his handwriting was improving remarkably, his Latin pronunciation was nearly perfect. I saw myself reflected in his bright eyes—not as Mrs. Westmore the governess, but as someone who mattered, someone whose opinion carried weight in his small world. He beamed under this attention, and I felt something dangerous and wonderful blooming in my chest: the intoxicating power of being essential to someone else's happiness.

Clara noticed, of course. How could she not? She was not a negligent mother, not the kind of woman who paid no attention to her children's daily lives. She saw how they sought me out, how they included me in their games and conversations, how they had begun to treat me less like a servant and more like a beloved aunt or family friend.

But what could she say? That her children liked me too well? That she was concerned about my competence, my dedication, the way I had seamlessly integrated myself into their routines. That would have sounded petty, jealous, the kind of complaint that reflected poorly on the complainant rather than the accused.

She said nothing, but I saw the way her eyes followed me when I was with Henry and Margaret, the slight tightening around her mouth when they laughed at something I had said, the careful way she reasserted her maternal authority after witnessing moments of particular closeness between her children and their governess.

Edward, meanwhile, remained largely a shadow in the daily operations of his household—coming and going with the unpredictable hours of a man whose business interests took him away from home more often than not, or perhaps whose domestic life had become something to escape rather than embrace. But I caught his gaze sometimes, across the breakfast table when he was home for the morning meal, quick glances that lasted only a moment before he returned his attention to his newspaper or his correspondence.

His eyes were curious, I thought, but not suspicious. I was careful never to hold his gaze too long, never to give him reason to look at me more closely than courtesy demanded. Instead, I played my role with flawless precision: modest but competent, efficient but never presumptuous, the kind of servant who made life easier without calling attention to herself, who solved problems before they became crises and managed domestic affairs so smoothly that her employers could take their comfort for granted.

In that carefully cultivated invisibility, I observed everything with the methodical attention of a scholar preparing a dissertation on the intimate workings of upper-class domestic life. I studied Clara's handwriting when she left notes for the cook or wrote letters to friends, memorizing the particular slant of her script, the way she formed her letters, the confident flourishes that marked her as someone who had received an expensive education.

I examined her books when I dusted the library, noting which volumes showed signs of frequent reading, which authors she favoured, what kinds of stories captured her imagination. I watched how she addressed envelopes; the formal courtesy she showed to social equals and the warmer tone she reserved for intimate friends.

Her monogrammed handkerchiefs became objects of particular fascination—fine linen edged with delicate lace, each one embroidered with her initials in silk thread the colour of spring leaves. The "C" was especially elaborate, with flourishes and curves that spoke of hours spent in girlhood practicing the art of beautiful penmanship. I memorized that flourish, traced it with my finger until I could reproduce it perfectly, practiced it late at night in the margins of my notebook until it became as natural as my own signature.

C. H. for Clara Harrowby.

C. W. for Clara Westmore—a combination that existed only in my imagination but felt increasingly real with each repetition.

E. A. for Eleanor Ashcombe—letters that seemed to fade a little more each time I wrote them, as if that woman were dissolving like morning mist in sunlight.

Eleanor Ashcombe no longer lived in this house, had never belonged in these elegant rooms with their silk wallpaper and Persian carpets. She had been a mistake, a rough draft of a person who had never understood her proper place in the world, who had been too proud and too stubborn to accept what was offered and too naive to understand what would be demanded of her if she refused.

But something new was growing in the space she had left behind, something constructed with infinite care from stolen moments and borrowed gestures, from the careful study of a woman who had everything Eleanor had wanted, and the systematic acquisition of every skill needed to replace her.

It was not imitation was surface, was mimicry, was the kind of shallow performance that could be detected by anyone with sufficient attention and interest. This was construction, was architecture, was the patient building of a new person from the foundation up, using materials scavenged from observation and desire and the terrible clarity that comes from having lost everything once and being determined never to let it happen again.

Every word I practiced, every gesture I perfected, every stolen scent and studied smile was a brick in a growing cathedral—not a church built to worship God, but a monument to the power of human will, to the possibility of becoming anyone you were desperate enough to become, patient enough to build, ruthless enough to inhabit completely.

And I was almost done laying the foundation. Soon, very soon, it would be time to begin construction of the walls that would house the woman Clara Harrowby would never see coming, the replacement who would step into her life so smoothly that even she might begin to wonder which of them was real.

The mirror in my room no longer showed me Eleanor Ashcombe's hollow-eyed desperation or Mrs. Westmore's careful respectability. Instead, it reflected something new and dangerous and infinitely more beautiful: the possibility of becoming someone who deserved everything she had ever wanted, someone who would never again be denied what was rightfully hers.

Someone who was almost ready to claim her inheritance.

# Chapter 12: The Husband's Glance

## "The Beginning of Notice"

There are different kinds of glances, and I have catalogued them all with the methodical precision of a naturalist studying species of birds—each type distinct in its purpose, its duration, its particular quality of attention or neglect.

The dismissive glance is perhaps the most common, especially toward women dressed in black serge and sensible shoes, the uniform of those who work for their living and are therefore beneath the notice of those who do not. It slides across you like water off glass, acknowledging your physical presence while denying your humanity, marking you as part of the furniture—useful when needed, invisible when not.

The indifferent glance is more habitual, more unconscious—the automatic sweep of eyes that sees without registering, the mechanical acknowledgment that trained servants learn to expect from their employers. It belongs to men wrapped in the comfortable cocoon of their own concerns, who look at governesses and housemaids the way they might glance at wallpaper: present but unremarkable, functional but forgettable.

Then there is the wary glance—Clara's, when she began to sense that I was not quite what I appeared to be, when some instinct she could not name started whispering warnings that her rational mind was not yet ready to hear. It carries the particular tension of someone who suspects they are being watched, studied, catalogued in return, though they cannot quite put their finger on why the feeling persists.

And then there was his.

Edward Harrowby had glanced at me perhaps a hundred times during my first weeks in his house—brief, automatic acknowledgments when we passed in hallways or when I was present during family meals, the kind of perfunctory notice that any well-bred gentleman would offer to any respectable servant in his employ. But these were not truly his glances, not expressions of his individual attention or interest. They belonged to a distracted father checking that his children were properly supervised, to a tired husband who had learned to trust that domestic arrangements would function smoothly without his direct involvement, to a man so wrapped in the comfortable tedium of responsibility and routine that he had stopped seeing the people who made his life possible.

Until one morning in late November, when London's habitual mist was falling like grey gauze against the conservatory windows, he saw me—really saw me—for the first time since that long-ago evening when I had refused his proposal and set both our lives on paths we could never have imagined.

I stood by the glass doors that opened onto the garden, Margaret nestled in my arms after a tumble that had left her cheek scraped and red from contact with the gravel path. Her small fingers were curled into the collar of my dress with the desperate grip that children use when they need comfort more than they need dignity, and I was murmuring the kind of soft, wordless sounds that mothers make to soothe hurt without drawing attention to weakness.

Edward entered the conservatory in his usual way—mid-step, mid-thought, his mind clearly occupied with whatever business matter had brought him home earlier than expected. But the moment his eyes found us, everything changed.

He stopped.

He stared.

It was not long—perhaps three seconds, maybe four, the kind of pause that could easily be dismissed as the natural reaction of a father checking on his injured child. But I felt it like a physical touch, that sudden sharp focus of masculine attention, the weight of scrutiny that had nothing to do with paternal concern and everything to do with the dangerous recognition of something that should not be there, something that demanded explanation.

His glance slid from Margaret's tear-stained face to mine and stayed a fraction too long—long enough for me to see the precise moment when casual notice transformed into something more complex, more troubling, more alive with possibility than either of us was prepared to acknowledge.

I kept my expression soft and maternal, the picture of a devoted governess tending to her young charge with appropriate concern and competence. But beneath that carefully constructed surface, I felt heat rise in the hollow of my neck, a flush of awareness that had nothing to do with the warmth of the conservatory and everything to do with the sudden, electric recognition that I was no longer invisible to him, no longer just another piece of domestic machinery that functioned smoothly in the background of his comfortable life.

He said nothing, gave no outward sign that anything had changed. After what felt like an eternity but was probably only a heartbeat, he simply walked on, continuing whatever errand had brought him to that part of the house. But the moment hung in the air between us like smoke, impossible to ignore even though we both pretended it had never happened.

Later that same day, fate or fortune arranged another encounter. I was descending the main staircase when he appeared at the bottom, his hand resting on the polished banister as he prepared to climb to his study. The afternoon light streaming through the tall windows caught the silver threading through his dark hair, and for just a moment he looked like the man who had proposed to me all those years ago—younger, more hopeful, less burdened by the weight of a life that had settled into comfortable but passionless routine.

I curtsied as I had been trained to do, modestly, with my eyes cast downward in the perfect pantomime of appropriate deference. It was an act I had perfected through countless repetitions, the precise balance of respect and self-effacement that marked a servant who knew her place without being servile about it.

But again, he paused.

"Mrs. Westmore," he said, and something in his tone made my name sound like a question, as if he were testing the weight of it on his tongue, as if he suspected it might not be quite what it claimed to be.

"Sir," I replied, lifting my eyes just enough to meet his gaze while maintaining the proper distance that should exist between employer and employee. I did not smile—not quite—but I allowed something warmer than mere politeness to colour my expression, a hint of the woman who existed beneath the governess's careful facade.

"You have done wonders with the children," he said, and there was genuine warmth in his voice, the kind of approval that any dedicated servant would treasure. "They seem... happier. More settled."

"Thank you, sir," I said, allowing a note of quiet pride to enter my voice. "They are... they were lonely, I think. But they are lovely children, truly. It is a privilege to help guide their education."

A silence stretched between us then, heavier and more charged than such a simple exchange should have warranted. His eyes held mine for a heartbeat longer than strict propriety allowed, and in that extended moment I saw something I had not expected: genuine interest, the kind of masculine curiosity that had nothing to do with children's education and everything to do with the woman who was providing it.

Then, as if suddenly remembering himself, he stepped aside to let me pass and continued up the stairs, leaving me to complete my descent with legs that felt less steady than they should have and a heart that was beating far too quickly for such an innocent encounter.

That night, lying in my narrow bed with the sounds of the sleeping house around me, I replayed every second of our brief conversation—the tone of his voice when he spoke my name, the almost-kindness in his expression, the way his eyes had lingered on my face as if trying to solve some puzzle he had not even realized he was working on. There had been something unspoken in that moment, something that hummed in the air between us like a tuning fork struck against crystal, the beginning of something neither of us was quite ready to acknowledge but both of us had felt.

I had not planned for this part of my campaign—not exactly. My obsession had always been Clara, the life she inhabited, the role I was destined to claim as my own. She was the prize, the life I had been cheated out of, the woman whose place I intended to take through whatever means necessary. But Edward was part of the architecture of that life, the foundation upon which everything else was built. He had constructed this house, sired these children, wrapped Clara in silk and safety and the comfortable assumption that she would always be cherished, always be protected, always be the centre of his domestic universe.

To truly become Clara, to claim not just her position but her reality, I could not ignore him. I could not treat him as merely an obstacle to be worked around or a problem to be solved through clever manoeuvring. He was the key to everything—the source of the money that made this life possible, the man whose love and attention transformed a woman from mere wife to beloved companion, the person whose approval or disapproval could make the difference between security and disaster.

To claim Clara's life completely, I would have to unravel him first.

I began small, with the subtle artistry that I had learned during my months of careful observation and patient transformation. Not seduction—that would have been too obvious, too crude, too likely to trigger the kind of alarm bells that would destroy everything I had worked toward. Instead, I gave him silence with just enough soul behind it to make him wonder what I might be thinking during those quiet moments when our paths crossed.

I arranged to be in places where he might overhear me laughing with the children, my voice bright with genuine affection and the kind of joy that adults often lose but remember wistfully when they encounter it in others. I walked the hallways at times when he might notice, moving with the particular grace I had learned from watching Clara, carrying myself like someone worthy of attention even when dressed in governess's grey.

I borrowed Clara's perfume—just a touch, just enough to leave a whisper of lavender and lemon verbena in the air when I passed, a scent that would register in his subconscious without his understanding why the governess suddenly seemed to carry with her the ghost of more expensive pleasures.

Most importantly, I made myself someone he could wonder about. Not obviously, not in ways that would seem inappropriate or threatening, but subtly, gradually, letting him glimpse just enough depth beneath the surface to make him curious about what else might be hidden there.

And he was curious. I could see it in the way his attention began to focus when I entered rooms where he was present, the way his conversations with Clara sometimes paused when I passed by, the growing frequency of those moments when our eyes would meet across the dinner table or in doorways and linger just a fraction longer than mere courtesy required.

The second time I caught his gaze studying me with real interest, it lasted noticeably longer than the first. He was watching me through the reflection in the dining room mirror while Clara spoke about some social engagement she was planning, his attention ostensibly on his wife's words but his eyes tracking my movements as I helped Margaret with her napkin, as I quietly corrected Henry's posture, as I performed the hundred small tasks that made family meals run smoothly.

He did not blink, did not look away when he realized I might notice his scrutiny. Instead, he simply continued watching with the frank appreciation of a man who had suddenly realized that something interesting was happening right under his nose, something that deserved closer examination.

I pretended not to see, of course. I continued my work with the children, maintained my conversations with Clara, played my role as the perfect governess who was far too focused on her duties to notice the master of the house studying her with increasing fascination.

The third significant encounter came in the library on a rainy Thursday afternoon when the children and I had sought refuge from the weather in the warm, book-lined sanctuary that was Edward's particular domain. I was reading aloud to Margaret—something from Grimm's fairy tales, my voice pitched low and melodic in the way that makes even familiar stories seem magical—when she gradually succumbed to the combined effects of the warm fire and my soothing narration, curling up in my lap like a kitten and drifting off to sleep.

Edward entered the room quietly, perhaps not wanting to disturb what he had heard from the hallway and lingered in the doorway for a long moment before stepping inside. I did not acknowledge his presence immediately, did not want to wake Margaret with sudden movement or conversation, but I was acutely aware of him watching us—the governess and the sleeping child, a picture of domestic tranquillity that might have stepped from a painting of idealized motherhood.

"Do you read often, Mrs. Westmore?" he asked finally, his voice pitched just above a whisper out of consideration for his sleeping daughter.

"Every day, sir," I replied softly, my hand moving in gentle circles on Margaret's back to keep her settled. "Children deserve stories more than anyone, I think. They still believe in the possibility of magic, of transformation, of lives that can be completely changed by courage and determination."

He nodded slowly, and when he smiled, it was with the kind of warmth that transforms a face from merely handsome to genuinely appealing. "You have a gift for it. I could hear you from my study—Margaret was completely entranced."

"She has a wonderful imagination," I said, allowing pride to colour my voice. "Both children do. They simply needed someone to nurture it, to help them see that the world is larger and more interesting than they had been led to believe."

Something bloomed inside me then dark and thrilling and infinitely dangerous. Not love, certainly not that. What I felt for Edward Harrowby had nothing to do with the tender emotions that poets celebrated and everything to do with power, with the intoxicating recognition that I was succeeding in ways I had hardly dared to hope.

It was not even desire, not in any simple physical sense. It was possibility—the slow, sweet realization that the man who had once asked for my hand, who I could have had if I had been less proud, less principled, less foolishly naive about the way the world really worked, was beginning to see me again not as a servant but as a woman worth noticing, worth wondering about, worth wanting.

Now, after years of watching his domestic happiness from the outside, after months of careful preparation and patient transformation, I could see his eyes beginning to follow me across rooms with the particular quality of attention that meant he was asking questions he could not yet put into words, questions about who I really was and why his governess seemed to carry with her hints of depths that no mere employee should possess.

But I had the answer to those unspoken questions.

I was the answer—the woman he should have waited for, the life he should have chosen, the future he had let slip away through his own impatience and Clara's convenient willingness to accept what was offered instead of demanding what she deserved.

And soon, very soon, he would see it too.

The careful architecture of Clara's life was beginning to shift, stone by stone, glance by glance, moment by charged moment. She still sat at his breakfast table and shared his bed and carried his name, but she was no longer the only woman in his world worthy of masculine attention.

Now there was Mrs. Westmore—mysterious, compelling, just familiar enough to trouble his dreams and just different enough to make him wonder why the governess seemed to understand his children better than their mother did, why her laugh sounded like music he had heard before but could not quite place, why her presence in his house had begun to feel less like employment and more like homecoming.

The first cracks were appearing in the foundation of his marriage, hairline fractures that Clara had not yet noticed but that I could see spreading with the satisfied attention of an architect watching her carefully planned demolition proceed exactly according to schedule.

Soon, very soon, those cracks would widen into chasms. And when they did, I would be there—patient, devoted, indispensable Mrs. Westmore—ready to offer him everything Clara never could, everything he had lost when he settled for second-best instead of waiting for the woman who would have been worth any price, any wait, any sacrifice he might have been asked to make.

The husband's glance had become the husband's attention.

Next would come the husband's heart.

And then, finally, everything else would follow.

# Chapter 13: Seeds of Doubt

## "The Gentle Undermining"

Doubt is not a hammer that shatters confidence with a single devastating blow—it is a whisper, soft and persistent as morning mist, seeping into the smallest cracks in a person's certainty about themselves and their world. It does not break the structure of a life with dramatic violence; instead, it seeps into the mortar that holds everything together, working its way between the stones of routine and assumption with the patient persistence of water finding weakness in a foundation.

It waits, growing quietly in the dark spaces where fear lives, feeding on small inconsistencies and minor failures until it becomes strong enough to work real damage.

And then, one day when you least expect it, when you have almost forgotten it was there at all, a wall cracks.

I began gently, with the delicate touch of a surgeon who understands that healing sometimes requires the precise infliction of controlled harm.

It started with something as simple as a misplaced appointment in Clara's leather-bound calendar—the kind of small domestic oversight that could happen to anyone, the sort of minor confusion that busy women experience when managing the complex choreography of upper-class social obligations. A dinner invitation moved from Thursday to Tuesday without her knowledge, leaving her to dress for guests who would not arrive. An afternoon tea with Lady Pemberton that somehow never made it into her daily schedule, resulting in an elderly woman sitting in the salon for twenty minutes while Clara remained upstairs, completely unaware that she was expected elsewhere.

I said nothing about these incidents, of course—not immediately. That would have been far too obvious, too crude an approach for the delicate work I was undertaking. Instead, I offered only the slightest tilt of my head when Edward asked about the confusion, a barely perceptible furrow of my brow that suggested sympathetic concern rather than accusation.

"You didn't remind me that Clara had changed the dinner to tonight?" he might ask, his voice carrying the particular exasperation of a man who prided himself on social punctuality, who understood that such oversights reflected poorly on his household's management.

And Clara, caught between confusion and growing fluster, would stammer her response: "I was certain I mentioned it. Didn't I tell you at breakfast? I could have sworn..." Her voice would trail off as she realized that her certainty was not shared by anyone else present, that her memory was being contradicted by the evidence of empty chairs and cold dishes.

I was always nearby during these moments—close enough to witness the confusion, to register the growing tension, to offer subtle support that somehow managed to highlight the problem even as it appeared to solve it. But I was never in the room when the actual failures occurred, never present at the moment when Clara forgot to pass along important information or failed to keep track of social commitments that had once been second nature to her.

When the children asked for their mother and she could not be found—perhaps because she was lying down with another of her increasingly frequent headaches, or because she had stepped out to the garden to clear her head and lost track of time—I appeared with the calm competence that crises demand. "She's resting, darlings," I would say in the soothing tone I had perfected, "and you know how important it is that Mama gets her rest. Why don't we take our reading lesson in the garden instead? The fresh air will do us all good."

Margaret began coming to me first when she scraped her knees or bumped her head, seeking comfort from arms that were always available, always ready to provide the immediate attention that small injuries require. Henry started bringing me questions that should have gone to Clara—about his lessons, about permission for various activities, about the thousand small decisions that make up a child's daily life. I always answered warmly, with the kind of engaged interest that children crave, but I was careful never to appear possessive or to suggest that I was deliberately usurping Clara's maternal role.

Let them drift naturally, I told myself. Let her feel the gradual erosion of her central position in their lives without being able to point to any specific transgression, any obvious manipulation that might explain why her children were slowly turning to someone else for the care and attention they had once sought from her.

Then came the stories—carefully crafted tales that carried meaning beneath their innocent surfaces like poison wrapped in sugar.

One evening, while Clara sat in the parlour with her head in her hands, suffering from what she increasingly called her "nerves"—those mysterious feminine ailments that seemed to strike women of her class with alarming frequency—I settled into the nursery for the children's bedtime story with deliberate purpose.

"Once upon a time," I began, my voice taking on the hypnotic cadence that made even familiar tales seem magical, "there was a beautiful queen who had everything a woman could desire—pearls that glowed like captured moonlight, gowns that rustled like autumn leaves, a golden cradle for her precious baby, and a palace filled with people who loved and served her faithfully."

Margaret snuggled deeper into my lap, her small body warm and trusting against mine, while Henry leaned forward with the intense concentration that children bring to stories that capture their imagination.

"But one day," I continued, my fingers moving in gentle circles through Margaret's silky hair, "the queen began to forget things. At first, it was only small details—the names of distant stars, the words to songs she had known since childhood. Her courtiers thought nothing of it, for queens have many important matters to occupy their minds, and such minor lapses seemed perfectly natural."

Henry's eyes were fixed on my face with the particular intensity that suggested he was listening to more than just words, that some part of him recognized the deeper currents running beneath this seemingly innocent tale.

"But as the days passed, the forgetting grew worse. The queen forgot the names of her dearest friends, lost track of important appointments, could not remember which of her beautiful gowns she had worn the day before. And one terrible morning, she woke up and could not remember how to find her way home through the corridors of her own palace."

"That's not a real story," Henry said, his young voice sharp with suspicion. At nine, he was old enough to recognize when adults were using fairy tales to communicate truths too complex or troubling for direct statement. "Queens don't forget their own homes."

I smiled at him with the particular warmth I reserved for children who showed signs of unusual intelligence. "Isn't it real? Sometimes the truest things we know sound exactly like stories, don't you think? And sometimes stories help us understand things that are too complicated to explain any other way."

When the children told Clara about the tale the next day—as I had known they would, with the innocent transparency that makes children such effective messengers—she laughed with the brittle, too-quick sound that had become increasingly frequent in her conversation.

"What a strange little tale," she said, her voice carrying an edge of nervous irritation that she probably thought she was concealing. "Rather... ominous for a bedtime story, don't you think?

Hardly the sort of thing to give children pleasant dreams."

"Children are drawn to mystery," I replied with the calm authority of someone who had spent considerable time studying child psychology. "They find comfort in stories that acknowledge that the world can be confusing and unpredictable, because it helps them make sense of their own experiences. They're much more resilient than we often give them credit for."

Clara frowned but said nothing more, though I could see the wheels turning behind her eyes, the growing recognition that perhaps there had been more to the story than innocent entertainment, that maybe the governess she had welcomed into her home was not quite as simple and straightforward as she had initially appeared.

Days passed, and I found increasingly creative ways to interfere with the smooth operation of Clara's daily routine. Her silver hairpins—the ones she always placed on her dressing table in a specific pattern that helped her prepare for social calls—would be moved just slightly, not missing but out of place in ways that made her question her own memory of where she had left them. Her silk slippers would not be where she remembered taking them off, appearing instead in locations that made no logical sense, that could not be explained by the normal movement of servants tidying the household.

Once, when I knew she was struggling with the increasing anxiety that was making sleep elusive, I replaced her nightly bottle of laudanum tincture—the mild opiate that Dr. Morrison had prescribed for what he diplomatically called her "feminine nervous complaints"—with a weaker preparation that would provide less relief from the racing thoughts that kept her awake until the early hours of the morning.

When she complained to Edward that someone had tampered with her medicine, that the usual dose was no longer effective, she accused the housemaid of either carelessness or deliberate interference. I stepped forward immediately to defend the girl, my voice warm with indignation at the injustice of such an accusation.

"Mary would never do such a thing," I said firmly. "She's been nothing but conscientious in all her duties, and she's far too experienced to make mistakes with medications. Perhaps Dr. Morrison prepared this batch differently, or perhaps the apothecary made an error in mixing the ingredients."

Clara apologized to the maid with obvious reluctance, then spent the remainder of the evening in wounded silence, her eyes following me with growing suspicion even as she could find no logical reason to blame me for problems that seemed to have simple, innocent explanations.

Edward's questions about his wife's behaviour became more pointed as these incidents accumulated, his concern sharpening into something that looked uncomfortably like doubt.

"She seems unusually tired lately," I offered gently when he sighed heavily after Clara forgot the names of two important luncheon guests, leaving him to stumble through introductions with the embarrassed awkwardness of a man who prided himself on social competence. "The children are demanding at this age, and I've known many ladies who suffer tremendously after childbirth—the effects can linger for years, affecting memory and concentration in ways that are quite distressing."

He gave me a long, searching look, his eyes studying my face as if trying to read some deeper meaning in my carefully neutral expression. "She's not losing her mind," he said—not really to me, not as part of our conversation, but more to himself, as if voicing the fear might somehow make it less real, less possible.

"No," I agreed softly, my voice warm with sympathy and understanding. "Of course not. She's simply... overwhelmed. It happens to the best of us when life becomes too much to manage all at once."

But the seed was there now, planted in the fertile soil of his growing concern, watered by each new incident of forgetfulness or confusion, nurtured by the growing contrast between his wife's increasing fragility and his governess's unshakeable competence.

I let it root slowly, feeding it with carefully timed glances and meaningful silences, with the occasional well-placed phrase delivered with just the right mixture of concern and discretion: "She seems very pale lately, don't you think? I'm sure it's nothing serious, but perhaps Dr. Morrison should be consulted." Or: "The children mentioned that she was crying again last night—poor darlings, I didn't want to worry them with questions, but they seemed quite distressed by it."

Each comment was designed to sound like the natural observation of a caring employee who had only the family's best interests at heart, someone who was perhaps more attuned to the subtle signs of distress than a busy husband whose attention was necessarily divided between domestic concerns and business obligations.

Clara began to pace during the long afternoon hours when social calls were impossible, and her various charitable committees were not in session. She would walk the corridors of her own house like a restless spirit, her steps quick and nervous, her hands fluttering from object to object without seeming to find the peace or occupation she was seeking. She forgot more names, more appointments, more of the thousand small details that had once been the foundation of her identity as a competent woman managing a complex household.

And most importantly—most dangerously for the careful life she had built—she began to notice me with the sharp attention that comes from sensing a threat you cannot quite identify or articulate.

"You're everywhere," she said to me one afternoon, her voice carrying an edge of accusation that she was not quite ready to voice directly. "Always watching. Always... smiling.

Sometimes I feel as though you know more about what's happening in my house than I do."

I widened my eyes with the innocent surprise of someone who could not imagine what she might mean by such a strange observation. "I'm only doing what you've asked of me, ma'am. Caring for the children, helping with household coordination when needed, trying to make your life easier rather than more complicated. Unless I've misunderstood my duties somehow?"

The question hung in the air between us, a challenge disguised as uncertainty, forcing her to either make specific accusations she could not support or retreat into the appearance of paranoid suspicion.

"No," she said after a long pause, her voice deflated by the recognition that she had no reasonable complaint to make against someone who had been nothing but helpful and professional. "No, I suppose not."

But her lips tightened with frustration, and her fingers twitched with the nervous energy of someone who knew something was wrong but could not put their finger on exactly what it might be.

And when Edward entered the room at that precise moment—as I had carefully timed his arrival by tracking the sounds of his movement through the house—and asked his usual question about the children's welfare and daily activities, he looked at me for his answer rather than at his wife.

It was only for a moment, barely perceptible to anyone not watching for such signs. But it was enough to mark the precise instant when the balance of power in that household shifted, when the man who had once trusted his wife to manage their domestic sphere began to rely on someone else for information about his own family's daily life.

Clara saw it too—I could tell by the way her breath caught, by the flush that rose in her cheeks, by the sudden tightening around her eyes that spoke of a wound deeper than any physical injury.

The seeds of doubt were not only planted now—they were beginning to sprout, sending up tender green shoots that would soon grow into the kind of suspicions that destroy marriages from within, that make people question not just their partners but their own perceptions, their own sanity, their own right to trust what they think they know about the people closest to them.

Soon, very soon, those fragile shoots would become strong enough to crack the foundation of everything Clara Harrowby believed about her life, her marriage, and her place in the world she had thought belonged to her.

And when that happened, I would be there—patient, understanding, indispensable Mrs. Westmore—ready to step into whatever space her collapse might leave behind.

# Chapter 14: The Poison in Petals

## "Slow Illness, Careful Hands"

They say a woman's mind can wither under the pressure of silence, that solitude and neglect can drive even the strongest spirit to madness through sheer isolation. But they are wrong about the mechanism, wrong about the precise nature of the cruelty that breaks a human soul.

It is not silence that destroys her.

It is being unbelieved.

It is the slow, systematic erosion of trust in her own perceptions, the careful dismantling of her confidence in what she knows to be true, the deliberate cultivation of doubt until she no longer trusts even her most basic senses. It is watching the people she loves most look at her with pity instead of concern, with dismissal instead of attention, with the particular brand of masculine patience that treats feminine distress as inherently unreliable, inherently suspect.

Clara began to fall ill in June, when the roses in her garden were at their most magnificent and the London air was soft with the promise of summer—though "fall ill" suggests a natural process, a random misfortune that struck without warning or cause. What happened to Clara was far more deliberate than illness, far more artful than accident.

It started with dizziness that came without explanation—a sudden loss of equilibrium that would strike her in the middle of conversations, leaving her gripping the back of chairs or the edges of tables while the room seemed to tilt around her like the deck of a ship in heavy seas. Then came the tremors, fine shaking in her hands that made her teacup rattle against its saucer, that caused her pen to skip across the page when she tried to write letters, that left her cursive looking like the work of someone much older or much sicker than she appeared to be.

The shivering fits were perhaps the most distressing—sudden waves of cold that would wash over her even when she sat in the bright afternoon sun streaming through the conservatory windows, leaving her wrapped in shawls and blankets while everyone around her complained of the heat. Her eyes began to take on a glassy quality that no one else seemed to notice, a distant look as if she were seeing things that existed just beyond the edge of normal vision.

She complained that the walls whispered to her in voices too soft to understand but too persistent to ignore. She said the floor shifted beneath her feet, that solid objects seemed to swim and waver when she tried to focus on them, that familiar rooms in her own house had begun to feel foreign and threatening.

Edward dismissed these complaints as nerves—the same feminine hysteria that physicians had been diagnosing for centuries whenever women reported symptoms that could not be easily explained or conveniently treated. Dr. Morrison, when summoned for consultation, concurred with this assessment after a brief examination that consisted mainly of taking her pulse and asking questions about her monthly cycles and emotional state.

"A common condition among ladies of her station," he pronounced with the confident authority of a man who had never experienced what he was so casually diagnosing. "The pressures of managing a household, raising children, maintaining social obligations—it can overwhelm the delicate feminine constitution. Rest, mild exercise, perhaps a tonic to strengthen the nerves."

But I believed her.

I told her I did, sitting beside her in the parlour with her trembling hand clasped in both of mine, my voice warm with sympathy and understanding.

"You must rest," I said with the gentle firmness of someone who genuinely cared about her welfare. "You're carrying too much, trying to be everything to everyone. It's no wonder your body is rebelling."

I brought her chamomile tea to soothe her nerves and warm milk laced with valerian to help her sleep through the nights that had become increasingly restless and full of strange dreams. I insisted she take her tonics regularly—the ones I had begun to alter so subtly that even I sometimes forgot which bottles contained the original preparations and which had been enhanced with my own additions.

Belladonna, extracted from the deadly nightshade that grew wild in the forgotten corners of London's parks and cemetery grounds. Not enough to kill—never enough to be obvious to anyone who might think to look for such things. But enough to blur the edges of reality, to make the boundary between waking and dreaming permeable, to create the kind of symptoms that could be dismissed as hysteria while slowly poisoning the mind from within.

The beautiful irony was that belladonna had once been used by fashionable ladies to dilate their pupils, to create the wide-eyed look that men found so alluring. Now I was using it to make Clara appear mad; to steal away her clarity one carefully measured drop at a time.

She began forgetting words—not important words, not the kind of memory loss that might have prompted immediate medical attention, but small failures of language that seemed like the natural result of stress and exhaustion. Common nouns would slip away from her just when she needed them most, leaving her grasping for sounds that had once come as naturally as breathing.

Once, in front of the children during their afternoon tea, she pointed at the tall grandfather clock that had stood in the hallway for as long as any of them could remember and called it "the loud chair." Henry blinked with the confusion of a child whose world has suddenly stopped making sense, while Margaret laughed with the cruel innocence that children bring to adult failures they don't understand.

I said nothing, but I felt my hands tighten around my teacup so hard that I was afraid the porcelain might crack, revealing the tremor of excitement I couldn't quite suppress. This was working. My careful campaign was succeeding beyond my most optimistic hopes, transforming Clara from the competent woman I had observed and envied into something fragile and unreliable, something that needed care rather than providing it.

Later that same day, I found her in the rose garden, barefoot and sobbing, crouched beneath the thorned archway that had been her pride when the season began. Her fine silk stockings were torn and muddy, her skirts stained with earth and grass, her carefully arranged hair fallen loose around her shoulders in a way that made her look wild, unhinged, dangerous to herself.

"They're lying to me," she whispered when she saw me approaching, her voice broken with the kind of despair that comes from being betrayed by everything you once trusted. "Even the plants. Even the roses. Nothing is what it seems."

I knelt beside her on the damp ground, heedless of what the moisture might do to my own dress and smoothed her hair back from her damp temples with the gentle touch of someone who genuinely cared about her suffering.

"No one is lying to you, Clara," I said softly. "You're ill, darling. Your mind is playing tricks on you, but that doesn't mean the people who love you are your enemies."

"You are!" she snapped with sudden fury, then immediately looked ashamed of the outburst, her face crumpling with the guilt that came from lashing out at the one person who seemed to believe her distress was real. "I didn't mean—I don't know why I said that—"

"Yes, you did mean it," I replied with the calm understanding that comes from recognizing truth even when it's inconvenient. "But it's the illness speaking, not you. The real Clara would never accuse someone who's trying to help her."

She recoiled from me just slightly at that word—illness. It struck her like a physical blow, the clinical term that transformed her from a woman experiencing something real and frightening into a patient whose perceptions could not be trusted, whose reality was suspect by definition.

That night, I brewed her a new tea blend, something stronger than what I had been giving her before, laced with extracts that would deepen the confusion and make her even more dependent on my care. I sat beside her bed while she drank it, humming a lullaby I had heard her sing to Margaret months ago, a sweet melody that she had used to soothe her daughter through nightmares and childhood fears.

She blinked slowly, her eyes struggling to focus on my face in the lamplight. "You know that song?"

"I must have heard it from you," I said with innocent surprise. "You hum it so often, especially when you're working in the garden or arranging flowers. It's become one of the sounds I associate with this house, with feeling safe and cared for."

She never had hummed that song outside the nursery, had probably forgotten she knew it at all. But she no longer trusted her memory, no longer felt confident about what she had or hadn't done, what was real and what might be the product of her increasingly unreliable mind.

By July, she had stopped attending the Sunday luncheons that had once been the highlight of her social week, the gatherings with other ladies of her class where she had found companionship and purpose in discussing charitable works and community concerns. Her friends began to whisper about her absence, creating explanations that ranged from financial troubles to marital difficulties to the kind of nervous breakdown that fashionable women sometimes suffered when the pressures of maintaining appearances became too much to bear.

Her own reflection in mirrors began to frighten her, as if the woman looking back was a stranger wearing her face, someone she didn't recognize and couldn't trust. She started avoiding the full-length glass in her dressing room, asking me to help her with her hair and dress without letting her see the results of our work.

She confided in me about the hallucinations that were becoming more frequent and more disturbing.

"Sometimes I see someone standing behind me when I look in the glass," she whispered, her voice barely audible, her eyes darting around the room as if checking for eavesdroppers. "A woman in dark clothes, watching me. But when I turn around, there's no one there. It's always just empty space."

I placed my hand over hers, feeling the tremor that had become constant, the fine shaking that spoke of a nervous system under siege.

"It's only shadows playing tricks," I said with gentle reassurance. "They can seem very real when one is tired and overwrought. Dr. Morrison said these kinds of experiences are quite common in cases of nervous exhaustion."

I began to escalate my campaign of small torments, replacing her beloved lavender oil with a harsh, acrid scent that made her recoil from her own pillows and linens. I moved her silver comb from its usual place on her dressing table, then replaced it in a different location with a few strands of unfamiliar hair wound around its teeth. Once, I burned the edges of a page from her private diary—nothing important, just idle thoughts about the weather and social calls—and placed it beneath her pillow where she would find it and wonder how it had gotten there, what it might mean, who might have access to her most private thoughts.

She began to question her sanity out loud, voicing the fears that had been growing in the dark corners of her mind.

"I think someone is doing this to me," she said one afternoon, her eyes wild with the particular desperation of someone who knows the truth but can't make anyone believe it. "Moving things, changing things, watching me. Someone wants me to think I'm losing my mind."

"You're safe here," I said, pulling a soft blanket up around her trembling shoulders, tucking it around her with the care one might show a child. "I'm here, and I won't let anything hurt you."

That part was true, in its way. I was always there—constant, vigilant, devoted to her care with the single-minded attention that she had been lacking from everyone else in her life. I was there when Edward was at his office, when the children were occupied with their lessons, when the servants were busy with their duties. I was there in the spaces between other people's attention, filling the gaps in her care with my own relentless presence.

One afternoon in late July, Edward came to me with the defeated expression of a man who had run out of explanations for what was happening to his wife.

"She's not herself," he said quietly, his voice heavy with grief and frustration. "She's... fading. Disappearing a little more each day. I don't know how to help her, and I'm not sure the doctors understand what's wrong."

"I'm so sorry," I whispered, allowing genuine sympathy to colour my voice. After all, I was sorry—sorry that it had come to this, sorry that Clara's strength had made such extreme measures necessary, sorry that there had been no other way to claim what should have been mine from the beginning. "I've done everything I can think of, but she seems to be fighting battles that the rest of us can't see."

His eyes were full of something I couldn't quite read—shame, perhaps, or grief, or the kind of guilt that comes from knowing you've failed someone who depended on you for protection.

"She used to be so sharp," he murmured, more to himself than to me. "So sure of herself, so confident in her judgments. Now she second-guesses everything, questions her own perceptions, acts as if she can't trust her own mind."

"She's still the same woman underneath," I said carefully, choosing my words with the precision of a surgeon selecting instruments. "But sometimes even the strongest people bend under pressure, especially when they feel alone in their struggle, when they don't have the support, they need to fight back."

He said nothing to contradict this gentle accusation, didn't deny the implication that his absence, his dismissal of her concerns, his failure to provide the understanding she needed had contributed to her decline.

He didn't deny it because he couldn't. Because part of him knew it was true.

And in that moment of recognition, I knew I had him. Not completely, not yet, but enough to continue the work I had begun, enough to ensure that when Clara finally disappeared entirely from the life she had built, there would be someone ready to step into the space she left behind.

By August, Clara had lost all appetite, pushing food around her plate without eating, growing thinner and more fragile with each passing day. Her skin had taken on a waxy quality that spoke of poor nutrition and chronic illness, while her fingers trembled constantly, like leaves in a wind that only she could feel.

I helped her dress in the mornings, my hands gentle and competent as I fastened buttons she could no longer manage, as I arranged her hair in styles that would hide the worst effects of her condition. I combed the tangles from her hair with infinite patience, watched her slip further and further from the surface of herself like someone drowning in slow motion.

"I don't know who I am anymore," she said to me one morning, tears streaming down her face as she stared at her reflection in the hand mirror I held for her. "I look at myself and see a stranger. I try to remember who I used to be, what I used to care about, and it's all just... empty. Like looking into a well with no bottom."

I touched her cheek with the tenderness of a mother comforting a frightened child, feeling the fever heat that had become constant, the result of a body trying to fight off poison it couldn't identify.

"You're tired, my dear," I said with infinite compassion. "So very tired. But you don't have to carry the burden of remembering everything right now. Rest and let me remember for you. Let me be strong enough for both of us until you're well again."

And she let me.

She let me take over the small decisions and then the larger ones, let me become the keeper of her memories and the guardian of her daily life. She let me step into the spaces that her illness was creating, filling the gaps in her competence with my own steady presence.

She was disappearing, and I was becoming visible in direct proportion to her fading. Soon, very soon, there would be nothing left of Clara Harrowby but a shadow, a whisper, a memory of someone who had once lived in this house but could no longer manage the demands of existence.

And when that happened, when the last traces of her had been erased by the careful application of poison and patience, Mrs. Westmore would no longer be the governess.

She would simply be the woman who had saved this family when no one else could, the woman who had stepped forward when she was needed most, the woman who deserved to be loved and cherished and given everything that Clara had been too weak to hold onto.

The poison was working. The petals of belladonna were doing their slow, patient work.

And soon, the garden would be mine to tend.

# Chapter 15: The Disappearance

## "Into Fog and Silence"

It happened on a morning wrapped in fog so thick and unyielding that it seemed as though the world itself was holding its breath, waiting for something terrible and inevitable to unfold. The mist pressed against the windows of the Harrowby house like gray silk, muffling sounds and softening edges until reality took on the quality of a half-remembered dream.

I rose before dawn, before the servants began their quiet preparations for the day, before the children stirred in their beds and called for water or milk or someone to chase away the shadows that lingered in the corners of their rooms. The floors beneath my slippers creaked softly as I moved through the darkened corridors, but the sounds were not protests—they were agreements, the house itself conspiring in what was about to occur.

The door to Clara's room stood slightly ajar, as it had for the past several nights. She had stopped bothering to close it completely, stopped caring about privacy or the appearance of control that a firmly shut door suggested. Sleep had become her enemy rather than her refuge, bringing with it dreams that were more vivid and terrifying than her waking hours, visions that blurred the line between nightmare and reality until she could no longer distinguish between them.

The laudanum I had been leaving for her—carefully measured doses that were just strong enough to create dependency but not strong enough to provide real relief—had made sure that rest remained elusive, that her nights stretched endlessly while her days blurred together in a haze of confusion and mounting panic.

She sat in her chair by the window like a ghost of herself, draped in the paisley shawl that had once been one of her favourite possessions but now seemed to dwarf her shrinking frame. Her eyes were half-lidded with exhaustion and chemical fog, their once-bright intelligence dimmed to a glassy stare that seemed to see through the visible world into some darker realm beyond it.

Her hair, which she had once arranged with such meticulous care that every pin served both function and beauty, now hung in limp coils over her shoulders, unwashed and unbrushed, the dark strands clinging to her pale skin like seaweed on a drowning woman.

"Can't sleep," she murmured as I entered the room, her voice barely above a whisper, hoarse from disuse and the constant low-level terror that had become her natural state. "The walls keep breathing. In and out, in and out, like they're alive. And there are voices behind them, whispering things I can't quite understand."

I knelt beside her chair with the fluid grace I had perfected over months of practice, my movements conveying compassion and concern while my mind calculated distances and timing with the precision of a mathematician solving a complex equation.

"Then come with me," I said, my voice warm with the kind of maternal comfort that she had been craving, the understanding that no one else had bothered to offer. "Fresh air will clear your head. You'll feel so much better once you're away from these close, stuffy rooms."

She blinked slowly, her pupils dilated from the various substances I had been feeding her, her thoughts moving like honey through her poisoned consciousness. "Where would we go?"

"Just for a walk through the garden," I replied, already helping her to her feet with gentle but firm hands. "The fog will lift soon, and you'll be able to see the roses. You always loved the roses, remember? You used to say they were the only things that made sense in a world gone mad."

She didn't resist when I helped her stand, didn't question why I wrapped her heavy winter coat around her shoulders instead of the lighter cloak she usually preferred for morning walks, didn't ask why I guided her toward the back of the house, through the conservatory and out the garden gate, instead of through the front door where the servants might see us leaving together.

The fog outside was thick and cold, pressing around us like the embrace of something that had never been alive, never been warm, never known the touch of sunlight or the comfort of human companionship. It clung to Clara's coat and hair with an intimacy that made me think of burial shrouds, of winding sheets, of all the ways that the dead are wrapped and hidden from the sight of the living.

We didn't speak as we walked, but I could feel her leaning on me more heavily than usual, her body weak and trembling from months of careful poisoning, her legs unsteady on the familiar garden paths that had once been as natural to navigate as the corridors of her own house. My arm around her waist was firm and supportive, guiding her steps while my mind remained sharper and more focused than it had ever been, every sense alert to the precise moment when opportunity would present itself.

When we reached the edge of the formal gardens, where the carefully tended flower beds gave way to the wilder growth that marked the boundary of the estate, she began to falter. The woods behind the Harrowby property stretched into the fog like something from a fairy tale—not the kind with happy endings, but the older stories, the ones where children disappeared and were never found, where the forest kept its secrets buried beneath layers of fallen leaves and twisted roots.

"This isn't the garden," she said, her voice carrying the first note of real alarm I had heard from her in weeks, a flicker of the intelligence that had once made her formidable returning like a candle flame in a dark room.

"No," I agreed, my voice calm and matter of fact, no longer bothering with pretence or gentle deception. "It isn't."

Her body went rigid against mine, every muscle tensing as some primitive instinct warned her that she was in mortal danger, that the woman who had been caring for her with such devotion was not what she appeared to be. Her breathing quickened, shallow and panicked, as her mind struggled to piece together fragments of suspicion and half-remembered warnings into something resembling understanding.

She turned to look at me then, and for the first time in months I saw her eyes clear completely, the fog of confusion and chemical interference lifting just enough to reveal the sharp intelligence that had once made her such a formidable manager of her household, such a devoted mother, such a worthy rival for the life I had always known should be mine.

"You," she whispered, the single word carrying with it the weight of terrible recognition, the awful understanding of exactly who had been destroying her from within, exactly whose hands had been feeding her poison disguised as medicine, exactly whose caring attention had been slowly erasing her from her own life. "You've been—you're the one who—"

"Yes," I said simply, allowing all pretence to drop away like a discarded mask, letting her see the truth of what I was, what I had always been, what I had become through months of patient work and careful planning.

There was no need to pretend anymore. No reason to maintain the fiction of Mrs. Westmore, the devoted governess, the woman who had appeared like an angel of mercy just when the family needed her most. Clara knew now, in these final moments of clarity, exactly what had been done to her and why, exactly who had been orchestrating her decline with such methodical precision.

She backed away from me, her feet tangling in the underbrush that grew thick and wild at the forest's edge, brambles catching at her coat and skirts like grasping fingers trying to hold her back from whatever fate awaited her in the grey depths of the woods.

"Why?" she asked, and her voice was stronger now, more like the woman she had been before I began my work of destruction. "Why did you do this to me? What did I ever do to deserve—"

I wanted to tell her the truth—that she had stolen the life that should have been mine, that she had married the man who had once asked for my hand, that she had claimed through passive acceptance what I had lost through stubborn pride. I wanted to scream at her that I could have been everything she was and more, that I would have loved Edward better, raised his children with more devotion, managed his household with greater skill and attention.

I wanted to explain that her only crime had been being in the right place at the right time with the right willingness to settle for whatever was offered instead of demanding what she deserved, that she had won by default what I had lost through the fatal mistake of believing that my worth should be recognized rather than simply accepted without question.

Instead, I simply said, "Because it's mine now."

The words fell between us like stones dropped into still water, creating ripples that would spread long after we were both gone from this place. She stared at me for a moment longer, her face cycling through expressions of disbelief, horror, and finally a kind of sad understanding that made her look older than her years, worn down by the recognition of how completely she had been betrayed by someone she had trusted.

She turned to run then, her survival instincts finally overriding the chemical confusion that had made her so easy to manipulate for so many months. But her legs betrayed her, weakened by poison and prolonged illness, unsteady on ground that seemed to shift and roll beneath her feet like the deck of a ship in heavy seas.

The belladonna and other substances I had been feeding her had done their work too well, leaving her body unable to respond to the desperate commands of her mind. She managed perhaps three steps before her knees buckled, sending her crashing to the forest floor with a muffled sound that was swallowed immediately by the thick fog and the patient silence of the trees.

Her hands scrabbled at the dirt and fallen leaves, trying to find purchase, trying to pull herself upright and continue her flight. But there was no strength left in her arms, no coordination in her movements, nothing but the desperate animal instinct to escape danger even when escape was no longer possible.

I stood over her fallen form and felt something that might have been pity if I had been a different person, if I had chosen a different path, if the world had arranged itself more fairly from the beginning. But pity was a luxury I could not afford, a weakness that would have made the necessary work impossible.

I didn't kill her—not directly, not with my own hands stained by obvious violence. That would have been crude, messy, the kind of thing that left evidence and raised questions that I was not prepared to answer.

Instead, I simply left her there.

I left her to the fog that pressed around us like a living thing, hungry and patient and utterly without mercy. I left her to the cold that was already seeping through her coat and into her bones, leeching away whatever warmth and strength remained in her failing body. I left her to the brambles and thorns that would wrap around her like a burial shroud as she tried to crawl—if she had the strength to crawl at all.

I walked back through the garden slowly, carefully, stopping to brush leaves and dirt from my skirts, to smooth my hair and compose my expression into something appropriate for the concerned employee returning from an early morning walk. Every step took me further from what I had done and closer to what I was about to become, each breath drawing me deeper into the new life that would begin the moment Clara's absence was discovered.

By the time the house began to stir with the familiar sounds of servants starting their daily routines and children waking to call for breakfast and attention, I was in the nursery, sitting in the rocking chair with Margaret in my lap while I brushed her fine hair into the neat plaits that would keep it tidy throughout the day.

When Edward came down to breakfast and asked where Clara was, I told him with perfect composure that she hadn't come down yet, that she had been having such trouble sleeping lately that perhaps it was best to let her rest until she woke naturally.

When the maid reported that Clara's bed was cold and untouched, that it appeared she had not slept there at all, I allowed my face to register appropriate concern while my mind calculated exactly how long to wait before suggesting that someone should look for her.

"She must have gone out early," I said, my voice carrying just the right note of worry. "You know how restless she's been lately, how the close air in the house seems to make her symptoms worse. Perhaps she needed some fresh air to clear her head."

We searched, of course. I made sure of it, organizing the servants into efficient teams that would cover every inch of the grounds, calling out Clara's name with apparent distress while pressing a handkerchief to my mouth as if I might weep from the strain of not knowing what had become of my dear mistress.

The police were summoned when our search proved fruitless. Neighbours were questioned about whether they had seen a woman in a dark coat walking alone in the early morning fog. But there was no trace of Clara Harrowby, no sign that she had ever existed except for the lingering scent of lavender in her bedroom and the silence that seemed to echo through rooms that had once been filled with her voice.

"She was not well," I said to Edward that evening as we sat in the parlour that had been Clara's domain, my eyes bright with unshed tears that spoke of genuine grief for a woman who had suffered so much before finding whatever peace awaited her in the foggy woods. "Her mind had been troubled for so long, and she spoke sometimes of feeling trapped, of wanting to escape from everything that was familiar. Perhaps she wandered off and became lost, or perhaps... perhaps she meant to leave us, to find some place where she could start over without the burden of her illness."

Edward shook his head with the stubborn denial of a man who could not accept that someone he loved might choose to abandon everything they had built together. "She wouldn't do that. Clara would never leave the children, no matter how confused or distressed she became. They were everything to her."

But his voice cracked as he spoke, betraying the doubt that was already growing in his mind, the terrible possibility that his wife's deteriorating mental state might have driven her to actions that the Clara he had married would never have contemplated.

I waited for the children to ask where their mother had gone, dreading and anticipating the moment when I would have to explain the inexplicable, when I would have to find words to comfort them for a loss, they were too young to understand. When Margaret finally voiced the question that had been building in her small chest like a sob waiting to escape, I gave her the smile I had been practicing, the expression of maternal warmth and infinite patience that a mother would wear when delivering news too terrible for complete honesty.

"She had to go away, darling," I said gently, gathering both children close to me on the sofa where Clara had once sat to read them bedtime stories. "Sometimes adults have to make very difficult choices, and your mama decided that she needed to find a place where she could get better, where her sickness couldn't hurt her anymore. But she loved you both so very, very much—more than all the stars in the sky, more than all the flowers in the garden."

They cried, of course. Great heaving sobs that shook their small bodies and left them gasping for breath between waves of grief that they could not yet name or understand. I held them against my chest and whispered the comforting lies that parents have been telling children since the beginning of time, the gentle fictions that make unbearable truths just bearable enough to survive.

That night, alone in the house that was now truly mine, I performed the ritual that marked my complete transformation from pretender to rightful occupant. I poured Clara's expensive French perfume onto my wrists and throat, feeling the cool liquid soak into my skin and carry with it the scent that would now be mine by right rather than theft.

I wrapped myself in her silk robe—the one embroidered with tiny roses that had been a wedding gift from Edward's mother, the one that had seemed like the height of luxury when I first glimpsed it hanging in her wardrobe. The fabric whispered against my skin like secrets, like promises, like the sound of a life finally claiming its proper place in the world.

I sat in her chair by the window, the one where she had spent so many hours gazing out at the garden she would never tend again and stared through the glass at the fog that still curled around the hedges like fingers reaching up from some underground realm where the displaced and forgotten made their home.

She was gone—lost in the mist and silence, claimed by the woods and the cold and the patient earth that accepts all offerings without judgment or question.

And I remained.

I remained to raise her children as my own, to comfort her husband in his grief, to step into the space she had left behind with such perfect seamlessness that soon even I might forget which of us had been born to this life and which had claimed it through will and patience and the kind of love that recognizes no boundaries between desire and destiny.

The fog outside was beginning to lift, revealing the familiar shapes of garden and house and the world beyond. But inside, in the warm lamplight of Clara's former sanctuary, everything had changed completely.

Mrs. Westmore the governess was gone, dissolved like mist in morning sunlight.

In her place sat the new mistress of the house unnamed as yet, undefined except by the absence she had created and the space she now filled. Soon enough, there would be discussions about what to call her, how to explain her presence to the children and the servants and the wider world that would need some story to make sense of the transformation.

But for now, in the quiet darkness of this first night of her new life, she simply existed—victorious, patient, and utterly, completely home.

# Chapter 16: Wearing Her Skin

## "Becoming the Ghost I Envied"

It's remarkable how quickly the world adjusts to an absence—how the space left by a missing person reshapes itself around whoever is willing to fill it, how memory becomes fluid when need demands adaptation, how the living unconsciously conspire to heal wounds they don't even realize exist by accepting whatever replacement presents itself with sufficient conviction.

Clara had not been gone a fortnight before the house began to reorient itself around me—subtly, quietly, like a compass needle finding true north after being disturbed by some temporary magnetic interference. The very architecture seemed to sigh with relief at having someone competent to organize its daily rhythms, someone who understood that homes require constant attention to maintain the illusion of effortless comfort that their inhabitants take for granted.

The children came to me first now with their scraped knees and troubled dreams, their innocent questions about why flowers die and where the sun goes at night. They sought my lap when thunder frightened them, my voice when bedtime stories were required, my judgment when disputes arose over toys or turns or the thousand small negotiations that make up childhood's social education. There was no conscious decision in this migration of trust—it simply happened, as naturally as water finding the lowest point in a landscape.

The servants, who had initially approached me with the careful uncertainty of people unsure about chain of command in a household suddenly without its mistress, gradually began to address me with a softness that bordered on reverence. They sensed something in my manner that commanded respect—not the brittle authority of someone grasping for power, but the quiet confidence of someone who had always belonged exactly where she found herself.

Mrs. Hartwell, the housekeeper who had served the family for nearly two decades, began bringing the daily domestic reports to me rather than waiting for Edward's sporadic attention to household matters. The cook consulted me about menus and special dietary requirements with the deference she had once reserved for Clara. Even the youngest housemaid curtsied when she passed me in the corridors, her eyes bright with something that looked suspiciously like admiration.

And Edward... Edward began to look at me as if I might be the only still point in his unravelling world, the one constant in a reality that had shifted so dramatically he no longer trusted his own perceptions of what was normal, what was expected, what was safe.

I wore her slippers—soft kid leather dyed the colour of cream, with tiny pearl buttons that caught the morning light streaming through the conservatory windows. They fit my feet as if they had been made for me, as if Clara and I had been cast from the same Mold and all these years of watching her had been preparation for this moment when I would step literally into her place.

I wore her gloves to morning calls and evening entertainments, fine cotton and silk confections that transformed my hands from the roughened appendages of someone who had once scrubbed floors into the pampered extremities of a woman who had never known manual labour. Her perfume became my signature scent, that distinctive blend of French lavender and expensive soap that now announced my presence in rooms before I spoke a word.

I moved into her bedroom—our bedroom now—not in a single bold gesture that might have shocked the household or raised uncomfortable questions, but in careful increments, like ink soaking through fine cloth, spreading so gradually that the change seemed natural, inevitable, right. First my books appeared on her bedside table, volumes of poetry and philosophy that suggested depths Clara had never possessed but that I wanted Edward to discover when he entered the room to retrieve forgotten items or simply to remember.

Then my silver hairbrush claimed space on her vanity, its monogrammed handle catching lamplight as I performed the nightly ritual of brushing my hair—my hair, which had grown longer and more lustrous during my months of proper nutrition and care, which now fell in waves that resembled Clara's but somehow seemed richer, more alive, more worthy of masculine attention.

The green silk dressing gown with the mother-of-pearl clasps had been Clara's favourite, a wedding gift from Edward's mother that spoke of approval and acceptance and a place in the family hierarchy that I had been denied through my own stubborn pride. Now it wrapped around my shoulders like liquid emerald, like armour made of beauty, like a memory of grace made flesh. When Edward glimpsed me wearing it in the hallway outside our bedroom, his step faltered for just a moment, his eyes widening with something that might have been recognition, might have been longing, might have been the beginning of a dangerous confusion about which woman he was looking at.

No one stopped me. No one questioned the gradual migration of my possessions into spaces that had belonged to Clara, the slow transformation of her sanctuary into our shared domain. The servants seemed to understand instinctively that nature abhors a vacuum, that empty spaces demand to be filled, that I was simply providing the stability the household needed to continue functioning in the absence of its former mistress.

When Clara's friends came calling—those polished, perfectly groomed women who had once measured me with wary eyes, who had whispered among themselves about the governess who seemed to know her place too well, who stayed too long, who smiled too knowingly at domestic arrangements that should have been none of her concern—I welcomed them into the Parlor that was now mine by right rather than permission.

I poured tea from Clara's best service with hands that trembled just enough to suggest deep emotion barely held in check, adding precisely the right amount of fragility to my manner to win their sympathy without appearing weak or unstable. These women understood the performance of grief, the social choreography of loss that required perfect balance between genuine sorrow and practical competence.

"She was never quite herself these past months," I murmured to Lady Pemberton, my voice pitched low enough to suggest intimate confidence while remaining loud enough for the other visitors to hear. "The strain of managing the household, caring for the children, maintaining all her various commitments—I fear it was simply too much for her delicate constitution. Her mind began to seem... fragile."

They nodded with the knowing sympathy of women who had all witnessed the particular pressures that could break even the strongest feminine spirit. They had suspected something was wrong with Clara's increasingly erratic behaviour, her forgotten appointments and strange conversations, her growing tendency to cancel social engagements at the last moment with vague excuses about headaches or nervous exhaustion.

"She was always so perfect, so poised," Mrs. Worthington observed, stirring her tea with the mechanical precision of someone performing a familiar ritual. "Perhaps that was part of the problem. When someone appears to have everything under such complete control, a crack becomes inevitable."

"She's fortunate to have had you during those difficult final months," Lady Hemsley added, reaching across the small table to pat my hand with the gesture of one woman comforting another. "You've been like a sister to her, truly. The children are so lucky to have someone who cares for them as you do, someone who understood their mother so well."

I smiled at them through invented tears that caught the afternoon light streaming through the lace curtains, allowing my voice to catch just slightly as I replied. "A sister, yes. That's exactly what I always felt like—what I tried to be for her when she needed someone to understand what she was going through."

A sister. The word hung in the air between us, heavy with implications they could never fully grasp. Yes, that was what I had always been— the sister who should have been born into this life, who would have worn these clothes and lived in these rooms and married this man if the world had arranged itself more justly from the beginning. The sister who had finally claimed her rightful inheritance through patience and determination and the kind of love that recognizes no boundaries between desire and destiny.

In the nursery, I read the children stories that Clara had never finished, tales of transformation and magic that took on new meaning when spoken by lips that now wore her rose-coloured lip balm, that carried her scent, that moved with her particular grace. Margaret would settle into my lap with the absolute trust that children reserve for those who have proven themselves worthy of complete faith, while Henry leaned against my shoulder and asked questions about plot and character that revealed an intelligence his mother had never properly nurtured.

"Tell us about the princess who forgot her own name," Margaret would whisper, her small fingers playing with the buttons on my dress—Clara's dress, altered to fit my slightly different proportions but otherwise identical in every detail that mattered.

And I would tell them about women who lost themselves and found something better in the losing, about transformations that seemed like tragedies but were actually triumphs, about the magical possibility of becoming someone entirely new while remaining fundamentally, essentially yourself.

When Margaret began calling me "Mama" in whispered experiments—testing the word like a secret, like a prayer, like something that might be too precious to say aloud—I didn't correct her. Instead, I gathered her closer and hummed the lullabies that Clara had sung, that I had memorized during my months of careful observation, that now belonged to me by right of survival, by virtue of being the one who remained when the singing was needed most.

Edward lingered in doorways now, watching me with expressions that shifted from grief to confusion to something that might have been the beginning of a dangerous new attention. We didn't speak of what was happening between us, not directly—that would have been inappropriate, premature, a violation of the mourning period that social convention demanded. But his behaviour spoke more clearly than words ever could.

His grief had made him solemn, certainly, but it had also softened him in ways that years of comfortable marriage had not achieved. He began to trust my judgment more than anyone else's, asking my opinion about business decisions and social obligations, deferring to my wisdom about the children's education and emotional needs. When he passed my chair at dinner, his hand would brush my shoulder briefly, a touch that lingered just long enough to suggest awareness, interest, the kind of unconscious intimacy that develops between people who share the burden of maintaining a household and protecting its vulnerable inhabitants.

One evening, as I sat in the drawing room that had become my domain, reading by lamplight while the children played quietly nearby, he appeared in the doorway and simply looked at me. Not with the detached appreciation that men show to competent servants, but with something deeper, more complex, more alive with possibility than mere gratitude.

His eyes travelled from my face to my hands holding the book, to the way the lamplight caught in my hair, to the familiar elegance of the dress I wore—Clara's dress, but somehow more beautiful on my frame, more suited to my colouring, more expressive of the woman who inhabited it.

"You remind me of her," he said finally, his voice rough with an emotion he probably couldn't name.

"I miss her too," I replied, and felt the truth of it resonate in my chest like a bell struck in a cathedral. "She was... she was everything I hoped to be."

And that was true, in ways he could never understand. I did miss Clara—not the woman she had been, exactly, but the idea of her, the life she had represented, the possibilities she had embodied that were now mine to explore and improve upon. I missed the Clara who had once stood between me and the existence I deserved, because her absence had created the space for me to become something far more remarkable than either of us had ever imagined possible.

I began to venture beyond the house wearing her clothing, visiting the tailor who had once fitted her for gowns I could only dream of owning, the milliner who had created hats that framed her face with such becoming elegance. Now I stood where she had stood, turned slowly before mirrors that reflected my image draped in fabrics that cost more than most people earned in a year, listened to shopkeepers offer the same obsequious compliments they had once directed toward my predecessor.

"The blue silk is exquisite with your colouring, madam," the dressmaker murmured, pins held between her lips as she marked alterations that would perfect the fit. "Mrs. Harrowby always had such excellent taste in fabrics."

I hosted tea parties in the Parlor that had been Clara's favourite, using her best China and silver service to entertain the women who had once been her closest friends. They seemed to find comfort in my presence, in my ability to maintain the familiar rhythms of their social circle despite the tragedy that had disrupted their small world. I provided continuity, stability, the reassuring proof that life could continue even after loss, that some changes might even represent improvements rather than mere substitutions.

In the privacy of my bedroom—our bedroom—I practiced Clara's signature with the devotion of a medieval monk copying illuminated manuscripts. Not out of necessity anymore, since there were no more documents that required her authorization, but for the pure aesthetic pleasure of watching her handwriting flow from my pen, of feeling her identity merge with mine in the most intimate possible way.

It wasn't mimicry anymore, wasn't the crude theatrical performance of someone pretending to be what she wasn't. This was inheritance, the natural claiming of a legacy that had always belonged to me by right if not by law. I had studied Clara so thoroughly, absorbed her mannerisms and preferences so completely, that inhabiting her life felt less like deception than like finally stepping into clothes that had been tailored specifically for my measurements.

I was the better Clara—more attentive to the children's emotional needs, more interested in

Edward's business concerns, more skilled at managing household staff, more gracious to guests, more deserving of the love and security this life provided. I had taken the Mold that society had used to shape her and cast something sharper, more enduring, more worthy of preservation in its place.

The woman who emerged from this transformation was not an imitation but an improvement, not a replacement but a fulfilment of potential that had been wasted on someone too weak to appreciate what she possessed, too fragile to defend what was precious, too naive to understand that some things must be fought for if they are to be kept.

One night, as winter settled over London and fog pressed against the windows like the breath of something vast and patient waiting in the darkness, I lay in the bed that was now mine by every right that mattered—by survival, by competence, by the simple fact that I was the one who remained when remaining required strength.

I ran my hands across the fine linen sheets that had once covered Clara's sleeping form, feeling the quality of the weave, the softness that spoke of money and care and a life lived in comfort. I pictured her body as it had been in those final weeks—hollow-boned and fading, skin like paper, eyes that had lost their focus and their hope.

I imagined her still out there somewhere in the fog that had swallowed her, crawling through underbrush on hands and knees too weak to support her weight, gasping for breath that came in shorter and shorter intervals, calling for help that would never come because no one was looking anymore, because her absence had been explained and accepted and accommodated by people who had already moved on to more pressing concerns.

The image should have disturbed me, should have filled me with guilt or remorse or at least some recognition of the magnitude of what I had done. Instead, I found myself smiling in the darkness, feeling a satisfaction so complete and perfect that it seemed to warm my bones from within.

Because I had become what she never knew I could be—what she never could have been, even if she had lived a hundred years and possessed every advantage that birth and breeding could provide.

I was the ghost in silk, the doppelganger who had replaced the original so completely that even I sometimes forgot which of us had been born to this life and which had claimed it through will and patience and the kind of love that transforms everything it touches.

The house slept around me, filled with people who depended on me for their comfort and security, who looked to me for guidance and care and the thousand daily kindnesses that make a house into a home. Children who called me Mama in their dreams, servants who spoke my name with respect and affection, a husband who was beginning to see me not as a substitute for what he had lost but as something entirely new and infinitely more precious than what he had never fully appreciated while he possessed it.

I was home at last, wrapped in silk and satisfaction, surrounded by love that had been earned rather than inherited, protected by a life that I had built with my own hands from the raw materials of desire and opportunity and the absolute refusal to accept that some people are simply born to want what others are born to have.

Clara Harrowby was gone, dissolved into fog and memory and the kind of story that people tell to explain away mysteries they prefer not to examine too closely.

In her place lay something far more dangerous and beautiful and enduring—a woman who knew exactly what she was worth and had proven herself willing to pay any price necessary to claim what belonged to her.

The ghost in silk smiled in her perfect bed and dreamed of all the tomorrows that stretched ahead, bright with promise and rich with the particular satisfaction that comes from winning a war that no one else had even realized was being fought.

I had not just taken Clara's place.

I had improved upon it.

I had become the woman she should have been, if she had possessed the strength and intelligence and ruthless clarity of vision to deserve what she had been given.

And now, finally, everything was exactly as it should be.

# Chapter 17: The Family Portrait

## "A Smile That Doesn't Fit"

The artist arrived on a Wednesday morning that felt heavy with significance, as if the universe itself understood that this day would mark something irrevocable in the careful fiction I had been constructing. He was a slight man in his fifties, wearing a well-tailored tweed coat that spoke of middle-class respectability, his fingers permanently stained with charcoal and paint, his portfolio worn smooth by years of carrying it from house to house, from one family's commissioned happiness to another's.

Edward had insisted on the portrait with the kind of quiet determination that had become characteristic of him since Clara's disappearance. He spoke of it as a necessity rather than a luxury, as if capturing this moment in oil and canvas might somehow make permanent what felt increasingly fragile, increasingly threatened by forces none of us dared to name aloud.

"A way to remember," he had murmured the night before, his voice heavy with meanings that layered beneath the simple words. "A way to anchor the present, to make it real."

He didn't say Clara's name. He never did anymore, as if speaking it might summon her ghost to interrupt this new life we were building from the ashes of her absence. But I could feel her presence in the gaps between his words, in the way his eyes sometimes searched my face as if looking for traces of someone else, in the careful distance he maintained even as he drew me deeper into the role that should have been hers from the beginning.

We arranged ourselves in the drawing room with the deliberate precision of actors taking their marks for a performance that would be viewed and judged by generations yet unborn. The artist requested natural light, so the heavy curtains were drawn back completely, flooding the space with the soft, grey illumination that London's autumn sky provided—not harsh enough to reveal flaws, but clear enough to capture truth, should any exist to be found.

I wore Clara's cream-colored gown, the one with the high lace collar and tiny jet buttons that had always given her trouble in the mornings when her fingers were stiff with sleep and morning nerves. The irony was not lost on me that it fit me better now than it had ever fit her—my body had somehow reshaped itself to accommodate her absence, had learned to fill the spaces she had left behind with such precision that even her clothes seemed to recognize me as their rightful owner.

The fabric whispered against my skin with familiar intimacy as I settled into the upholstered armchair that would serve as the portrait's centre, the chair where Clara had once sat to read to the children, to receive visitors, to pose for photographs that would never capture what this painting promised to preserve. The silk lining had absorbed years of her lavender perfume, and now it released those ghostly fragrances with each movement I made, surrounding me with the scent of a woman who no longer existed anywhere but in memory and stolen moments like this.

Edward stood behind my chair with his hand resting on my shoulder—not possessively, but protectively, the gesture of a man who had learned to guard what remained of his family against further loss. I could feel the weight of his palm through the fabric, warm and substantial, anchoring me to this moment even as part of me wanted to float away from the intensity of what we were attempting to capture and preserve.

Margaret sat beside me on the small velvet stool that had been brought in specifically for the portrait, her legs folded neatly beneath her pale blue dress, her small hand gripping the edge of my sleeve with the unconscious need for connection that children display when they sense undercurrents they cannot understand but know instinctively, they should fear. Henry stood beside his father, straight-backed and solemn beyond his years, his dark eyes holding the particular gravity that comes to children who have learned too early that the adults who are supposed to protect them are not immune to the kind of suffering that leaves permanent marks.

The artist—Mr. Pemberton, he had introduced himself, no relation to our butler despite the shared name —adjusted his easel with the practiced efficiency of someone who had performed this ritual countless times, in countless drawing rooms, for countless families who believed that oil paint and canvas could somehow stop time, could preserve moments of happiness against the inevitable erosions of memory and change.

He sketched the basic outlines first, his charcoal moving across the paper with confident strokes that seemed to capture not just our physical arrangement but something more ephemeral—the weight of the silence between us, the careful way we held ourselves as if afraid that any natural movement might shatter the illusion we were trying to create.

"Try not to smile too widely," he said gently, his words directed not specifically to me but to the room in general, to the atmosphere of controlled performance that filled the space like incense. "Something softer would be more appropriate. More... maternal."

I nodded, understanding immediately what he meant. This was not meant to be a portrait of individual personalities but of a family unit, a cohesive whole where each member served a specific function in the larger composition. I was to be the mother figure—warm but not overly familiar, elegant but not intimidating, present but somehow eternal, the kind of woman who would look down from the wall at future generations and represent all the values and stability that such families were built upon.

Softness. Yes. I could do that. I had been practicing softness for months, learning to modulate my expressions until they matched what people expected to see when they looked at someone in my position. The difficulty was not in achieving the expression itself, but in maintaining it while fighting against the other emotions that threatened to surface—satisfaction at how completely I had succeeded in my deception, contempt for how easily they had all been fooled, and underneath it all, a growing anxiety that perhaps I was succeeding too well, that I was disappearing into Clara's identity so completely that I might never find my way back to whoever I had been before this elaborate masquerade began.

But as I held my pose, something began to ache beneath my carefully constructed surface, something that made my skin feel tight and foreign, as if I were wearing a mask that had been crafted by someone who had never quite understood the shape of my face.

It was Margaret.

The child kept glancing at me—small, furtive movements of her eyes that she probably thought were undetectable but that I felt like pinpricks against my consciousness. Not with open suspicion, exactly, but with something I couldn't quite name, something that made my throat constrict with a fear I hadn't experienced since those first terrifying days when I had been certain that someone would see through my performance and expose me for what I truly was.

Her brow would furrow slightly as she looked at me, then smooth out when she noticed me noticing, but not before I caught glimpses of something troubling working behind her bright eyes. Once, she opened her mouth as if to speak, her small face turning up toward mine with the beginning of what might have been a question, then thought better of it and subsided back into posed silence.

Children see things that adults have trained themselves to overlook. They notice inconsistencies in behaviour, changes in scent, the subtle alterations in familiar voices that come from years of careful practice rather than natural habit. Margaret had been Clara's constant companion, had absorbed her mother's rhythms and mannerisms with the unconscious thoroughness that only children possess, and now she was beginning to sense that something was not quite right about the woman who had taken Clara's place at the centre of their family constellation.

I smiled more gently, softening my expression in response to what I imagined she was seeing, trying to project the kind of maternal warmth that would soothe whatever doubts were beginning to form in her developing mind. But even as I did so, I felt the smile sitting strangely on my face, as if it belonged to someone else, as if I were borrowing an expression that had never quite been mine to wear.

The artist paused in his sketching, his head tilted slightly as he studied my face with the kind of professional attention that made me feel exposed, analysed, reduced to a collection of lines and shadows that might not add up to the person I was pretending to be.

"You have a very particular expression," he said finally, his voice carrying the thoughtful tone of someone trying to solve a puzzle that interested him professionally. "Elegant, certainly, but... distant. Not unkind, mind you. Just somehow far away, as if you're looking at something the rest of us can't see."

The observation struck me like a physical blow, so accurate that I had to fight to keep from reacting visibly. He had seen something in my face that I had been trying so hard to hide, had identified the exact quality that made my performance imperfect, that revealed the gap between who I was and who I was pretending to be.

"I've been told I carry sorrow in my eyes," I offered, hoping that this explanation would satisfy his curiosity while also accounting for whatever it was, he had detected in my expression. "Loss has a way of marking a person, doesn't it? Even when we try to move forward, something of what we've endured remains visible."

Edward said nothing to this, but I felt his hand tighten almost imperceptibly on my shoulder, a response that could have been sympathy or something more complex recognition, perhaps, of the truth that lay beneath my carefully chosen words.

The session lasted nearly two hours, during which the children gradually grew restless despite their best efforts to remain still and composed. Margaret's hand relaxed its grip on my sleeve as her attention wandered to the sounds of life continuing in other parts of the house—servants moving about their duties, the distant sound of horses' hooves on cobblestones, the ordinary rhythms of a world that continued to function despite our attempts to freeze this particular moment in time.

Henry shifted his weight from foot to foot with increasing frequency, his young body rebelling against the unnatural stillness that portraiture required, though his face maintained the serious expression that had become his default since his mother's disappearance. Edward's shoulder sagged slightly with fatigue, and I could sense rather than see the way his attention drifted between the present moment and whatever business concerns occupied his thoughts during the long hours when he was not actively engaged in the performance of domestic happiness.

But I held myself steady throughout it all, every line of my body shaped to Clara's remembered grace, every breath calculated to maintain the illusion that I belonged in this tableau, that I was the natural and inevitable centre around which this family organized itself. I was the still point in their turning world, the maternal figure whose presence made everything else possible, the woman who deserved to be immortalized in oil paint as the heart of this household.

When the artist finally declared himself satisfied with his preliminary work and began packing away his materials, promising to deliver the completed portrait within the month, I remained in the drawing room, watching the afternoon light fade through the tall windows and feeling something like relief wash over me as the performance finally ended.

Edward lingered in the doorway after the children had been dismissed to their nursery, and the artist had been shown out by the butler. I could feel him watching me, studying my profile as I sat in the chair that had served as my throne during the portrait session, still wearing Clara's cream-colored gown, still surrounded by the faint scent of her perfume that seemed to cling to everything she had once touched.

"You were... perfect," he said finally, after a silence that stretched long enough to become meaningful in itself.

I turned to face him slowly, allowing the movement to be graceful and measured, the kind of gesture that a woman comfortable in her own beauty might make when acknowledging a compliment. "Do you mean that?"

He gave me what might have been a smile, though it carried more weight than simple pleasure—satisfaction, perhaps, or the kind of relief that comes from seeing a difficult situation resolved in a way that serves everyone's interests. "You've held this family together, Eleanor. Through everything that's happened, through all the uncertainty and grief, you've been the constant. I don't know what we would have done without you."

He almost never said my name aloud anymore, and hearing it felt strange, almost jarring, like a word in a language I had half-forgotten. It didn't fit the woman I had become, didn't match the role I had been playing with such dedication and skill. Eleanor Ashcombe belonged to a different life, a different story, a woman who had made different choices and suffered different consequences.

I wanted to ask him why, if I had been so perfect, if I had held his family together so successfully, he still maintained the careful distance that kept us from becoming what we both knew we could be. I wanted to demand an explanation for why he looked at me with gratitude rather than desire, why he spoke to me as if I were an especially competent employee rather than the woman who had stepped into his wife's place and made it her own through sheer force of will and careful attention to detail.

Then why haven't you kissed me yet? The question burned in my throat, demanding to be spoken, but I swallowed it back because I already knew the answer.

He still saw her in me—but not enough. Not completely. Not in the way that would allow him to forget what he had lost and embrace what he had found to replace it.

I was close, so close to achieving everything I had worked toward, but something still hovered between us like a ghost that refused to be laid to rest. Guilt, perhaps, over how quickly he had been comforted after Clara's disappearance. Doubt about the propriety of replacing one woman so seamlessly with another. The past, with all its complications and unresolved emotions. And always, always, her—Clara's memory, Clara's claim on his heart, Clara's stubborn refusal to be completely erased despite everything I had done to eliminate her from this life that should have been mine from the beginning.

That night, after the children had been tucked into their beds and the house had settled into its familiar patterns of creaking wood and shifting shadows, I crept down to the study where the artist had left his preliminary charcoal sketch—a rough but recognizable rendering of the family portrait that would soon become a permanent fixture on the drawing room wall.

The lines were faint but clear, capturing with surprising accuracy the arrangement we had held for so many hours, the relationships and hierarchies that defined our little group. Edward, solid and protective behind the chair. The children, positioned with careful attention to both artistic composition and family dynamics. And me, at the centre of it all, the focal point around which everything else was organized.

I studied my own face in the sketch, examining the delicate tilt of my chin, the way my eyes seemed to look both at the viewer and beyond them, the small, careful smile that the artist had captured with just a few economical strokes of his charcoal. It was undeniably me—not Clara, not the woman whose life I had claimed, but Eleanor Ashcombe wearing Clara's dress and sitting in Clara's chair and pretending to be Clara's replacement.

And I hated it.

I hated the way my own features showed through despite months of practice at arranging my face into Clara's expressions. I hated the way my natural bone structure refused to be completely disguised by borrowed mannerisms and studied grace. Most of all, I hated the way the sketch revealed the truth that I had been trying so desperately to hide—that I was an imposter, a replacement, a woman playing a role rather than living an authentic life.

The rage that filled me was pure and clean, the kind of anger that comes from seeing your carefully constructed illusions exposed for what they truly are. I took a match from the silver box on the mantelpiece and struck it, watching the small flame flare to life with hypnotic intensity. For a moment, I held it beneath the paper's edge, watching the corner begin to curl and blacken, smoke unfurling like a ghost into the still air of the study.

The fire would solve the problem, would eliminate this evidence of my imperfection, would ensure that no one else would ever see what the artist had seen when he looked at me with his professional eye and captured something I had never intended to reveal. The flames would consume the sketch and leave nothing behind but ash, allowing me to continue my masquerade without this troubling reminder of how far I still had to go before my transformation would be complete.

But just before the flames reached the line that represented my eyes, I stamped the match out, pressing it against the wooden surface of the desk until the fire died and left only the acrid smell of sulphur and burnt wood.

Not yet.

Let the world see what I had become, even if what I had become was not yet perfect, not yet complete. Let them frame the lie and hang it on their wall, a permanent reminder of this moment when I had stood at the centre of their family and claimed my rightful place in their lives.

The portrait would serve as evidence of my success, proof that I had achieved what I had set out to do when I first began watching Clara from the shadows, learning her habits, studying her weaknesses, planning her replacement with the methodical patience of someone who understood that the greatest victories required the greatest sacrifices.

And if the painting also revealed something of Eleanor Ashcombe beneath the surface of Clara's stolen life—well, perhaps that was as it should be. Perhaps the world deserved to know that the woman in the cream-colored gown was not who she appeared to be, that beneath the maternal smile and gentle manner lay someone harder, more determined, infinitely more dangerous than anyone suspected.

The sketch would become a painting, and the painting would hang in the drawing room for years to come, a testament to the power of will over circumstance, of desire over morality, of the human capacity for reinvention when the stakes were high enough and the need was great enough.

Let them frame the lie, I thought as I made my way back upstairs to the bedroom that had once been Clara's, to the bed where I now slept surrounded by her scent and her memories and the ghosts of the life she would never live again.

Let them hang it on their wall and call it truth.

I would know better. But I would also know that I had won.

# Part III: The Haunting

*You can steal a name. But not peace.*

# Chapter 18: Whispers in the Walls

## "A Thread Unravels"

The first time I heard it, I convinced myself it was only the wind—London's eternal wind that found its way through every crack and crevice of even the most well-maintained houses, that carried with it the scents and sounds of a thousand other lives being lived in parallel to this careful fiction I had constructed.

A faint sound behind the nursery walls—so soft it might have been imaginary, so subtle that it lived in that space between perception and doubt where the mind manufactures meaning from nothing. A shuffle, perhaps, or the ghost of a breath, or a murmur that never quite formed into words but carried with it the suggestion of human presence, of consciousness existing where none should be.

The kind of sound that lives between sleep and waking, in those liminal moments when the boundaries between reality and dream become permeable, when the rational mind loses its grip on the careful categories that usually keep terror at bay. Dismissible, certainly. Almost.

But it returned.

Night after night, the sound followed me through the house like a patient predator, appearing in different rooms as if it were mapping the territory of my life, learning the routines and rhythms that had become so essential to my sense of security. Behind the marble fireplace in the drawing room, where Clara had once sat to read her correspondence by lamplight. Under the polished floorboards of the dining room, where her footsteps had once created their own familiar percussion. In the breathless silence between the measured tick of the longcase clock that had counted the hours of her marriage, that now counted the hours of my usurpation.

At first, I ignored it with the determined rationality of someone who understood that acknowledging such phenomena would be the first step toward madness. I told myself it was nothing more than the natural creak and settle of a house that had stood for decades, that had absorbed generations of human emotion and was now releasing it back into the atmosphere like moisture evaporating from old wood.

I reminded myself that guilt could play tricks on the mind, could create phantom sounds and imaginary threats from the raw material of conscience and regret. I was overtired, overstressed, adjusting to the demands of my new life with its complex web of deceptions and performances. It was only natural that my mind would rebel against the constant vigilance required to maintain such an elaborate masquerade.

But doubt is a seed that grows with terrible speed in the fertile darkness of a guilty conscience, and once planted, it spreads through the mind like poison through water, contaminating every thought, every perception, every moment of what should have been peaceful satisfaction with my success.

The whispers—for that's what they were, I realized with growing dread, not random house sounds but something far more purposeful and personal—began to follow patterns that suggested intelligence, intention, the deliberate attempt of something to communicate with me across whatever barrier separated the living from whatever Clara had become.

One morning in late October, when the autumn air carried the scent of dying leaves and the promise of winter's approach, I found evidence that my torment was not confined to the invisible realm of sound and suggestion.

There, clinging to the iron bars of the garden gate like some grotesque flower that had bloomed overnight, was a scarf. Tattered and mud-stained, sodden with moisture that could have been dew or rain or something more sinister, it hung from the black metal as if it had grown there, as if it were part of the gate's original design rather than something that had been placed with deliberate intent.

Pale blue silk, expensive and delicate despite its current condition. The colour of forget-me-nots, of spring skies, of the dress Clara had worn to her first dinner party as Edward's wife.

Clara's scarf. I recognized it immediately, though I had been certain it was buried with her in whatever unmarked grave the woods had provided, whatever shallow depression in the earth had accepted her body and kept it hidden from the searches that had combed the countryside for weeks after her disappearance.

My breath caught so violently in my throat that I tasted iron, felt the sharp metallic flavour of blood where my teeth had caught my tongue in shock. For a moment that stretched like eternity, I stood frozen in my morning dress and robe, staring at this impossible artifact, this piece of evidence that should not exist, could not exist, unless—

I forced myself to look around with the systematic attention of someone trained in deception, someone who understood that panic was the enemy of rational thought. The hedge that bordered our property stood undisturbed, its leaves showing no signs of recent passage. The lane beyond was empty, marked only by the wheel ruts of yesterday's traffic and the hoofprints of horses that had passed hours ago. The trees that lined the path showed no broken branches, no disturbance of the undergrowth that would suggest someone had hidden there to watch, to wait, to deposit this terrible message.

No one visible. No footprints in the soft earth around the gate. No rational explanation for how Clara's scarf had come to be hanging from our garden gate like a flag of surrender or a declaration of war.

I took it inside with hands that shook despite my efforts to maintain control, and I burned it in the drawing room hearth, watching the delicate silk curl and blacken and finally dissolve into ash that the chimney carried away into the grey London sky. But even after the flames had consumed every thread, even after I had swept the ashes into the dustpan and disposed of them in the kitchen fire, the scent of her perfume lingered on my hands like an accusation, like a mark that no amount of scrubbing could remove.

Later that week, as I was attempting to return to the normal routines that had once provided structure and meaning to my days, Elsie the housemaid knocked hesitantly on the drawing room door. She was a timid creature, barely eighteen, with the kind of pale, nervous demeanour that marked her as someone who had learned early that survival depended on making herself as invisible and inoffensive as possible.

"Beg pardon, ma'am," she said, her voice barely above a whisper, her hands twisting the hem of her apron with the unconscious gesture of someone delivering news she knew would not be welcome. "But someone's moved the attic ladder. It was folded against the wall yesterday when I dusted the upper landing, but this morning it's been pulled down, and the hatch is standing open."

The blood turned to ice in my veins. No one was allowed in the attic—I had established that rule early in my tenure, claiming that the space contained delicate family documents and heirlooms that required careful handling. In truth, it was there that I had hidden the few remaining traces of my transformation from Eleanor Ashcombe into the woman who now sat in Clara's chair and wore Clara's clothes and answered to whatever name the family chose to call her.

I had locked the attic myself, had placed the key in a location known only to me, had checked and double-checked that my secrets were safe from discovery by curious servants or children who might stumble upon evidence that would destroy everything I had worked so hard to achieve.

I dismissed Elsie with a tight smile and a half-crown for her discretion, but my hands trembled as I climbed the narrow stairs to investigate this impossible breach of my security. Each step felt like walking toward my own execution, toward the moment when my carefully constructed world would collapse and reveal the terrible truths that lay beneath its pretty surface.

The attic key was exactly where I had left it—tucked behind the China vase on Clara's writing desk, the hiding place I had chosen because it was too obvious to be suspicious, too simple to attract attention from anyone who might be looking for hidden secrets. And yet, when I examined the lock with the careful attention of someone whose life depended on such details, I could see fresh scratches around the keyhole, thin silver lines that suggested someone had forced the mechanism with something small and sharp, someone who had known exactly what they were looking for and where to find it.

Inside, the air was stale and cold, thick with the particular mustiness that accumulates in spaces where human presence is rare, and memories gather like dust in the corners. The trunks that contained my old life stood exactly where I had placed them, their contents apparently undisturbed. The window shutter remained bolted from the inside, eliminating the possibility that someone had entered from the outside.

But something was wrong. Something had changed in ways that my rational mind struggled to identify but that my deeper instincts recognized immediately as evidence of violation, of intrusion, of presence where no presence should have been possible.

A boot print on the dust-covered floor. Clear and distinct, pressed into the fine grey powder that coated everything in that forgotten space. The outline of a woman's boot, small and delicate, with the particular shape of expensive leather carefully maintained and lovingly polished.

And it was not mine.

I knelt beside the print, studying its dimensions, measuring it against my own foot, hoping desperately to find some innocent explanation that would restore my sense of security and control. But there was no denying what I saw, no rational way to explain how Clara's footprint had come to be impressed in the dust of an attic she should never have been able to reach, in a house where she no longer lived, in a world where she was supposed to be nothing more than memory and scattered bones in some forgotten corner of the woods.

That night, I slept lightly, fully dressed beneath my nightgown, a kitchen knife hidden beneath my pillow where I could reach it quickly if the whispers in the walls finally took on physical form. Every creak of the house settling, every sigh of wind against the windows, every distant sound from the street beyond became a potential threat, a possible harbinger of the reckoning that seemed to be approaching with inexorable patience.

I began to see her in reflections—not clearly, never directly, but in fleeting glimpses that vanished the moment I tried to focus on them. A flicker of movement in the mirror as I brushed my hair, there and gone so quickly that I could never be certain whether I had seen Clara's face looking back at me or merely the product of my own deteriorating mental state. A silhouette behind the sheer curtains of the morning room, gone when I rushed to investigate but leaving behind the impression of a familiar figure, a beloved shape that haunted my dreams and now seemed determined to invade my waking hours as well.

The whispers grew louder, more distinct, more clearly directed at me personally rather than being random manifestations of a guilty conscience or an overactive imagination. They followed me through my daily routines, commenting on my actions with a voice that carried the particular cadence of someone who had known me intimately, who understood exactly which words would cut deepest and leave the most lasting wounds.

Once, as I sat in the drawing room attempting to focus on some household correspondence, I was certain I heard my name spoken with perfect clarity, the syllables carrying across the room like stones thrown with deadly accuracy.

Not Clara's name, which would have been disturbing enough. Not "Mrs. Harrowby" or whatever other identity I had claimed for myself in this house where I had never truly belonged.

My name. My real name. The name I had tried so hard to leave behind, to bury along with the woman who had worn it in another life.

"Eleanor..."

Soft as silk, sharp as winter ice, carrying with it the weight of recognition and accusation and something that might have been bitter amusement at my attempts to escape what I had been, what I had done, what I could never stop being no matter how perfectly I performed the role of someone else.

The sound sent terror through me so pure and immediate that I knocked over my teacup, sending hot liquid spreading across Clara's mahogany desk, staining the papers I had been pretending to read while my mind catalogued every sound, every shadow, every possible sign that my past was finally catching up with me in the form of a woman who should have been dead but seemed determined to reclaim what I had stolen from her.

I began checking locks compulsively—twice, then three times, then so often that I lost count of the repetitions. I started keeping a detailed journal of the hours I slept and the hours I remained awake, looking for patterns that might explain when the manifestations were strongest, when I was most vulnerable to whatever force was haunting the edges of my carefully constructed reality.

I watched the servants with the paranoid attention of someone who suspected conspiracy in every gesture, who searched for signs of disloyalty or collusion in every sideways glance or whispered conversation. I read the children's drawings as if they were coded messages, looking for hidden meanings in their innocent sketches of family life, evidence that they had seen or heard something that would expose the truth about their missing mother and her replacement.

Most disturbingly of all, I began speaking aloud to Clara's portrait in the drawing room—the one that had been painted shortly after her marriage, when her face still held the soft glow of new happiness and unburdened hope. I would stand before it in the late evening hours when the house was quiet and demand that she stays dead, that she stops tormenting me with her persistent refusal to accept what had been done to her.

"You lost," I would whisper to the painted eyes that seemed to follow me wherever I moved in the room. "You were weak, and careless, and too trusting, and you lost everything because you didn't fight hard enough to keep it. This is my life now. This is my family, my house, my husband. You have no claim here anymore."

But the painted Clara only smiled her gentle, enigmatic smile, and the whispers in the walls continued their patient commentary on my deteriorating grip on the reality I had worked so hard to create and control.

Was she here? Could she be? Was it possible that I had made some mistake in those crucial moments in the fog-shrouded woods, that she had somehow survived what should have been her final disappearance into the mist and undergrowth, that she had been watching and waiting for the right moment to reclaim what had been taken from her?

No. No—impossible. I had been careful, methodical, thorough in my planning and execution. I had seen her fall, had watched the weakness in her limbs as the poison did its work, had left her in a place where discovery was unlikely and survival was impossible. She was gone, had to be gone, must be gone if there was any justice or logic left in the world.

And yet...

I found myself staring longer at the garden gate where the scarf had appeared, searching for other signs of her presence, other evidence that the boundary between the living and the dead was more permeable than I had allowed myself to believe. I watched the rosebushes she had once tended with such care, looking for disturbances in the soil that might suggest someone had been digging there, searching for something that had been buried and forgotten.

When the fog crept in at dusk, as it did with increasing frequency as winter approached, I would stand at the windows and peer into its grey depths, half-expecting to see a familiar figure emerging from the mist like something from a ghost story, like the materialization of guilt given form and substance and the power to destroy everything I had built on the foundation of her absence.

She was gone. She had to be gone. I repeated this truth like a prayer, like an incantation that might have the power to make reality conform to my desperate needs.

But even as I spoke the words, even as I tried to convince myself that what I was experiencing was nothing more than the natural consequence of stress and guilt and the enormous psychological pressure of maintaining such an elaborate deception, I could not escape the growing certainty that something was fundamentally wrong with the world I had created.

There are whispers in the walls of this house that should have been my sanctuary, voices that speak my name with intimate knowledge and barely concealed contempt. Sometimes, in the moments between sleeping and waking when the mind is most vulnerable to truths it prefers to ignore, I think I can hear laughter in those whispers—soft, bitter laughter that speaks of patience rewarded, of justice delayed but not denied, of reckonings that come for everyone eventually, no matter how cleverly they think they have escaped the consequences of their actions.

The thread is unravelling. The careful weave of lies and deceptions that I used to construct this new life is beginning to come apart, pulled loose by forces I cannot see or understand but that seem to know exactly where to apply pressure to cause the maximum damage.

And somewhere in the gathering darkness, in the spaces between the walls where whispers live and grow and multiply, Clara is waiting.

Clara is waiting, and she is no longer alone.

# Chapter 19: The Housemaid's Eyes

## "A Witness in the Dark"

She had been watching me.

I should have noticed it sooner—should have recognized the particular quality of attention that marks someone who has seen too much, who has begun to piece together fragments of truth that were never meant to be assembled. But I had been so focused on the larger threats, the whispers in the walls and the impossible appearance of Clara's belongings, that I had failed to notice the more immediate danger lurking in the shadows of my own household.

Elsie's glances lingered too long when she thought I wasn't looking, her pale eyes studying my face with the intensity of someone searching for answers to questions she was afraid to ask aloud. Her footsteps had developed a careful quality, too light and deliberate for a girl with nothing to hide, moving through the corridors of the house like someone navigating a minefield where any misstep might trigger consequences she could not imagine.

She was one of the newer maids, barely eighteen, with the kind of forgettable face that made her invisible to most of the household—thin and pale, with mousy brown hair always perfectly arranged beneath her white cap, her movements quick and efficient in the way that marked her as someone who had learned early that survival depended on competence and discretion. The sort of girl who should have been grateful for her position, who should have kept her head down and her mouth shut and never noticed anything beyond the dust she was paid to clean and the fires she was expected to tend.

But I noticed her now, with the sharp attention of a predator who had suddenly become aware that she was being stalked by something smaller but potentially more dangerous. I saw how she avoided direct eye contact when we passed in the corridor, how she hesitated for just a fraction too long before answering even the simplest questions about household routine, how her hands trembled slightly when she served my morning tea, as if the very act of being in my presence had become a source of barely controlled terror.

Most disturbing of all, I had caught her standing outside Clara's former bedroom—not working, not moving, just standing with her hand hovering near the door handle as though she were listening for something, waiting for some signal that would tell her whether it was safe to enter or whether she should flee from whatever presence she sensed on the other side of that threshold.

The sight had sent ice through my veins, because I recognized in her posture the same quality of fearful anticipation that I had been experiencing myself, the growing certainty that Clara's absence was not as complete or as permanent as I had believed it to be.

That night, driven by an anxiety that had been building for weeks, I made the decision to follow her, to discover what she knew and how much danger her knowledge posed to the carefully constructed life I had built on the foundation of Clara's disappearance.

She left her cramped chamber in the servants' quarters just after midnight, when the house had settled into the deep quiet that comes in the hours before dawn. Her bare feet were silent on the narrow stairs, and she carried a single candle cupped protectively in her hands, the flame casting dancing shadows on the walls as she made her way through corridors she knew by heart, moving with the practiced stealth of someone who had done this before, who had established a routine of nocturnal activity that no one else in the household suspected.

She moved like a girl with secrets—dangerous secrets that could destroy lives and reshape the future in ways that would serve no one's interests except perhaps those of justice, that abstract concept that I had been running from since the moment I decided that Clara's life was less important than my own desires.

I stayed far enough behind that the darkness could conceal me, matching my footsteps to hers, pausing when she paused, breathing when she breathed, becoming her shadow in a house that suddenly felt full of shadows, full of watchers and watched, full of the kind of tension that precedes either revelation or violence.

She led me through a route I had never used myself—down the back stairs that the servants employed to move through the house without disturbing the family, through the small hallway that connected the pantry to the servants' washroom, into spaces that existed for the convenience of people like her, people whose labour made possible the comfortable lives of people like me but who were expected to remain invisible, to conduct their business in the margins where their betters would never have to acknowledge their existence.

There, tucked behind the large linen cabinet where sheets and towels were stored between washings, she reached for something that had been carefully hidden, something that she retrieved with the reverent care of someone handling a religious relic or a piece of evidence that could change the course of history.

A small parcel, wrapped in brown paper and tied with string, the sort of innocent-looking package that might contain anything from a love letter to a death warrant. She unwrapped it with painstaking slowness, her fingers trembling with either anticipation or fear, revealing its contents to the flickering candlelight like a priest unveiling sacred mysteries to a congregation of one.

A scarf. Another one. The same pale blue silk as the one I had found hanging from the garden gate, the same delicate fabric that had once adorned Clara's throat, that had carried her scent and absorbed her warmth and served as testimony to her existence in a world that was supposed to have forgotten her completely.

But this one was different—cleaner, less weathered, as if it had been recently acquired rather than recovered from some forgotten hiding place where it had waited for months to be discovered. And nestled within its folds was something even more disturbing: a folded piece of paper covered with handwriting I could not read from my hiding place, but which caused Elsie's breath to catch in her throat as she unfolded it and held it close to the candle flame.

I watched as her lips moved silently, reading words that seemed to confirm her most impossible hopes, and then—worse, far worse than anything I could have imagined—I heard her speak aloud the words that shattered my world like glass:

"She's alive."

The words struck me with physical force, each syllable a blow that left me reeling with the implications of what I had just witnessed. Clara was alive. Somehow, impossibly, she had survived what should have been her final disappearance into the fog and undergrowth, had found a way to communicate with the outside world, had been leaving signs of her continued existence like breadcrumbs in a fairy tale, waiting for someone to follow the trail and discover the truth about what had happened to her.

And Elsie—simple, overlooked Elsie—had been the one to find those breadcrumbs, to piece together the evidence of Clara's survival, to become the link between the woman who should have been dead and the world that believed her gone forever.

I stepped forward from my hiding place, my voice cutting through the silence like a blade. "Elsie."

She spun toward me with the panicked grace of a deer that has suddenly found itself in the sights of a hunter, nearly dropping the candle in her shock, her face going white as bone in the flickering light. "M-ma'am—I—I didn't see you there—I was just—I wasn't doing anything wrong—"

"Where did you find that?" I gestured toward the scarf with calm precision, though inside I felt as if I were falling through empty space, as if the ground beneath my feet had suddenly revealed itself to be nothing more than carefully painted canvas stretched over an abyss.

She pressed the scarf to her chest as if it could protect her from whatever she saw in my face, her voice barely above a whisper. "I—I wasn't snooping, I swear on my mother's grave. It was outside, by the stables, just lying there in the dirt. I thought maybe... maybe Mrs. Clara had left it there, maybe she's been hiding somewhere, maybe she's hurt and can't come home and she's trying to tell us where she is—"

Her words tumbled over each other with the desperate speed of someone who knows she has stumbled into something far more dangerous than she had ever imagined, someone who is beginning to understand that knowledge can be a death sentence when it concerns the wrong secrets, the wrong people, the wrong crimes.

Her eyes widened as she took in my silence, the way I stood perfectly still in the candlelight, and in their depths, I saw something that made my blood run cold with the recognition of how completely my careful plans had been compromised.

Hope.

She still believed Clara could be saved, still imagined that this discovery meant rescue rather than disaster, still thought she was uncovering a story with a happy ending rather than digging up evidence of a murder that had only been delayed, not prevented.

"She's dead," I said with the calm finality of someone stating an obvious fact, though every word required tremendous effort to keep my voice steady, controlled, free of the panic that was clawing at my throat like a living thing. "You're confused, dear. Grief does strange things to the mind, makes us see connections that don't exist, find hope where none remains."

"But I saw—" she began, then stopped herself, perhaps finally recognizing the danger she was in, the trap she had walked into by revealing what she knew.

"What exactly did you see?" I asked, taking a step closer, close enough that she would be able to see every detail of my expression in the candlelight, close enough that she would understand that her next words might determine whether she lived to see another sunrise.

Elsie's mouth opened as if to speak, then closed without sound, her throat working as she swallowed whatever truth she had been about to reveal. The silence stretched between us like a taut wire, vibrating with tension that seemed to fill the small space with the potential for violence.

"Nothing," she whispered finally, the lie so obvious that it felt like an insult to both our intelligences. "I didn't see anything at all."

She turned to leave, clutching the scarf and note to her chest, moving with the quick, nervous steps of someone who has suddenly realized that discretion is not just the better part of valour but the only thing standing between her and consequences too terrible to imagine.

I let her take two steps, let her believe for just a moment that she might escape the conversation with her secrets intact and her life still her own to live.

Then I reached forward and grabbed her wrist.

My fingers closed around the delicate bones of her forearm with just enough pressure to communicate that resistance would be both futile and dangerous, that she was no longer in control of when this conversation would end or how it would conclude.

"Elsie," I said softly, my voice carrying the particular gentleness that predators use when they want their prey to remain calm until the moment of the killing strike. "There's something I need you to understand."

She looked up at me, and I watched fear bloom in her face like a bruise spreading beneath pale skin, watched the exact moment when she finally comprehended that she had not discovered a mystery that needed solving but had instead stumbled into the presence of something that would kill to protect its secrets.

"Please," she whispered, and the word carried with it all the desperate hope of someone who still believed that mercy was possible, that explanation might lead to understanding, that the woman she had served faithfully for months might choose compassion over self-preservation.

"Loyalty," I said, savouring the way the word felt on my tongue, the way it seemed to carry weight in the flickering candlelight, "is the most valuable quality in a house like this. More valuable than cleverness, more valuable than curiosity, certainly more valuable than the kind of amateur detective work that leads well-meaning servants to make discoveries that would be better left unmade."

She trembled under my grip, her entire body shaking with the kind of terror that comes from the sudden understanding that you have been living in close proximity to something monstrous without ever realizing the danger, that the woman whose tea you have been serving and whose floors you have been scrubbing has been capable of violence beyond your imagining.

"I won't say anything," she promised, her voice breaking with desperation. "I swear on the Bible, on anything you want, I'll never tell anyone what I found. I'll burn it all, pretend I never saw anything, never speak of it again as long as I live."

I smiled then, and I saw in her eyes the moment when she realized that her promises meant nothing, that her life had become a problem to be solved rather than a precious thing to be preserved, that the woman holding her wrist was capable of making decisions that would prioritize convenience over conscience without a moment's hesitation.

And then I pushed her.

It didn't require much force—she was small and off-balance, standing at the top of the narrow servants' stair that descended steeply into darkness, her skippered feet finding no purchase on the polished wood as gravity took hold and pulled her down into the shadows below.

The wooden steps were unforgiving, each one striking her falling body with sounds that seemed impossibly loud in the nighttime quiet of the house. She screamed once—a brief, sharp sound that was cut off almost immediately as her head struck the banister with the sickening crack of skull meeting solid wood.

Then silence.

Her body crumpled at the bottom of the stairs in a configuration that spoke of broken things, of damage that could not be repaired, of the particular stillness that comes when life begins its final departure from the flesh that has housed it.

I waited, listening with every fibre of my being for sounds that would indicate her fall had awakened others, that servants or family members would come running to investigate the noise, that my careful solution to the problem of Elsie's knowledge would bring new problems that I had not anticipated.

But the house remained quiet, wrapped in the deep sleep that comes to those whose consciences are clear and whose secrets are safely buried.

I descended the stairs slowly, each step deliberates and careful, until I reached the place where Elsie lay motionless in the pooling light of the candle that had somehow survived her fall, its flame still dancing bravely despite the violence that had just occurred above it.

I knelt beside her broken form and checked for the pulse at her throat, finding it weak and irregular but still present, still fighting against the darkness that was gathering at the edges of her vision. Her eyes were open but unfocused, looking at something beyond the narrow confines of the stairwell, perhaps seeing visions that belonged to the border country between life and death.

Not dead. Not yet.

But close enough that it would not take much to complete what the fall had begun, to ensure that her secrets died with her and that my own secrets remained safe in the darkness where they belonged.

A silver candlestick rested nearby, knocked from its place on a small shelf during her tumbling descent. I picked it up and weighed it in my hand, feeling the substantial heft of polished metal, the way it balanced perfectly as if it had been designed for exactly this purpose.

Heavy enough to finish what needed to be finished. Solid enough to ensure that there would be no miraculous recovery, no deathbed confessions, no last-minute revelations that would destroy everything I had worked so hard to build.

I looked down at Elsie's face, at the trust that still lingered in her dying eyes, the innocent belief that the woman she had served faithfully would not be capable of completing this act of calculated murder. She was still hoping for mercy, still believing that human decency would triumph over self-interest, still clinging to the naive faith that had led her to imagine she could uncover dangerous truths without facing dangerous consequences.

Then I did what was necessary.

The candlestick rose and fell with mechanical precision, ending her hopes and her breathing and her potential to destroy the life I had killed to claim. The sound it made was final, decisive, the period at the end of a sentence that had been building toward this conclusion since the moment she first found Clara's scarf and allowed herself to believe that lost things could be recovered, that the dead could return to reclaim what had been taken from them.

When I returned to my room, my hands were shaking with a tremor that had nothing to do with the physical effort of what I had just accomplished and everything to do with the recognition that I had crossed another line, had added another weight to the burden of guilt that I would carry for the rest of my life.

I poured water from the pitcher on my washstand and drank deeply, trying to wash the taste of violence from my mouth, trying to cleanse myself of the lingering sense that I had just done something that would change me in ways I could not yet understand. I forced myself to breathe slowly and steadily, to regain the composure that would be essential when morning came, and the household discovered what appeared to be a tragic accident.

In the morning, I rang the bell with appropriate timing and informed the assembled household that poor Elsie seemed to have fallen down the servants' stair during the night. They found her exactly where I had left her, her neck bent at an angle that spoke eloquently of the violence of her fall, the candlestick positioned nearby as if it had been knocked from its shelf during her tumbling descent.

No one questioned the obvious explanation. Servants fell downstairs with depressing regularity—tired from long hours of work, navigating narrow passages in inadequate light, carrying heavy loads that affected their balance. It was a tragedy, certainly, but not a mystery. A slip, an accident, the sort of thing that happened in houses like this where the lives of those who served were considered far less valuable than the comfort of those who were served.

Edward placed a comforting hand on my back when the constable finished his perfunctory investigation and declared the death accidental, his touch warm and reassuring in the way that grieving men seek comfort from the women who remain constant in their lives.

"These things are hard on the children," he said, his voice heavy with the kind of masculine concern that focuses on practical matters rather than emotional ones. "But they'll manage. You'll see to it that they understand these things happen, that it wasn't anyone's fault."

I nodded, accepting this responsibility along with all the others that came with my position in his household, my role as the woman who made difficult things manageable and tragic things bearable through her steady presence and unshakeable composure.

The scarf, the note, the candle—all of it disappeared into the kitchen fire where such things belonged, reduced to ash and smoke that the chimney carried away into the grey London sky where secrets went to die. Buried so deep that even the rats in the walls would never find traces of the evidence that had nearly destroyed everything I had worked so hard to achieve.

But that night, as I lay in the bed that had once been Clara's, wrapped in sheets that still carried the faint scent of her perfume, I heard it again with a clarity that made my blood freeze in my veins.

A whisper from behind the walls, soft as silk but sharp as broken glass, carrying with it the weight of accusation and the promise of consequences that could not be avoided forever.

"She saw."

The words seemed to come from everywhere at once—from the walls themselves, from the spaces between the floorboards, from the darkness that pressed against the windows like something alive and patient and utterly without mercy.

Elsie had seen. Had known. Had been silenced.

But her silence had not ended the whispers, had not stopped the evidence from appearing, had not solved the fundamental problem that Clara seemed determined to remain a presence in this house even though her body was supposed to be rotting in some forgotten corner of the woods where no one would ever think to look for her.

If anything, the whispers seemed stronger now, more insistent, as if Elsie's death had somehow added to their power rather than diminished it, as if the act of murder had opened a door that I had never intended to unlock, had invited into my carefully ordered world forces that recognized no boundaries between the living and the dead, between justice and revenge, between what had been done in darkness and what would eventually be revealed in light.

I closed my eyes and tried to sleep, but the whispers followed me down into dreams where Clara and Elsie walked hand in hand through fog that never lifted, where they spoke in voices that carried across impossible distances, where they watched me with eyes that saw everything and forgave nothing and waited with infinite patience for the moment when all debts would finally come due.

She saw.

And now she would never stop seeing, never stop remembering, never stop whispering to whoever might be listening that the woman sleeping in Clara's bed was not who she claimed to be, that the peace of this house had been purchased with blood, that the whispers in the walls were only the beginning of a reckoning that would continue until justice was finally served.

The housemaid was dead.

But her eyes were still watching from whatever place the dead go when they refuse to stay buried, when they have witnessed truths too terrible to carry silently into whatever darkness awaits beyond the borders of life.

And they were not the only eyes watching now.

Something was gathering in the shadows of this house, something that grew stronger with each act of violence, each lie told to preserve the fiction of my innocence, each life taken to protect the secret of what I had become and what I was willing to do to remain what I had chosen to be.

The whispers were no longer just Clara's voice.

They were becoming a chorus.

# Chapter 20: A Visitor from the Past

## "The Sharp Edge of Memory"

The letter arrived with the morning post on a Tuesday that had begun like any other, nestled among the usual collection of social invitations and business correspondence that marked the routine communications of a respectable household. Its envelope was thick, expensive, the sort of quality paper that spoke of education and refinement, and the handwriting across its face was unfamiliar but precise—the careful script of someone who had been taught penmanship as an art form rather than mere utility.

Edward opened it over breakfast, his coffee growing cold as his brow furrowed with the concentration of someone trying to place a name that belonged to memories from a different phase of his life, a time when Clara had been the centre of his world in ways that seemed increasingly distant from the reality we now inhabited.

"Charlotte Linton," he said aloud, glancing toward me with the particular expression men wear when they expect women to be more interested in social connections than they themselves pretend to be. "Clara's childhood friend from Yorkshire. She's returning to England after years abroad. Wishes to call on us to pay her respects."

I set my delicate China teacup down with the careful precision that had become second nature to me, though inside I felt as if the porcelain might shatter in my suddenly unsteady hands. "How kind of her to remember us in our time of grief."

"She was always fond of Clara," Edward added with the absent tone of someone whose attention was already drifting toward the business concerns that would occupy his day. "The two were nearly inseparable at school thick as thieves, Clara used to say. They kept up correspondence for years, though I haven't seen Charlotte since before Margaret was born. She went to Italy with her aunt, if I remember correctly. Something about her health requiring a warmer climate."

A chill passed through me that had nothing to do with the morning air filtering through the breakfast room windows, a coldness that seemed to settle in my bones and spread outward until I had to fight to keep my expression composed, my voice steady, my hands from trembling as I reached for my napkin.

I remembered Clara speaking of Charlotte, though the memory felt like something observed through thick glass—distant and distorted but unmistakably real. It had been during one of those evenings when Clara read her correspondence aloud to Edward, her voice bright with pleasure at news from friends scattered across the globe, that insufferable little laugh punctuating anecdotes about people I had never met but whose happiness seemed to mock my own isolation and longing.

Charlotte Linton, the friend who had known Clara before society had shaped her into the perfect wife and mother, before marriage had given her the security and status that I had been denied, before children had provided her with purpose and meaning that filled the spaces where my own life remained empty and aching. Charlotte, who had been present during Clara's formation into the woman I had both envied and ultimately destroyed, who possessed memories of her that predated every mask and performance, every carefully constructed social persona that I had spent months learning to inhabit.

She would remember Clara too well. She would know things about her childhood, her dreams, her fears, her unconscious habits and natural reactions that no amount of careful observation and meticulous study could have taught me. She would be able to detect inconsistencies in my performance that even Edward and the children had failed to notice, gaps in my knowledge that could expose the fundamental fraud at the heart of my assumed identity.

I wrote back immediately, before Edward could take it upon himself to handle the correspondence, using Clara's personal stationery and adopting the warmly gracious tone that would be expected from a family friend receiving news of an old companion's return.

*Dearest Charlotte,*

*\*How wonderful to hear from you after all these years, though I confess the circumstances of your visit bring me both joy and sorrow. Edward and I would be delighted to receive you at your convenience. The children often ask about their dear mother's school friends, and I know Clara would have wanted us to maintain the connections that were so precious to her.*

*With warmest regards and anticipation of your visit,*

*Mrs. Eleanor Westmore*

The letter was a masterpiece of careful ambiguity, positioning me as the family friend who had stepped into the breach after Clara's tragic disappearance rather than claiming any identity that might be tested against Charlotte's intimate knowledge of the woman I was pretending to have replaced. It bought me time, space, the possibility of navigating whatever challenges her presence might bring without immediately exposing myself to the kind of scrutiny that could destroy everything I had worked so hard to achieve.

But even as I sealed the envelope and arranged for its immediate posting, I felt the familiar anxiety that had become my constant companion since the first whispers had started echoing through the walls of this house that should have been my sanctuary but was increasingly feeling like a trap of my own construction.

When Charlotte arrived three days later, announced by the sound of carriage wheels on cobblestones and the butler's respectful knock on the drawing room door, the very air seemed to shift in response to her presence, as if reality itself were adjusting to accommodate someone whose relationship to this household predated my own carefully orchestrated insertion into its history.

She was tall and thin, dressed in the kind of understated elegance that spoke of good breeding and comfortable circumstances without the need for ostentation or display. Her traveling dress was well-cut but not fashionable, practical rather than decorative, the choice of someone who valued substance over style and had learned to navigate the world based on intelligence rather than beauty.

But it was her eyes that made my breath catch in my throat—sharp, fox-coloured eyes that seemed to take in everything at once, missing nothing of significance, cataloguing details with the methodical attention of someone trained to notice discrepancies, to spot the small inconsistencies that revealed larger truths.

She embraced Edward with the gentle affection of someone who had known him during happier times, who remembered him as Clara's devoted husband rather than the grieving widower he had become. Her greeting to the children was warm but not presumptuous, the careful kindness of an adult who understood that young hearts heal differently than mature ones and required delicate handling in the aftermath of loss.

And then she turned to me with a smile that was perfectly polite, socially appropriate, and utterly devoid of warmth—the expression of someone who was prepared to be civil but had not yet decided whether genuine friendship would be possible or advisable.

"Mrs. Westmore," she said, her voice carrying the particular cadence of someone who had been educated to speak with authority and precision, "it is an honour to finally meet the woman who has done so much for this family during such a difficult time. Clara's letters spoke so warmly of your dedication to the children and your support of Edward during her... difficulties."

The pause before that final word was so slight that anyone else might have missed it, but I heard it like a bell tolling, marking the space where doubt lived, where questions had been raised but not yet answered.

"The honour is entirely mine," I replied, extending a gloved hand with the practiced grace that months of living Clara's life had made automatic. "Clara spoke of you often, always with such fondness. I know she would have been delighted to know you had returned safely to England."

Charlotte's handshake was cool and brief, her fingers making contact just long enough to fulfil social requirements before withdrawing, as if prolonged physical contact might reveal something she was not yet prepared to know.

We took tea in the sitting room, the three of us arranged around the low table in a tableau that should have represented domestic harmony but felt instead like a scene from a play where each actor was performing a different drama, working from scripts that had never been properly coordinated.

Charlotte asked about Clara with the systematic thoroughness of someone conducting an investigation disguised as social conversation. What had she said in her final weeks? How had she seemed when she left the house that last morning? How were the children coping with the uncertainty of not knowing what had become of their mother?

I answered each question with perfect composure, drawing on months of practice at discussing Clara's disappearance with the appropriate mixture of regret and carefully modulated sorrow. I had rehearsed these responses until they felt natural, until I could deliver them without the slightest tremor in my voice or hesitation in my manner.

"She had been unwell for some time," I said softly, allowing my voice to carry the particular sadness that comes from watching someone you care about struggle with demons too powerful for ordinary comfort to address. "Withdrawn, increasingly troubled by thoughts she rarely shared with others. I fear her heart was burdened by sorrows that ran deeper than any of us fully understood, though she tried so hard to maintain her usual cheerful demeanour for the sake of the children."

Charlotte studied me for a moment that stretched longer than comfort allowed, her fox-coloured eyes examining my face with the intensity of someone reading a document written in a language she was still learning to decipher.

"She never wrote to me of any such troubles," she said finally, her voice carefully neutral but carrying undertones that suggested surprise, concern, and perhaps the beginning of suspicion. "Her letters were always so full of life, so focused on domestic happiness and the joy she found in her role as wife and mother. Even her most recent correspondence, which arrived only weeks before I learned of her disappearance, spoke of plans for the children's education, excitement about improvements to the garden."

The information hit me like cold water, a shock of recognition that Clara's performance of contentment had extended far beyond her household, that she had been maintaining the fiction of happiness even in private correspondence with friends who might have been trusted with more complex truths.

"She rarely wrote at all toward the end," I said, improvising desperately to account for this discrepancy between Charlotte's memories and the narrative I had constructed to explain Clara's state of mind. "But perhaps you knew her in ways that the rest of us never could. Childhood friendships often preserve insights that later relationships cannot match."

Charlotte tilted her head slightly, a gesture that reminded me uncomfortably of a bird of prey assessing potential victim, deciding whether the movement below represented threat or opportunity.

"Perhaps," she agreed, but the single word carried weight that suggested volumes of unspoken reservation.

The rest of the afternoon passed like a blade drawn slowly across silk, each moment creating the potential for damage while maintaining the appearance of harmless social interaction. Our conversation was polite but stilted, punctuated by laughter that sounded forced and unnatural, as if we were all playing roles in a drama that none of us had properly understood when we agreed to participate.

Charlotte's questions were subtle but barbed, designed to test my knowledge of Clara's history, her preferences, her habits and reactions in ways that seemed casual but carried the weight of examination. She mentioned shared memories from their school days, referenced conversations they had supposedly had during visits that I could not have witnessed, spoke of Clara's opinions on subjects that had never come up during my careful observation of her daily life.

I navigated these challenges as best I could, deflecting some inquiries with claims of incomplete knowledge, answering others based on logical deduction from what I had observed during my months in the household. But I could feel the ground shifting beneath my feet with each exchange, sense Charlotte's growing certainty that something was fundamentally wrong with the picture I was presenting, that the woman sitting across from her sharing Clara's tea service and wearing Clara's jewellery was not who she claimed to be.

The moment that crystallized my danger came when Charlotte's gaze fell on the sapphire brooch I wore at my throat—one of Clara's favourite pieces, selected that morning because its elegance seemed appropriate for receiving an important visitor. Without warning, Charlotte reached across the small space between our chairs and touched the jewellery with familiar fingers, her expression shifting into something that looked almost like recognition of an old friend.

"Clara always complained about this piece," she said conversationally, but her eyes never left my face as she spoke, watching for reactions that might confirm or contradict whatever theory was forming in her mind. "She loved the stones, but the clasp mechanism irritated her skin terribly. She said it felt like tiny claws digging into her throat every time she wore it, but the brooch had been her grandmother's, and she couldn't bear to have it altered."

The words hung in the air between us like an accusation disguised as reminiscence, a test designed to reveal whether I possessed the intimate knowledge of Clara's physical responses that any woman who had lived in her body would naturally possess.

I smiled with what I hoped appeared to be gentle understanding, though inside I felt as if the ground were opening beneath my chair. "I wouldn't know about that particular sensitivity. The clasp has never bothered me at all—perhaps we simply have different types of skin."

A pause that seemed to last for hours.

A flicker in Charlotte's gaze that spoke of recognition, revelation, the moment when suspicion crystallizes into certainty.

Then she smiled as well, but her expression carried something cold and calculating that had not been present earlier in our conversation.

"No," she said softly, as if speaking to herself rather than to me, "I suppose it wouldn't bother you. Different skin entirely."

The words carried layers of meaning that made my blood freeze, implications that she understood exactly what I was and what I had done, that my performance had been insufficient to deceive someone who possessed the kind of intimate knowledge that comes from years of true friendship.

After she left, I watched her carriage from the drawing room window as it disappeared into the fog that was beginning to gather with the approach of evening, my fingers digging into the heavy velvet drapes until my knuckles went white with the force of my grip.

She knows.

Or at the very least, she suspects strongly enough to pose a threat that could not be ignored or dismissed as easily as I had dealt with poor Elsie's dangerous curiosity.

I could feel the weight of her knowledge in the way she had walked through the halls during her visit, the careful attention she had paid to the family portrait in the entrance hall, the subtle questions she had asked the servants about household routines and recent changes in the family's circumstances. Her presence had filled the house with a kind of electric tension, an awareness that someone was watching, analysing, drawing conclusions that could prove fatal to everything I had worked so hard to achieve.

Later that night, after Edward had retired to his study and the children had been settled in their beds, I retrieved Clara's correspondence from the locked drawer where I kept documents that required careful handling. Every letter Charlotte had sent over the years; every folded page covered with news and affection and the kind of casual intimacy that exists only between people who have known each other since childhood.

I studied Charlotte's handwriting until I could reproduce it with reasonable accuracy, memorized her style of expressing herself, her preferences for certain phrases and constructions. If circumstances required me to forge correspondence that would support my version of recent events, I needed to be prepared to create documents that would pass even careful scrutiny.

But even as I practiced writing farewell notes and confessional letters in Charlotte's hand, preparing for whatever desperate measures might become necessary to protect my secret, something else gnawed at me with cold insistence—an awareness that threats were multiplying faster than my ability to address them, that the careful balance I had maintained for months was beginning to collapse under the weight of accumulating lies and mounting evidence.

A piece of paper had been slipped under my bedroom door while I worked, appearing sometime during the hours I had spent hunched over Clara's desk practicing penmanship and preparing for possibilities I hoped would never become necessary.

One sentence, written in handwriting I did not recognize, words that struck me like physical blows:

"You're wearing her skin, but her bones still rattle."

The message was unsigned, undated, offering no clue about its origin or the identity of whoever had composed it and delivered it with such stealth that I had not heard a single footstep in the corridor outside my room.

But its meaning was unmistakable, its implications clear enough to send terror racing through my veins like poison.

Someone knew. Someone understood exactly what I had done and how I had done it, someone who possessed knowledge that went beyond suspicion or speculation into the realm of certainty, someone who was prepared to use that knowledge in ways that could destroy not just my carefully constructed life but my very freedom, perhaps even my life itself.

Charlotte's visit had been the beginning, not the end, of a reckoning that was gathering force like a storm building on the horizon. The sharp edge of memory had cut through my defences, had revealed the gaps and inconsistencies in my performance that I had hoped would remain hidden forever.

And now, somewhere in the darkness that pressed against the windows of this house that had never truly been mine, forces were aligning that recognized no boundary between justice and revenge, between what had been done in secret and what would eventually be revealed in the harsh light of truth.

The bones were rattling.

And soon, very soon, they would dance.

# Chapter 21: Blood in the Garden

## "The Roses Remember"

It began with a stench that arrived on the morning wind like a messenger bearing news that no one wanted to receive—subtle at first, just a sourness threading through the crisp November air that infiltrated even the most carefully sealed rooms of the house.

I was sitting in the breakfast room, maintaining the quiet ritual that had become so essential to my sense of control over the domestic sphere I had claimed as my own, when the Odor first reached me. It was carried through the open windows that I always insisted remain partially ajar despite the servants' concerns about the chill, because fresh air seemed the only antidote to the oppressive atmosphere that had been building in the house since Charlotte's visit and the discovery of that terrible note slipped beneath my door.

I paused with my delicate China teacup halfway to my lips, the warm liquid growing cold as I tried to identify what my senses were telling me, what part of my carefully ordered world had developed this corruption that seemed to seep into everything like smoke from a hidden fire.

"Something's gone off," Edward muttered from behind his morning newspaper, glancing toward the butler who stood waiting to refill his coffee cup. His voice carried the particular irritation of a man whose domestic comfort had been disrupted by forces beyond his control. "Perhaps something in the cellar has spoiled, or there's been a problem with the drains. See to it, would you?"

I said nothing, but my hand trembled slightly as I set the teacup back on its saucer, because somewhere beneath the layers of rational thought and careful composure, a primitive part of my mind had already recognized what my conscious awareness was still refusing to acknowledge.

I knew that smell.

It was the scent of secrets that refuse to stay buried, of crimes that insist on returning to the surface despite all efforts to keep them hidden in the darkness where they belonged. It was the particular sweetness that comes from flesh returning to the earth, the biological process that reduces all human ambition and desire to the basic elements from which they arose.

But I had been so careful. I had disposed of my evidence with methodical precision, had chosen burial sites far from the house and its carefully tended grounds. Whatever was producing this Odor should not have been anywhere near the rose garden that had been Clara's particular pride, the sanctuary she had created with her own hands and tended with devotion that bordered on obsession.

By midday, when the sun had climbed high enough to warm the air and intensify whatever corruption was fouling the atmosphere, the source could no longer be ignored or explained away as a minor household mishap that could be resolved with better ventilation and careful cleaning.

Old Thomas, the head gardener whose stooped back and tobacco-stained teeth marked him as someone who had spent his entire life working with soil and plants and the patient rhythms of growing things, came knocking at the kitchen door with his hat clutched in hands that shook with more than age.

He was white as milk, his weathered face drained of all colour except for the broken veins that mapped his cheeks like rivers on an ancient landscape. When he spoke, his voice carried the particular quality of someone who had discovered something that challenged his understanding of how the world was supposed to work.

"Begging your pardon, ma'am," he said to me, though his eyes refused to meet mine, as if direct contact might somehow implicate him in whatever horror he had uncovered. "There's something under the roses. Something what shouldn't be there, something that's been disturbing the earth and making the plants sick. The smell's been getting worse for days now, and today... today I had to know what was causing it."

I followed the growing crowd out into the back garden, my heart hammering against my ribs with such force that I was certain everyone could hear it, my stomach hollow with the kind of fear that comes from knowing that your most carefully buried secrets are about to be exposed to daylight and examination.

The Harrowby rose garden had been Clara's masterpiece, her contribution to the beauty of a world that had given her so much comfort and security. She had planned every bed and border with artistic precision, had chosen varieties that would bloom in succession throughout the growing season, creating a display that drew admiring comments from every visitor and filled the house with fragrance during the warmer months.

Lush with creamy whites and deep pinks the size of a curled hand, heavy with blooms that seemed to embody all the domestic happiness and marital contentment that I had worked so hard to claim for myself, the garden had been a testament to Clara's ability to create beauty from bare earth, to nurture living things into flourishing abundance.

Now, the earth had been turned and churned, soil scattered across the carefully maintained paths like evidence of violence done to something sacred. One of the prize bushes—the magnificent white rose that grew near the marble bench where Clara had spent so many peaceful hours reading or simply enjoying the work of her hands—lay uprooted and dying, its petals scattered across the dark earth like fragments of broken skin, like pieces of something that had once been beautiful but was now only a reminder of destruction.

The smell was infinitely worse here, concentrated and inescapable, a sweetness so cloying that it made breathing difficult, that seemed to coat the inside of my throat with corruption and made my eyes water with involuntary tears.

Edward stood to one side of the disturbed ground, his face pale and set with the expression of a man trying to maintain composure in the face of something that threatened to destroy his understanding of his own life. He kept his distance from the excavated area, as if proximity might somehow contaminate him with whatever evil had taken root in his wife's beloved garden.

The children had been kept indoors, thankfully, though I could see their faces pressed against the nursery windows, their young minds trying to make sense of the unusual activity that had disrupted their normal routines and filled the air with tension that even they could sense.

Charlotte—damn her, damn her presence and her timing and her terrible intuition—had returned that morning, arriving just as the discovery was being made, just in time to witness the moment when my carefully constructed world began to crumble like a castle built on sand. She stood among the gathered servants and constables with her arms folded across her chest, her face unreadable but her eyes alert with the kind of attention that suggested she understood the significance of what was happening far better than anyone else present.

The constables worked with grim efficiency, treating the garden like a crime scene, which of course it now was, though not in ways that any of us had anticipated. They found fabric first—

scraps of material that had once been clothing but were now stained and partially rotted, evidence of a body that had been concealed beneath the earth with the expectation that it would remain hidden forever.

Then they found something more substantial, something that made even the experienced investigators step back with expressions of distaste and professional concern.

I watched from the drawing room window, my hands pressed so tightly against the sill that I could feel the wood cutting into my palms, as the chief inspector lifted what appeared to be a soiled bundle wrapped in some kind of shrouding material. His gloved hands moved with careful precision as he unwrapped part of the package, revealing what lay beneath the improvised burial cloth.

Bone. White and clean where the earth had not stained it, unmistakably human despite the corruption that surrounded it. A length of rib, perhaps, or part of an arm—I was not anatomist enough to be certain, but the sight made my vision blur with the kind of shock that comes from seeing proof that your worst fears have materialized in forms even more terrible than imagination had suggested.

Charlotte stood in the garden below, watching the proceedings with the focused attention of someone who understood that she was witnessing the resolution of mysteries that had been troubling her since her arrival. When she glanced up toward the window where I stood frozen, I saw something in her expression that made my blood turn to ice in my veins.

Accusation. Certainty. The look of someone who had suspected terrible truths and was now watching them be confirmed by physical evidence that could not be explained away or dismissed as coincidence.

She wanted it to be Clara. She was hoping that the bones emerging from the rose garden would provide answers to questions that had been tormenting her since she learned of her childhood friend's disappearance, would offer closure and explanation and perhaps even justice for whatever crime she was increasingly certain had been committed.

But I had never buried Clara beneath the roses. I had been more careful than that, more methodical in my disposal of evidence. Clara's body lay somewhere far from here, in the woods beyond the estate where fog and undergrowth had concealed my crime and would continue to protect my secret long after her bones had been scattered by animals and weather and the patient work of time itself.

So, what was this? Who had been interred beneath Clara's beloved roses with such apparent haste and carelessness that the burial had begun to advertise its presence to anyone with functioning senses?

The answer came to me with sickening clarity as I remembered another night, another death, another problem that had required immediate solution without time for careful planning or methodical execution.

Elsie.

The memory returned with vivid intensity—her broken body at the bottom of the servants' stair, the need to dispose of evidence before morning brought questions that could destroy everything I had worked to achieve. In my panic, I had chosen expedience over security, had selected the nearest available location rather than the carefully chosen sites I had used for more significant crimes.

The rose garden. Clara's sanctuary, transformed into a graveyard for the girl whose only crime had been seeing too much, knowing too much, threatening to expose truths that were supposed to remain buried forever.

Yes. It had to be Elsie.

But the realization brought no comfort, only fresh terror at how quickly my careful plans were unravelling, how many different threats were converging on the life I had built through such careful deception and patient violence.

Still—this was too close to the house, too likely to be discovered, too soon after Charlotte's arrival to be coincidental. Someone was orchestrating these revelations, guiding investigations toward evidence that would destroy my carefully constructed identity and expose me to consequences I was not prepared to face.

The inspector questioned everyone with methodical thoroughness, treating each member of the household as both potential witness and possible suspect. The staff, the children—though gently, given their ages and obvious distress—and even Edward, who submitted to interrogation with the weary patience of a man who had grown accustomed to having his life disrupted by investigations that never seemed to provide the answers he desperately needed.

I was summoned last, ushered into Edward's study like an honoured guest at my own potential downfall, asked to sit in the leather chair that faced the inspector's borrowed desk while he arranged his notes and prepared to determine whether I was merely another witness or something far more dangerous.

"Mrs. Westmore," he said with professional courtesy, tipping his hat in the gesture that police officers used to establish their respect for social hierarchy even while pursuing investigations that might destroy the very foundations of respectable society. "You've been with the Harrowby family for how long now?"

I smiled with what I hoped appeared to be cooperative helpfulness, though every muscle in my body was tense with readiness to defend myself against accusations I could not predict or prepare for in advance.

"Nearly a year," I replied, choosing words that would establish my position in the household without claiming intimacy or knowledge that might be tested against evidence I could not control.

"And before that?" he continued, his pencil poised over the notebook where he was recording responses that might later be used to build cases or eliminate suspects from consideration.

"I was living in Kent with my late husband," I said with practiced smoothness, drawing on the fictional biography I had constructed during my months of preparation for this role. "He passed from consumption, and I found myself in need of employment. The Harrowby's were kind enough to offer me a position when their previous governess left to marry."

"And you knew Mrs. Harrowby well during your time here?"

The question was casual, but I heard in it the potential for deeper investigation, the beginning of inquiries that might reveal inconsistencies in my story or gaps in my knowledge that would expose the fundamental deception at the heart of my presence in this house.

"As well as anyone might know their employer," I replied carefully. "She was... a private person, given to keeping her own counsel rather than confiding in servants, however trusted they might be."

He nodded as if this confirmed expectations based on other testimony he had gathered. "And there's been no sign of her since her disappearance? No communication, no indication of where she might have gone or why she might have chosen to leave?"

"Nothing at all," I whispered, allowing my voice to carry the sadness that any devoted employee would feel at the continued absence of a beloved mistress. "It has been a source of great distress to all of us, particularly the children, who continue to hope for her return."

He narrowed his eyes slightly, studying my face with the kind of attention that suggested he was looking for signs of deception, inconsistencies between my words and my expressions that might indicate knowledge I was not sharing willingly.

"But now we find a body buried on the grounds," he said, making the transition from missing person to murder investigation with the casual efficiency of someone accustomed to following evidence wherever it might lead. "This changes the nature of the questions we must ask."

My gaze dropped to my folded hands, the picture of someone overwhelmed by the implications of what had been discovered, someone struggling to process how the disappearance of a cherished employer might be connected to the presence of human remains in what should have been a place of beauty and peace.

"It's a tragedy beyond comprehension," I said softly. "I can only hope that this discovery will somehow bring us closer to understanding what happened to Mrs. Harrowby, will provide answers that have been so desperately needed by all who loved her."

He tapped his pencil against his lip, a gesture that suggested he was considering how much information to share, how many details of the investigation could be revealed without compromising the pursuit of justice.

"This body," he said finally, "is that of a young woman, small in stature, probably no more than twenty years of age. But it's not Mrs. Harrowby."

I blinked with what I hoped appeared to be genuine surprise, though inside I felt a complicated mixture of relief and growing terror. "Not...?"

He watched my reaction carefully, as if my response to this information might reveal something significant about my relationship to both the discovered remains and the missing woman whose disappearance had brought him here in the first place.

"No. The height is wrong, the bone structure completely different. We'll know more once the examination is complete, but this is definitely not the woman we've been searching for."

Relief flooded through me like cold water, but it brought with it a chill that seemed to settle in my bones and spread outward until I felt as if I were drowning in ice. If the body was not Clara, and if I had not buried Elsie in the rose garden, then whose remains had been disturbed by Thomas's digging?

Who had been interred beneath Clara's beloved roses, and why had their resting place been chosen with such apparent deliberation, as if someone had wanted the discovery to occur at precisely this moment, when Charlotte's presence and growing suspicions would ensure that every detail of the investigation would be scrutinized for connections to larger mysteries?

I hadn't buried anyone there. I was certain of it. My crimes had been committed with far more care and forethought than this crude interment suggested, my disposal of evidence conducted with the kind of methodical precision that would prevent exactly this kind of exposure.

So, who had? And why?

That night, long after the constables had departed and the household had settled into the uneasy quiet that follows the disruption of tragedy, I stood alone in the garden, staring down at the raw wound in the earth where Clara's prize rose bush had once bloomed.

The soil was dark and freshly turned, like an open grave waiting to receive whatever additional secrets the investigation might uncover. The moonlight made everything appear silver and insubstantial, transformed the familiar landscape into something alien and threatening, a place where normal rules might not apply and impossible things might manifest with terrifying reality.

Wind tugged at my skirts and hair, carrying with it the lingering scent of corruption that no amount of fresh air seemed able to cleanse completely. The moon hung high and cold and utterly without sympathy, illuminating but not warming, revealing but not explaining.

I stood there in the silver light, trying to make sense of events that seemed to be spiralling beyond my control, when something changed in the quality of the air around me. Not dramatically, not in ways that anyone watching might have noticed, but with the subtle shift that announced the presence of something that should not have been there, something that defied rational explanation but could not be dismissed as imagination or overwrought nerves.

The air grew heavier, colder, thick with familiarity that made my skin crawl with recognition even as my rational mind rejected what my deeper instincts were telling me.

I didn't hear footsteps or the rustle of clothing that would announce another person's approach. But I felt her as clearly as if she had called my name, felt the particular presence that had been haunting the edges of my consciousness for weeks, growing stronger and more insistent with each passing day.

Clara.

I turned slowly, my heart hammering with such force that I was surprised the sound didn't echo across the disturbed garden, expecting to see her standing among the shadows cast by the bare trees and darkened house.

Nothing.

No figure in white moving through the moonlight, no ghostly apparition materializing from the mist that was beginning to rise from the damp earth. Just the empty garden and the raw hole where her roses had once grown, the evidence of violence done to something she had loved.

But in the silence that followed my turning, in the space between one heartbeat and the next, I heard something that made my blood freeze in my veins and my breath catch in my throat like a trapped bird.

A voice. Soft as silk, gentle as memory, but carrying with it the weight of authority that comes from beyond the boundaries of life and death.

So soft it might have been imagination, so quiet it could have been the wind sighing through bare branches or the settling of old wood in the cooling night air.

But unmistakably real, unmistakably hers, unmistakably directed at me with intimate knowledge of exactly what I had done and what I was still hiding in the darkness of my guilty conscience.

"Dig deeper."

The words hung in the air like smoke, like breath made visible, like the manifestation of truths that had been buried but refused to stay dead.

Dig deeper.

Into the earth where more secrets lay waiting to be discovered, where additional evidence of my crimes might be festering in the soil like seeds planted by someone who understood exactly how to orchestrate my destruction.

Or deeper into the mystery of who had been buried beneath Clara's roses, who had placed that body there and why, what connection existed between the discovered remains and the larger web of violence and deception that had consumed my life since the moment I decided that Clara's existence was less important than my own desires.

The voice faded into silence, leaving me alone with questions that multiplied like shadows in the moonlight, but the words continued to echo in my mind long after the garden had returned to its deceptive peace.

Dig deeper.

Someone was orchestrating these discoveries, guiding investigations toward revelations that would expose not just my recent crimes but perhaps older secrets, darker truths that I had convinced myself were buried so deeply they would never resurface to threaten the life I had built on their foundation.

The roses remembered. The earth remembered. And somewhere in the spaces between life and death, Clara remembered everything.

The reckoning I had been dreading was finally beginning, not with dramatic confrontation or obvious accusation, but with the slow, patient excavation of truths that had been planted like time bombs in the soil of my assumed life.

And I was running out of places to hide.

# Chapter 22: The Mask Slips

## "The Crack in the Glass"

Edward watches me now.

The change began subtly, in ways that only someone who had spent months studying every nuance of his behaviour would have noticed. But I had made myself an expert in reading the faces of this household, in interpreting the smallest shifts in expression and posture that might signal threats to the life I had constructed with such meticulous care.

He thinks I don't see it—the way his gaze lingers on me now with a quality it had never possessed before, no longer the appreciative attention of a man grateful for feminine comfort in his time of loss, but something sharper, more analytical, touched with the kind of wariness that suggested he was beginning to see me as a puzzle that required solving rather than a blessing to be accepted without question.

The shift in his regard was like watching sunlight fade from a room, gradual but inexorable, casting shadows where none had existed before. His polite silences carried weight now, pregnant with questions he was not yet ready to voice aloud but which I could feel pressing against the carefully maintained façade of domestic tranquillity that had protected us both from truths too dangerous to acknowledge.

He had grown careful around me, hesitant in ways that made every interaction feel like a performance where neither of us was quite certain of our lines. Our conversations, once easy and natural, now carried undercurrents of tension that made even the most mundane exchanges about household matters feel loaded with significance.

But most damning of all, most revealing of the fundamental change in how he perceived my presence in his home, he had begun locking his study door again—something he had stopped doing months ago when trust had replaced suspicion, when my position in his life had seemed secure enough that privacy was no longer necessary.

The sound of that key turning in the lock each evening was like a death knell for everything I had worked so hard to achieve, a return to the days when I had been an outsider looking in rather than an integral part of the family structure I had fought so desperately to join.

Something had turned in him. I could pinpoint the exact moment when suspicion had begun to replace trust, when gratitude had curdled into doubt. It was after the discovery in the garden, after the police had finished their excavation of the rose bed that had once been Clara's pride and joy, after the questions and examinations and careful documentation of evidence that pointed toward crimes none of us was supposed to have committed.

He hadn't said anything outright—Edward was too much the gentleman, too committed to maintaining the forms of civilized discourse even when civilized assumptions no longer applied. But I could feel his growing unease like a physical presence in the house, a chill that seemed to follow me through hallways that had once felt warm and welcoming.

He was wondering, with the persistent curiosity of a man who had discovered that his comfortable assumptions about his own life might be fundamentally incorrect, what else I might have buried in the carefully tended soil of his domestic sanctuary. If one body could be hidden beneath the roses his wife had planted with such loving attention, what other secrets might be festering in places he had never thought to look?

Charlotte's extended presence in the house did nothing to ease the mounting tension. What should have been a brief condolence visit from an old friend had stretched on with the relentless persistence of a season of drought, each day bringing new opportunities for observation and inquiry that made my skin crawl with the sensation of being dissected while still alive.

She lingered in the Parlors where Clara had once entertained visitors, questioned the maids with the casual authority of someone who had every right to seek information about household routines and recent changes. Her conversations with the staff were conducted in half-truths and leading questions that suggested she was assembling a picture of our family life that might not match the version I had so carefully constructed and maintained.

Every time I passed her in the corridors or encountered her in rooms where she had no particular business being, I felt the heat of her stare against the back of my neck, the weight of attention that was far more intense and focused than casual interest would account for. She was studying me with the methodical patience of a naturalist observing some new species, cataloguing my behaviours and responses for future analysis.

The conversation that shattered my sense of security came during what should have been a peaceful family dinner, one of those quiet evening meals that had become precious rituals of domestic normalcy in the months since Clara's disappearance. Charlotte had positioned herself with strategic precision, her chair angled so that she could observe both Edward and me while appearing to focus her attention on the simple pleasure of well-prepared food and civilized company.

Her question, when it came, was delivered with the casual tone of someone making idle conversation, but its implications struck me like a physical blow:

"Don't you think it strange, Edward, how little any of us really know about Mrs. Westmore's life before she came to you? I mean, one would expect someone who has become so integral to your family's welfare to have more... substantial connections to her past, wouldn't you say?"

The words hung in the air like smoke from a fire that threatened to consume everything I had built, and I felt my carefully maintained composure begin to crack under the pressure of what I knew was coming.

Edward didn't answer immediately. The silence stretched between question and response, growing heavier with each passing second, filled with the sound of cutlery against China and the careful breathing of people who understood that they were participating in something more significant than dinner conversation.

And that silence—God help me, that terrible, weighted silence—said everything that needed to be said about the direction his thoughts had been taking, the conclusions he was beginning to draw about the woman who had appeared in his life at such a convenient moment, who had filled the space left by his wife's disappearance with such perfect timing and seamless efficiency.

It was after midnight when he finally came to my room, when the house had settled into the deep quiet that comes in the hours before dawn and the servants were safely asleep in their quarters, when no one would witness whatever confrontation had been building between us for days like storm clouds gathering on the horizon.

I had just finished taking down my hair, the long tortoiseshell pins scattered across Clara's vanity like small silver weapons, the weight of the elaborate style finally released from my aching scalp. The ritual of undressing had become one of my few moments of genuine privacy, when I could drop the constant performance of being someone else and simply exist in the space between one day's deceptions and the next day's necessities.

He didn't knock. That should have warned me that this visit was different from any that had come before, that the rules of courtesy and propriety that had governed our interactions were no longer in effect. He simply opened the door and stepped inside, closing it behind him with the deliberate care of someone who understood that what was about to occur could not be allowed to reach other ears in the household.

"Edward?" I asked, modulating my voice to convey the appropriate mixture of surprise and concern that any respectable woman would feel at such an unconventional late-night visit.

He stepped further into the room, and I studied his reflection in the mirror while pretending to continue the domestic ritual of preparing for sleep. His face was pale and strained, marked by the kind of exhaustion that comes not from physical effort but from wrestling with thoughts too terrible to accept, conclusions too dangerous to voice aloud.

When I turned to greet him properly, to offer whatever comfort or explanation might be required to restore the harmony that had been so essential to my sense of security, I saw that he held something in his hand.

A letter. No—a single page, carefully folded, the paper bearing the distinctive watermark and texture that marked it as part of Clara's personal correspondence, the expensive stationery she had used for her most private communications.

"I found this in the garden room," he said, his voice carrying the controlled tone of a man who was working very hard to remain calm in the face of evidence that challenged everything he thought he knew about his own life.

I stood slowly, my mind racing through possible explanations, plausible stories that might account for whatever he had discovered without implicating me in crimes that could destroy not just my assumed identity but my very freedom.

"It must have been misplaced somehow," I said, allowing concern to colour my voice. "The children have been playing throughout the house since the weather turned cold, and they sometimes move papers from room to room without thinking about where they belong—"

He cut me off with the sharp gesture of someone who had already considered and rejected such innocent explanations.

"This is Clara's handwriting," he said, holding up the page so that I could see the familiar script that I had studied so carefully, had practiced imitating during the long nights when I prepared for the possibility that forgery might become necessary to maintain my deception. "But the date doesn't make sense. According to this, it was written months after she supposedly disappeared."

I moved toward him, my heart hammering with such force that I was certain he could hear it, my mind scrambling for some rational explanation that would satisfy his growing suspicions without revealing the true extent of my knowledge about Clara's fate.

"Edward, there must be some error in the dating," I began, reaching out as if to examine the document more closely. "Perhaps she misdated it, or perhaps it was written earlier and became separated from its proper sequence—"

But he was not finished with his catalogue of evidence, his methodical destruction of the careful lies that had protected me for so many months.

"You wore her sapphire brooch to Charlotte's first visit," he said, his voice growing stronger as he gained confidence in his accusations. "Even though you told me weeks ago that Clara never allowed servants to borrow her jewellery, that she was very particular about who was permitted to handle her personal possessions."

I felt the blood drain from my face as I realized how many small inconsistencies I had failed to account for; how many casual lies had accumulated into a pattern that anyone with sufficient motivation could recognize as evidence of larger deceptions.

"You called the east wing 'her' sanctuary," he continued relentlessly, "referring to it as if you had intimate knowledge of Clara's private habits. But only I knew she used that room for reading, only I was aware that she kept a personal diary hidden in the windowsill drawer where she thought no one would think to look for it."

As he spoke, he held up another item that made my breath catch in my throat like a trapped bird—a small journal bound in cracked brown leather, its pages yellowed with age and filled with Clara's most private thoughts, the secret record of her inner life that I had discovered during my systematic exploration of every corner of the house that might contain useful information.

"You broke into her private spaces," he said, his voice now carrying the weight of certainty rather than suspicion. "You read this diary, studied her personal correspondence, learned intimate details about her thoughts and feelings that no governess should have possessed. You knew things you had no right to know, things that could only have been discovered through deliberate violation of her privacy."

The accusations came like blows, each one landing with devastating accuracy, exposing the careful research and methodical preparation that had made my impersonation possible. I had been so proud of my thoroughness, so confident that my attention to detail would protect me from exactly this kind of scrutiny.

"Edward, please," I said, allowing desperation to enter my voice, hoping that an appeal to his lingering affection might provide some protection against the momentum of his investigation. "I was only trying to understand her better, to preserve her memory for the children, to ensure that her spirit remained alive in this house even after her physical presence was gone—"

He flinched as if I had struck him, his face contorting with disgust at what he clearly perceived as the manipulation of his love for his children to serve my own purposes.

"Don't," he said sharply. "Don't use them. Don't hide behind their innocence to justify whatever you've done here."

Silence fell between us then, heavy and breathless, filled with the weight of accusations that could no longer be avoided or explained away. I watched his face with the fascination of someone observing her own execution, saw confusion fold into horror as the full implications of what he had discovered began to penetrate his conscious understanding.

"Tell me, "He said finally, his voice shaking with the effort required to voice the question that had been building in his mind for days, "what really happened to Clara?"

The moment cracked like glass under pressure, like the final breaking point in a structure that had been strained beyond its capacity to endure. My mouth opened to deliver whatever lie might still provide protection, whatever story might preserve some remnant of the life I had built on the foundation of his wife's disappearance.

But the voice that emerged didn't feel like my own, didn't carry the careful modulation and practiced innocence that had served me so well for so many months. Instead, it carried the bitter honesty of someone who had finally grown tired of pretending, who had decided that truth might be more liberating than continued deception.

"She left you," I said, the words seeming to come from some deep well of resentment that I had never fully acknowledged even to myself. "She was unhappy here, desperately lonely despite all the comfort and security you provided. She felt invisible in her own life, unnoticed and unappreciated by the man who was supposed to love her above all others."

His brow furrowed with the confusion of someone whose fundamental assumptions about his marriage were being challenged in ways he had never considered possible.

"That's not an answer," he said. "That's not what I asked you."

But the dam had broken now, and the words poured out of me with the force of water too long contained, carrying with them all the rage and frustration and bitter envy that had motivated every choice I had made since the night I decided that Clara's life was less important than my own desperate need for the happiness she had taken for granted.

"She didn't want this life anymore," I continued, my hands trembling with the intensity of emotions I had kept locked away for so long. "She saw how easily you looked past her, how little attention you paid to her thoughts and feelings and needs. When I came here, I didn't have to lie about who I was or pretend to be someone else. I simply became what you had always wanted her to be—grateful, devoted, content with whatever scraps of affection you chose to offer. And you didn't even notice the difference."

He stared at me then with an expression I had never seen before, not like a man looking at someone he had grown to care for, not like a husband or a friend or even a casual acquaintance. He looked at me as if I were a complete stranger who had somehow infiltrated his home, a dangerous intruder wearing a familiar face but concealing intentions too terrible to contemplate.

"Who are you?" he whispered, and the question carried with it the weight of every fear that had been building in his mind since Charlotte's arrival had forced him to examine his assumptions about the woman who had become so central to his family's functioning.

In that moment, I felt something slip loose inside me, some final tether to the carefully constructed identity I had maintained for so many months finally snapping under the pressure of exposure and accusation. The sensation was almost physical, like the breaking of chains I had not even realized were binding me to a performance that had become increasingly exhausting to maintain.

I laughed.

Not with cruelty or malice, not with the dramatic intensity that might have been expected from someone whose carefully laid plans were crumbling around her. Just a hollow sound, empty of everything except the bitter recognition of how completely my elaborate deception had failed to provide the satisfaction I had expected it to deliver.

The laughter felt as though it had been trapped in my chest for years, waiting for this moment of release when pretense was no longer possible or necessary, when the truth could finally be acknowledged without the protective layers of fiction that had made survival possible but genuine expression impossible.

"Who am I?" I echoed, savoring the question that I had been asking myself in various forms since the day I first glimpsed Clara through the windows of this house and decided that her life would serve my purposes better than my own ever could. "I was the shadow standing beside her when you walked past without seeing either of us. I was the echo behind your perfect domestic life, reflecting back all the contentment and gratitude that she was too spoiled to provide. I was everything you never noticed, everything you took for granted, everything you failed to appreciate until it was too late to matter."

His face grew pale as the implications of my words penetrated his understanding, as he began to grasp not just what I had done but why I had been driven to such extremes, what combination of need and opportunity and bitter resentment had motivated me to construct such an elaborate and ultimately unsustainable deception.

"You're mad," he said, but his voice carried less conviction than fear, the recognition that madness might be an insufficient explanation for the calculated nature of whatever crime I had committed against his family.

"Maybe I am," I agreed, feeling a strange sense of liberation in the admission, a relief that came from finally dropping the mask of sanity and respectability that had required such constant effort to maintain. "Or maybe I'm finally free to be exactly what I've always been—someone who refused to accept that other people's happiness was more important than my own, someone who was willing to take what I wanted instead of waiting for it to be offered freely."

He left the room like a man fleeing a fire, his footsteps echoing through the corridor with the urgent rhythm of someone who had suddenly realized that he was sharing his home with something far more dangerous than he had ever imagined. I heard him lock his own door that night, the sound of the key turning in the mechanism carrying across the house with the finality of a judgment rendered.

Good, I thought with savage satisfaction. He should be afraid. He should understand that the comfortable assumptions that had allowed him to take his domestic peace for granted were no longer valid, that the woman who had been caring for his children and managing his household was capable of actions he had never suspected.

But deep in my bones, in the spaces where truth lives regardless of what stories we tell ourselves about who we are and what we deserve, something twisted with an emotion I could not quite identify.

Because the more I stared at my own reflection that night—at the carefully painted lips and perfectly arranged curls, at the sapphire brooch resting just so against the hollow of my throat—the more I began to see not the Eleanor Ashcombe who had infiltrated this house with such careful planning and methodical execution.

Instead, I saw her.

Clara, looking back at me from the depths of the mirror with an expression of gentle amusement, as if she found my attempts to inhabit her life more pathetic than threatening, more deserving of pity than fear.

And in that reflection that should have shown my own features transformed by months of careful impersonation and practiced mannerisms, Clara was smiling with the serene confidence of someone who knew that no amount of stolen identity could change the fundamental truth of who I was and what I would always be.

A shadow. An echo. A pale imitation of something real that I had destroyed but could never truly replace.

The mask had slipped, and what lay beneath was not the triumphant woman who had claimed her rightful place in the world through courage and determination.

It was still just Eleanor Ashcombe, wearing someone else's clothes and someone else's jewelry and someone else's life, but remaining essentially herself—desperate, envious, and ultimately empty despite all the beautiful things she had surrounded herself with.

The crack in the glass was spreading, and soon the entire illusion would shatter, leaving nothing but fragments of a dream that had never been real and a woman who had lost herself so completely in the process of becoming someone else that she no longer knew where Clara ended and Eleanor began.

But for now, in the silver light of the mirror that showed truths I was not yet ready to accept, I could only watch as Clara's smile grew wider, more knowing, more satisfied with whatever justice was finally beginning to unfold in the house that had never truly been mine to claim.

The reckoning was coming.

And Clara would be there to witness it all.

# Chapter 23: The Return of Clara

## "The Woman at the Gate"

The house had gone quiet in the days following Edward's confrontation, but it was not the peaceful silence of domestic contentment or the natural hush that settles over a well-ordered household as evening approaches. This was a different kind of stillness entirely heavy with unspoken accusations and trembling beneath its own weight, as if the very walls were holding their breath in anticipation of some terrible revelation that would shatter the last pretense of normalcy.

Even the children had grown wary, their natural exuberance dampened by an atmosphere they could not understand but instinctively feared. They spoke in whispers now when they thought I might be listening, their bright voices subdued to murmurs that carried undertones of confusion and growing anxiety. When they looked at me, their eyes were full of questions they didn't dare ask aloud, as if they sensed that the answers might be more frightening than the uncertainty they were living with.

Margaret had begun to flinch when I reached out to smooth her hair or adjust her dress, small movements of withdrawal that cut me more deeply than any direct accusation could have. Henry watched me with the particular intensity that children bring to adults whose behavior has become unpredictable, as if he were trying to solve a puzzle that might determine his own safety and well-being.

Edward had stopped speaking to me altogether except when absolute necessity required some form of communication about household matters or the children's needs. He moved through his own home like a ghost, polite but utterly distant, avoiding my gaze with the determination of someone who could no longer bear to look directly at something that had once brought him comfort but now inspired only revulsion and fear.

His correspondence had increased dramatically in the past week, letters arriving daily that he read in the privacy of his locked study, responses written in sessions that stretched long into the night. I caught glimpses of unfamiliar handwriting on envelopes, legal letterheads that suggested he was consulting with barristers, perhaps even reaching out to distant relatives who might provide guidance about how to handle a situation that had moved far beyond the realm of ordinary domestic crisis.

He was making arrangements. For what, I could only speculate, but the possibilities ranged from simple dismissal from my position to more serious legal consequences that might follow from whatever conclusions he had drawn about my role in Clara's disappearance and the mysterious body that had been discovered beneath her roses.

I could feel the noose tightening around my throat with each passing day, each silent meal, each averted glance that confirmed my growing isolation from the family I had worked so hard to join. The life I had constructed with such meticulous care was crumbling around me, and I was powerless to stop the process of disintegration that seemed to accelerate with each new piece of evidence, each fresh suspicion, each moment of recognition that dawned in Edward's increasingly hostile eyes.

And then, on an evening when the autumn air carried the particular chill that spoke of winter's approach and the early darkness that would soon engulf the shortened days, came the knock that would destroy everything I thought I knew about the world and my place in it.

It was that peculiar time of day when dusk settles over London like a gray shroud, when the light fails gradually and windows begin to sweat with condensation that blurs the boundary between inside and outside, between the comfortable certainties of domestic life and the unknown dangers that lurk in the gathering darkness beyond carefully tended gardens and locked doors.

The butler—a man who had always been quiet and efficient but who had grown increasingly nervous in recent days, as if he too sensed that something fundamental had shifted in the household's equilibrium—appeared at the drawing room door with his hands clenched so tightly that his knuckles stood out white against his dark skin.

His voice, when he spoke, carried the particular quality of someone delivering news that he knew would change everything, words that would mark the end of one era and the beginning of something else entirely, something that might be better or worse but would certainly be different from anything that had come before.

"There's... a woman at the gate, ma'am," he said, his usual professional composure cracking under the weight of what he had seen, what he had been asked to announce to a household already strained to the breaking point by secrets and suspicions and half-acknowledged truths. "She says... she says she's Clara Harroway."

The words struck me like ice water poured down my spine, like a physical blow that left me gasping for breath and struggling to maintain my balance in a world that had suddenly shifted on its axis. For a moment that seemed to stretch into eternity, I could not process what he had said, could not force my mind to accept the implications of those simple words that carried with them the power to destroy every assumption I had built my life upon.

I rose from my chair too quickly, the sudden movement sending my needlework tumbling to the floor in a cascade of silk thread and careful stitches that would never be completed. My voice, when I managed to speak, sounded foreign to my own ears, hollow and desperate with the need to deny what could not possibly be true.

"Impossible," I said, though even as the word left my lips I could feel its inadequacy, its futile attempt to hold back a tide of reality that would not be stopped by wishful thinking or desperate denial.

"She insists, ma'am," the butler continued, his own voice shaking now with the effort of maintaining his professional demeanor in the face of what he clearly believed to be either a miracle or a manifestation of something far more sinister. "And she... she looks exactly as you might expect someone to look who has been through terrible hardships, but the resemblance is unmistakable. She knows details about the house, about the family, that no stranger could possess."

I didn't let him finish his description, couldn't bear to hear any more details that would make real what my mind was still struggling to reject. Instead, I pushed past him and flew toward the front door, my silk skirts rustling with the urgency of movement driven by panic and disbelief and the terrible need to see for myself what waited beyond the threshold of the life I had constructed with such careful attention to every detail.

My mind was a storm of conflicting thoughts and emotions, fragments of memory and desperate calculation swirling together in patterns that made no sense, that offered no explanation for how this moment could be happening when I had been so certain, so absolutely convinced, that Clara was dead and buried in some forgotten corner of the woods where her bones would never be found.

Each step toward the front door felt like walking deeper into the past, as if the house itself were folding in on itself, pulling me back through months of careful deception and assumed identity to the moment when everything had begun, when I had first glimpsed Clara through these very windows and decided that her life would serve my purposes better than she would ever deserve.

The front hallway stretched before me like a tunnel leading toward judgment, the familiar furnishings and carefully arranged portraits taking on an ominous quality in the dying light that filtered through the tall windows. Every surface seemed to mock me with reminders of the domestic happiness I had stolen, the family life I had appropriated through violence and deception and the methodical elimination of anything that stood between me and the security I had craved for so long.

And there, beyond the heavy oak door that had once seemed like the barrier between my old life and my new one, waited the answer to questions I had never wanted to ask, the resolution of mysteries I had convinced myself were already solved.

I fumbled with the brass handle, my hands shaking so violently that I could barely manage the simple mechanical action of opening a door I had passed through countless times before. The metal was cold against my palm, solid and real in a way that seemed to anchor me to the physical world even as my understanding of that world was beginning to collapse around me.

The door swung open with a creak that seemed impossibly loud in the stillness of the evening, and I stepped outside onto the front steps that Clara had once climbed as the mistress of this house, stones that had supported her feet during happier times when she had been alive and unaware of the danger that watched her from the shadows.

And there she stood.

The sight of her hit me like a physical blow, like the collision between an unstoppable force and an immovable object that sends shock waves through everything in its vicinity. For a moment, I could not accept what my eyes were showing me, could not reconcile the reality of her presence with everything I thought I knew about what had happened in those fog-shrouded woods months ago.

She was thin to the point of emaciation, her once-plump cheeks now hollow with suffering and hardship, her skin bearing the particular pallor that comes from prolonged illness or exposure to conditions that push the human body beyond its normal limits of endurance. A long scar curved beneath her left eye like a cracked petal, a mark that spoke of violence survived rather than succumbed to, of healing that had taken place in circumstances far removed from medical care and comfortable recovery.

Her hair, once so carefully arranged in the elaborate styles that befitted her station as Edward's wife, had been cropped unevenly, probably with whatever sharp implement had been available when the decision was made to sacrifice beauty for practicality. The irregular lengths and jagged edges spoke of desperate measures taken in desperate circumstances, of choices made when survival was more important than appearance.

Her hands shook against the wrought iron of the gate, fingers that had once been soft and white now marked with calluses and small scars that testified to manual labor, to the kind of work that ladies of her class were never supposed to perform. But despite the physical evidence of suffering, despite the obvious toll that her ordeal had taken on her body, her eyes remained unmistakably hers—sunken now, perhaps, darkened with shadows that spoke of sleepless nights and constant vigilance, but still alight with something that had refused to die despite everything that had been done to extinguish it.

Recognition. Intelligence. And beneath it all, a flame of determination that had sustained her through whatever hell she had endured, whatever trials she had faced in the long months since I had left her broken and poisoned in the woods beyond the estate.

When she spoke, her voice carried the particular quality of someone who has been to the edge of death and returned with knowledge that the living are not supposed to possess. It was still recognizably Clara's voice, but changed, tempered by suffering into something harder and more implacable than it had ever been during the comfortable years of her marriage.

"Eleanor," she said, and my name in her mouth was like a blade drawn across my throat, sharp and cold and carrying with it the promise of justice delayed but not forgotten.

The sound of my real name—not the careful fiction of Mrs. Westmere, not the assumed identity I had constructed to gain access to her life, but the name I had been born with and tried so hard to leave behind—sent terror racing through my veins like poison. She knew who I was. Had always known, perhaps, or had learned through whatever means had kept her alive and brought her back to reclaim what I had stolen.

I opened the gate with fingers that trembled so violently I could barely manage the simple latch, the metal feeling foreign and unfamiliar beneath my touch despite the countless times I had performed this same action during my months as the mistress of this household.

"Clara," I whispered, and her name felt strange on my lips, like a word in a language I had once known but had not spoken in so long that it no longer came naturally. "You're... you're supposed to be..."

"Dead?" she finished for me, her scarred lips curving into something that might have been a smile if it had contained any warmth or forgiveness. "I told you, Eleanor. You couldn't kill me. Not with poison, not with abandonment, not with all your careful planning and methodical cruelty. I am stronger than you ever imagined, more determined than you ever understood."

Her words hit me like physical blows, confirming what I had never wanted to acknowledge—that my crime had been incomplete, that my victim had survived to bear witness against me, that everything I had built on the foundation of her supposed death was nothing more than a castle constructed on sand that was already shifting beneath my feet.

My legs buckled at the implications of her presence, at the recognition of what her survival meant for my carefully constructed life, and I gripped the iron gate to stay upright, feeling the cold metal bite into my palms through the delicate lace gloves that had once been hers, that I had claimed along with everything else that had defined her existence.

She was real. She was alive. She had survived everything I had done to her, had found the strength to crawl back from whatever abyss I had pushed her into, had endured months of hardship and suffering for the sole purpose of returning to expose my crimes and reclaim what I had stolen.

Behind me, I heard the creak of the front door opening wider, heard footsteps on the stone threshold that marked the boundary between the house and the outside world. A child's voice—Henry's voice, bright with desperate hope and disbelief—called out across the distance that separated him from the mother he had mourned, the parent whose absence had left a wound in his young heart that no amount of care from a substitute could heal.

"Mama?" he said, and the single word carried with it all the longing and confusion and desperate love that had sustained him through the dark months of not knowing what had become of the woman who had given him life, who had been the center of his small universe before I had arrived to disrupt everything he thought he understood about his family.

Clara looked past me then, her attention shifting from the woman who had destroyed her life to the child who represented everything she had fought to return to, everything that had given her the strength to survive when survival seemed impossible. Her expression transformed in that moment, the hard mask of vengeance and determination melting away to reveal something softer, more vulnerable, infinitely more powerful than any desire for revenge.

Love. Pure, uncomplicated, maternal love that had transcended death itself, that had pulled her back from whatever darkness she had inhabited during the long months of absence, that had sustained her through trials I could not imagine and brought her home to the children who needed her more than they would ever need anyone else.

"My darling," she choked, her voice breaking with emotion that had been too long suppressed, too carefully controlled during whatever journey had brought her back to this moment. "My sweet, precious boy—"

He ran then. Without hesitation, without the caution that might have been expected from a child who had learned that the adults in his life could disappear without warning, leaving behind only questions and grief and the inadequate comfort offered by strangers who could never truly replace what had been lost.

He ran to her with the absolute trust and joy that children reserve for the people they love most in the world, throwing his small arms around her waist with a force that nearly knocked her backward, clinging to her as if he could prevent her disappearance through the sheer strength of his embrace.

She held him with desperate intensity, dropping to her knees in the gravel of the drive without regard for the damage to her already worn dress, burying her face in his hair and breathing in the scent of her child as if it were the most precious perfume ever created. Her tears came then, great heaving sobs that seemed to carry with them all the grief and longing and desperate hope that had accumulated during their separation.

"I'm here," she whispered over and over, like a prayer or an incantation that could make the words true through repetition. "I'm here, I'm here, I'm here. I came back to you. I will never leave you again."

Margaret appeared next, her smaller figure framed in the doorway like a portrait of childhood uncertainty. Her eyes widened as she took in the scene before her—the woman who looked like the mother she remembered but bore scars that spoke of suffering beyond her understanding, the brother who was crying with joy and relief, the strange tableau of reunion that was both wonderful and frightening in its intensity.

She clutched at my skirts with small hands that sought comfort and stability in a world that had suddenly become unpredictable again, looking up at me with confusion and a need for explanation that I was utterly unable to provide.

"She came back," she whispered, more to herself than to me, as if speaking the words aloud might help her make sense of what she was witnessing. "I knew she would. I never stopped believing she would come home."

I couldn't move, couldn't speak, couldn't do anything but stand frozen in place as the family I had tried to claim as my own was reunited before my eyes, restored to its proper configuration in ways that made my presence not just unnecessary but actively harmful. I was a witness to my own obsolescence, watching as the life I had constructed with such care crumbled into irrelevance.

Clara gathered both children into her arms, holding them with the fierce protectiveness of someone who had learned exactly what it meant to lose everything precious and who would never again take such gifts for granted. Her tears mixed with theirs as she whispered endearments and promises, rebuilding the bonds that had been stretched but never broken by the long months of separation.

Then Edward stepped outside, and the sight of him made my heart contract with a pain I had not expected to feel. His face went through a progression of emotions so rapid and intense that it was like watching years of grief and guilt and desperate hope compressed into a single moment of recognition.

Disbelief gave way to wonder, wonder to joy, joy to the particular kind of anguish that comes from understanding how completely one has failed someone who deserved protection and care. He looked at his wife—his real wife, not the pale imitation I had provided—and I saw in his expression the full weight of what my deception had cost him, what he had lost during the months when he had been grieving a woman who was actually fighting for her life somewhere beyond his ability to help.

He didn't run to her as Henry had done. He was too overwhelmed by the magnitude of what he was seeing, too crushed by the implications of her survival and return. Instead, he moved with the careful steps of someone afraid that sudden movement might shatter a vision that was too precious to risk disturbing.

When he reached the small group gathered on the gravel drive, he dropped to his knees beside them as if the weight of what he saw had literally crushed his ability to remain standing. His hand reached out with infinite gentleness to touch the scar beneath Clara's eye, tracing the mark of suffering with fingertips that trembled with a combination of reverence, sorrow, and self-recrimination that was painful to witness.

"Clara," he said, and her name in his mouth carried all the love and regret and desperate gratitude that words could contain. "My God, what have I done? How could I have let this happen? How could I have failed you so completely?"

His question hung in the air like an accusation directed not at me but at himself, at his failure to recognize the danger that had been living in his house, caring for his children, wearing his wife's clothes and jewelry while the real Clara fought for survival in circumstances he was only beginning to imagine.

And me? I stood at the center of it all, still dressed in the life I had stolen, still wearing her sapphire brooch and her lace gloves and her carefully applied perfume, still maintaining the physical appearance of the woman whose place I had usurped through violence and deception and the systematic elimination of anything that stood between me and the security I had craved.

I looked down at my trembling hands, encased in gloves that had never truly belonged to me, and realized that everything I was wearing felt foreign now, like a costume that no longer fit, like the remnants of a performance that had been exposed as fraud and could never again be convincing to any audience.

Clara looked up at me then, over Edward's shoulder, past the children who clung to her as if she might disappear again if they loosened their grip. Her eyes met mine with the direct intensity of someone who had returned from the dead with a specific purpose, who had endured unimaginable hardships for the sole purpose of reaching this moment of confrontation.

And she smiled.

It wasn't a kind smile, wasn't the gentle expression of forgiveness or understanding that might have been expected from someone who had suffered so much at the hands of another. This was something far more complex and infinitely more terrifying—the smile of a woman who had clawed her way out of hell itself and returned with the absolute certainty that justice would finally be served, that accounts would be balanced, that debts would be paid in full regardless of the cost to those who owed them.

It was the smile of someone who had won a victory that had seemed impossible, who had proven that love and determination and sheer stubborn refusal to surrender could triumph over even the most carefully planned cruelty. It was the smile of a mother reunited with her children, a wife restored to her husband, a woman reclaiming her rightful place in the world after it had been stolen from her through treachery and violence.

But beneath all of that, it was also the smile of someone who understood exactly what my presence in her family had meant, what I had done to achieve my position in her household, what prices had been paid for the months of deception that were now coming to an end.

She said nothing more that evening, made no accusations or demands for explanation, issued no threats or promises of retribution. She simply rose from the gravel where she had been reunited with her family and walked past me with her children in her arms, Edward beside her like a man who had finally remembered what love truly felt like when it was freely given rather than carefully performed.

They moved toward the house that had always been hers by right rather than theft, the home where she belonged in ways that I never could, no matter how perfectly I had learned to imitate her mannerisms or how completely I had convinced myself that I deserved the life she had taken for granted.

I was left standing at the open gate, still wearing her clothes and her jewelry but no longer able to maintain the illusion that these external trappings could transform me into something I was not, someone I could never be. The elaborate fiction I had constructed was collapsing around me, revealing the truth that had always existed beneath the careful layers of deception.

I was not a shadow in silk, not a woman who had successfully claimed her rightful place in the world through courage and determination. I was not a mother or a wife or even a competent governess who had earned her position through skill and dedication.

I was nothing but the echo of a lie that was finally unraveling in the dark, the hollow remnant of a dream that had never been real and a scheme that had always been doomed to failure because it was built on the fundamental impossibility of becoming someone else through the simple act of eliminating them from existence.

The gate swung shut behind Clara and her family with a finality that seemed to mark the end of everything I had worked for, everything I had believed I could achieve through careful planning and ruthless execution. The sound of the latch clicking into place was like the closing of a book, the conclusion of a story that had always been heading toward this moment of reckoning.

Inside the house, lights began to appear in windows that had been dark, evidence of life returning to rooms that had been empty for too long, of a family being restored to its proper configuration after months of existing in a state of incomplete mourning and inadequate substitution.

I could hear voices through the walls—excited chatter from the children, deeper tones from Edward, and underneath it all, Clara's voice weaving through the conversation like a melody that had been missing from the symphony, the essential element that made everything else complete and meaningful.

They were home. All of them, together again in the way they were meant to be, in the way they would have been if I had never inserted myself into their lives with my poison and my lies and my desperate conviction that I deserved their happiness more than they did.

And I was outside, where I had always belonged, where I would always belong—looking in at a life that had never truly been mine, watching through windows that reflected only my own face, my own isolation, my own complete and utter failure to become anything more than what I had always been.

Eleanor Ashcombe, standing alone in the darkness, wearing stolen clothes and stolen jewelry and the remnants of a stolen identity that had never fit properly and could never be made to feel natural no matter how much time and effort I devoted to the performance.

The woman at the gate had returned to claim what was hers.

And I had become what I had always been—nothing but a shadow, an echo, a lie that had finally been exposed to the light and found wanting in every possible way.

The reckoning had come.

And I had lost everything.

# Chapter 24: The Trial

## "The Papers Called Me Monster"

I sat in the dock with my hands folded neatly in my lap, dressed in the same black mourning attire that had become my uniform during the months when I had played the role of the devoted family friend grieving Clara's mysterious disappearance. The irony was not lost on me—I was still in mourning, though the death I grieved was not Clara's, but my own, the slow dissolution of everything I had worked so hard to become.

No one had died, not officially. Clara sat in the gallery, very much alive, her scarred face serving as living testimony to the failure of my carefully planned crime. But something had died in that courtroom—my dreams, my assumed identity, my belief that I could reshape reality through sheer force of will and methodical elimination of obstacles.

The courtroom was packed beyond capacity, rows upon rows of curious strangers who had come to witness the spectacle of a woman's complete moral collapse played out for public consumption. The trial had captured London's imagination in ways that more conventional crimes never could, offering as it did a glimpse into the dark possibilities that lurked beneath the surface of respectable domestic life.

Reporters filled the front rows, their pencils moving frantically across their notebooks as they captured every detail of the proceedings for newspapers that would transform my story into entertainment for breakfast tables across the Empire. They sketched my profile, recorded my expressions, noted the quality of my dress and the way I held myself, creating a narrative that would outlive any memory of the actual truth.

Friends of the Harroways occupied the more expensive seats, their faces carefully composed to hide their fascination behind masks of appropriate moral outrage. They tried not to stare too openly, but I could feel their eyes upon me, nonetheless, studying the woman who had lived among them for months, who had attended their parties and shared their confidences, who had proven that the boundaries between civilization and savagery were far more permeable than any of them wanted to acknowledge.

The air was thick with the scent of ink and sweat, old wood and the acrid tang of judgment rendered by people who had never faced the kind of desperate choices that had driven me to actions they could barely comprehend. The very atmosphere seemed to pulse with anticipation, as if the building itself were holding its breath, waiting for revelations that would either satisfy or disappoint the crowd's hunger for moral clarity in a case that defied simple categorization.

The judge, the Honorable Mr. Justice Pemberton, did not look at me with anything approaching kindness or even professional neutrality. His eyes held the particular coldness reserved for criminals who had violated not just the law but the fundamental assumptions upon which civilized society operated. To him, I was not a woman who had made desperate choices under impossible circumstances, but a monster who had proven that evil could wear a familiar face and speak in gentle tones while destroying lives with methodical precision.

The prosecutors—led by Sir Reginald Hawthorne, a man whose reputation for theatrical oratory had made him the Crown's weapon of choice in cases that required not just legal victory but public spectacle—painted me as a creature of pure calculation, a predator who had inserted herself into an innocent family with the sole purpose of destroying it from within.

"She was not driven by passion or temporary madness," Sir Reginald declared to the packed courtroom, his voice carrying the particular resonance that had made him famous for his ability to sway juries through emotional manipulation disguised as legal argument. "This was not a crime of the moment, born of circumstances beyond the defendant's control. Instead, we see evidence of planning that stretches back months, of systematic study and preparation that reveals a mind capable of the most cold-blooded calculation."

He gestured toward the evidence table, where items from my former life were displayed like artifacts from an archaeological expedition into the depths of human depravity.

"She inserted herself into the Harroway family like a parasite seeking a host," he continued, his words chosen for maximum impact on both jury and gallery. "She studied Clara Harroway's habits, her mannerisms, her relationships with her children and husband. She learned to imitate not just the external forms of domestic life, but its most intimate details, wearing a woman's life like clothing that she had stolen from its rightful owner."

The metaphor sent murmurs rippling through the courtroom, and I saw several jury members lean forward with the kind of attention that suggested Sir Reginald's strategy was working exactly as intended.

"She turned husband against wife through systematic poisoning, through the careful cultivation of doubt and suspicion that destroyed a marriage that had weathered sixteen years of shared joy and sorrow. She drugged a mother in her own home, rendering her helpless to protect her children from the predator who had gained their trust through months of patient deception. She locked Clara Harroway away in a private sanitarium under a false name, forging documents and bribing officials to ensure that her victim would disappear so completely that even her own family would never think to look for her there."

Each accusation hit me like a physical blow, not because they were untrue, but because they reduced my complex motivations and desperate circumstances to simple acts of cartoon villainy. The prosecutors had no interest in understanding why I had acted as I did, what combination of longing and rejection and systematic exclusion from happiness had finally driven me to claim by force what had been denied to me by circumstance.

"And when a simple maid threatened to expose her crimes," Sir Reginald concluded with devastating effectiveness, "she murdered the girl and buried her beneath the roses that Clara Harroway had planted with her own hands, turning a symbol of love and beauty into a grave marker for innocence destroyed."

The courtroom erupted in gasps and murmured expressions of disgust, and I felt the weight of their collective judgment pressing down on me like a physical force. They saw me not as a woman who had made terrible choices for comprehensible reasons, but as a monster whose actions defied rational explanation.

Lies wrapped in truth, or truth wrapped in lies—after months of living in the space between Clara's identity and my own, I could no longer tell the difference. The facts were accurate, but the interpretation stripped away all context, all recognition of the impossible position I had found myself in, all acknowledgment that my crimes had been born of desperation rather than simple malice.

They read passages from my diary, the private journal I had kept during my months as Mrs. Westmere, never imagining that it would be discovered and transformed into evidence against me. I had hidden it carefully, or so I thought, but the police had been thorough in their search, motivated by the knowledge that they were dealing with someone whose capacity for deception ran far deeper than anyone had initially suspected.

The entries had not been written for public consumption, had never been intended to explain or justify my actions to an audience that would judge them according to moral standards I had been forced to abandon. They were ritual, pure and simple—the obsessive documentation of my transformation from Eleanor Ashcombe into someone worthy of the life I had always deserved.

Scraps of Clara's handwriting that I had traced over and over until my muscles remembered the precise curves and angles that marked her as educated, refined, deserving of respect. Detailed notations of her daily habits, her preferences in food and clothing and entertainment, the small routines that defined her domestic existence and would need to be replicated perfectly if my impersonation was to succeed.

Drawings of her face from every angle, studied with the intensity of an artist preparing a masterpiece, though my purpose had been far more practical than aesthetic. Transcriptions of conversations I had overheard between Clara and her children, between Clara and Edward, between Clara and the servants who respected her authority and sought her approval.

Most damaging of all, my attempts to rewrite Clara's own words in my voice, to practice the kinds of responses she might give to various situations until they became so natural that I would never hesitate, never reveal through inappropriate reaction that I was not who I claimed to be.

The prosecutors read selected passages aloud, their voices dripping with the kind of theatrical disgust that played well to audiences hungry for moral clarity:

"She doesn't deserve them. She takes their love for granted, treats it as her natural right rather than the precious gift it truly is. She has no idea how fortunate she is, how blessed, how envied by those of us who have been denied such happiness through no fault of our own."

Gasps rippled through the courtroom, and I saw a woman in the gallery press her handkerchief to her eyes as if the words themselves were weapons that had drawn blood.

"She left them long before I removed her," another entry proclaimed when read in Sir Reginald's resonant baritone. "Her body might have been present in their home, but her heart and mind had already departed. She was going through the motions of domestic life without any real engagement, any genuine appreciation for what she possessed. I simply made official what had already occurred in reality."

The logic that had seemed so clear to me during those long nights of writing now sounded hollow and self-serving when subjected to public scrutiny. What had felt like profound insight into the nature of human relationships and moral responsibility now appeared to be nothing more than elaborate rationalization for the unforgivable.

Edward sat in the front row of the gallery, his hand resting protectively atop Clara's in a gesture that spoke of reconnection, of gratitude for a second chance that few couples are fortunate enough to receive. He would not look at me, could not bear to meet the eyes of the woman who had taken advantage of his grief and vulnerability to insert herself into the most intimate spaces of his life.

Clara was thinner than she had been during our confrontation at the gate, her ordeal in the private sanitarium having taken a toll that would probably never be fully healed. Her eyes were hollowed by experiences that no respectable woman should ever have to endure, her movements carrying the particular brittleness that comes from having one's sanity questioned by medical professionals who possess the power to determine whether one deserves freedom or continued confinement.

But she was whole in ways that mattered more than physical appearance. She was seen, recognized, acknowledged as the rightful center of her family's existence in ways that my months of careful impersonation had never achieved. Every smile she gave Edward, every gentle touch she shared with her children, was a knife driven directly into my heart, proof that authentic love could not be manufactured or stolen, only earned through genuine connection and mutual choice.

My solicitor, Mr. Grimsby, was a decent man doing his best with an impossible case. He attempted to argue diminished capacity, temporary madness brought on by circumstances beyond my control, trauma from years of poverty and social exclusion that had finally driven me to actions that no rational person would contemplate.

"Ladies and gentlemen of the jury," he said in his closing argument, his voice carrying the particular weariness of someone who knew he was fighting a battle that could not be won, "we ask you to consider not just what Miss Ashcombe did, but why she was driven to such desperate measures. Here was a woman who had lost everything—her parents, her husband, her social position, her economic security. She found herself utterly alone in a world that offers few opportunities for women in such circumstances to rebuild their lives with dignity intact."

It was a valiant effort, but I could see in the jury's faces that they were not moved by appeals to understanding or compassion. They had heard the evidence, had seen the photographs of Elsie's broken body, had listened to Clara's testimony about the months of drugged stupor and systematic gaslighting that had nearly destroyed her sanity permanently.

They wanted justice, not psychology. They wanted clear moral lines, not complex explanations that might force them to acknowledge their own capacity for similar choices under similar circumstances.

When the judge asked if I had anything to say before sentencing, I stood slowly, feeling the weight of hundreds of eyes upon me, knowing that my words would be recorded and reproduced in newspapers across the Empire, that they would become part of the permanent record of my destruction.

My voice, when I spoke, was calm and controlled, almost serene—the tone of someone who had finally been freed from the exhausting burden of pretending to be someone else.

"I never harmed the children," I said, directing my words not to the judge or jury but to the gallery where Edward and Clara sat with their hands joined, where the truth of my statement could be verified by people who had witnessed my devotion to Henry and Margaret during the months when I had been their primary caregiver.

"I loved them with a depth and consistency that few adults in their lives had ever matched. I cared for them not because it was my duty or because I was paid to do so, but because they deserved the kind of attention and affection that their natural mother was too distracted to provide consistently."

More gasps from the gallery, murmured expressions of shock and disgust that anyone could speak so callously about crimes that had destroyed a family's peace and nearly cost a woman her life and sanity.

"I took nothing that wasn't already being discarded," I continued, allowing a faint smile to curve my lips as I spoke what I knew would be perceived as the most damning words of all. "Clara Harroway had already left her family in every way that mattered. She was drifting through her domestic responsibilities like someone walking in her sleep, going through the motions of maternal devotion and wifely duty without any genuine engagement or appreciation for the precious gifts she had been given."

The judge's eyes narrowed with the particular coldness reserved for defendants who showed no remorse, who insisted on justifying the unjustifiable even when faced with the full weight of legal and moral condemnation.

"You took a woman's place through systematic deception and attempted murder," he said, his voice cutting through my carefully constructed justifications like a blade through silk. "You drugged her repeatedly, forged documents to have her committed to a private sanitarium under a false identity and told her family that she had disappeared without a trace. These are not the actions of someone saving a woman from her own inadequacies, but of a predator who eliminated competition for resources she was not entitled to claim."

"I gave her rest," I interrupted, clinging to the interpretation that had sustained me through months of careful planning and methodical execution. "I removed her from a life that was making her miserable, that was slowly crushing her spirit through its demands for constant performance of domestic contentment she could no longer genuinely feel."

"And murdered a servant who threatened to expose your crimes," the judge concluded with devastating finality.

My breath caught in my throat, because this was the accusation I could not answer, could not explain in ways that preserved my self-image as someone motivated by noble purposes rather than simple self-preservation.

Elsie had known too much, had seen too much, had threatened to destroy everything I had worked so hard to achieve. She had appeared at my door on the night of Clara's disappearance, her young face bright with excitement and terrible knowledge, ready to share information that would have exposed my crime before I had time to establish the alternative narrative that would protect me from suspicion.

Her fear had betrayed her even as she tried to bargain for silence and safety. She had chosen to threaten me, to demand payment for her discretion, not understanding that she was sealing her own fate through her attempt at extortion.

I had only finished what she started, had simply eliminated a problem that she herself had created through her decision to involve herself in matters beyond her understanding or ability to control safely.

But the jury would not appreciate such complexity, would not be interested in the moral ambiguities that had forced me to make impossible choices under desperate circumstances. They wanted simple narratives of good and evil, clear lines between victim and perpetrator that would allow them to render judgment without being forced to examine their own capacity for similar actions.

They returned with their verdict in under two hours—barely enough time to review the evidence properly, let alone engage in the kind of thoughtful deliberation that such a complex case deserved.

Guilty on all counts.

I was to be held indefinitely in Broadmoor Criminal Lunatic Asylum, not hanged for my crimes or transported to some distant colony where I might eventually rebuild my life. The judge had determined that I was mad, that my actions could only be explained by mental illness that rendered me unfit for normal legal punishment but too dangerous to be released into civilized society.

It was, I realized, the outcome that would be easiest for everyone to accept. A sane woman capable of such calculating cruelty challenged too many comfortable assumptions about human nature and the reliability of social bonds. It was far more palatable to believe that I had suffered some form of mental breakdown that had temporarily transformed me into something monstrous, rather than acknowledging that ordinary people were capable of extraordinary evil when circumstances aligned in particular ways.

"She must have gone mad," I heard whispered throughout the courtroom as the verdict was announced. "No woman in her right mind could do such things to another woman, to innocent children, to a family that had shown her nothing but kindness and trust."

But I wasn't mad, despite what the legal system had determined. I had never been more clear-headed, more rational, more capable of analyzing complex situations and making difficult decisions based on realistic assessments of available options.

I had seen a hollow life being wasted by someone too privileged to appreciate its value, and I had filled it with purpose and genuine devotion that its original occupant had never been capable of providing. My crime was not insanity but clarity, not madness but the willingness to act on truths that others were too cowardly or too comfortable to acknowledge.

The press devoured the story with an appetite that seemed to grow with each new revelation, each fresh detail that emerged during the trial proceedings. The headlines grew more sensational with each edition: "The Governess Who Became the Wife," "The Shadow in Silk," "A Modern Medea Who Stole Rather Than Killed Her Children."

My photograph appeared on front pages across the Empire, my face becoming synonymous with a particular kind of feminine evil that combined calculation with domestic deception, that proved that the most dangerous predators were often those who appeared most harmless, most devoted to traditional virtues of care and service.

The case became a cautionary tale about the need for vigilance in hiring domestic staff, about the importance of thoroughly investigating the backgrounds of people admitted to the intimate spaces of family life. New laws were proposed requiring more extensive documentation and verification of employment histories, more careful screening of applicants for positions that granted access to vulnerable family members.

I had become not just a criminal but a symbol, a warning about the dark possibilities that lurked beneath the surface of respectable society, the reminder that evil could wear familiar faces and speak in gentle voices while systematically destroying everything that made life worth living.

And through it all, Clara watched from her seat in the gallery like a queen presiding over the final judgment of a usurper who had briefly challenged her rightful authority. Her presence was both vindication and accusation, proof that justice could eventually triumph over even the most carefully planned deception, that truth had a way of surfacing despite all efforts to keep it buried.

I found myself wondering, as the proceedings drew to their inevitable conclusion, whether she had ever truly feared me during those months when I had worn her identity like borrowed clothes, when I had slept in her bed and cared for her children and received her husband's gratitude for services she was supposed to have been providing.

Had she suspected, even in her drugged stupor, that something was fundamentally wrong with the narrative she was being told about her own mental state? Had some part of her recognized the woman who stood at her bedside in the sanitarium, speaking in soothing tones about the need for rest and recovery while systematically erasing her from her own life?

Or had she been so thoroughly convinced of her own madness, so completely gaslit by medical professionals who assured her that her memories and perceptions could not be trusted, that she had genuinely believed herself to be suffering from delusions that transformed a kind caregiver into a malevolent replacement?

I would never know, because Clara and I would never have the opportunity for honest conversation, never be able to discuss the complex motivations and desperate circumstances that had brought us to this moment of final reckoning.

But as they led me away from the dock toward the beginning of a confinement that would likely last the rest of my life, I caught her eye one final time and saw in her gaze not hatred or vindictive satisfaction, but something far more disturbing.

Pity.

She looked at me with the particular sadness reserved for those who have destroyed themselves through choices that seemed reasonable at the time but proved catastrophic in retrospect. She saw me not as a monster who deserved punishment, but as a woman who had lost herself so completely in the pursuit of someone else's life that she had forgotten what her own might have been worth preserving.

It was, perhaps, the cruelest judgment of all—not condemnation, but compassion for someone who had proven incapable of earning or accepting it through any legitimate means.

The papers called me monster, but Clara knew better.

I was just a woman who had wanted something desperately enough to destroy everything she touched in the pursuit of it, including herself.

And in the end, that was the most terrible truth of all.

# Chapter 25: The Final Reflection

## "The Woman in the Glass"

They call it Bedlam still, though it has been rechristened Broadmoor Criminal Lunatic Asylum and subjected to a dozen other bureaucratic renamings that attempt to soften the fundamental truth of what this place represents—a warehouse for broken minds, a repository for souls that have strayed too far from the acceptable boundaries of human behavior to ever find their way back to the light.

The halls creak with the accumulated weight of suffering, their ancient floorboards groaning beneath the footsteps of attendants who move like ghosts through corridors that have witnessed more despair than any building should be asked to contain. The sounds that echo through these passages might be the settling of old wood, the expansion and contraction of materials subjected to decades of London's damp and cold, or they might be something more ethereal—the restless spirits of patients who have passed through these rooms and left fragments of their anguish embedded in the very walls.

It is impossible to tell the difference between structural decay and supernatural presence when you live in liminal space between sanity and madness, between the person you once were and the person you have been declared to be by medical professionals who wield the power of definition like gods determining the boundaries of reality itself.

The air carries a perpetual scent of vinegar and carbolic acid, the cleaning agents used to maintain the illusion of cleanliness in a place where moral contamination seeps through the stones like moisture through poorly mortared joints. Beneath these chemical attempts at purification lies something more primal and disturbing—the metallic tang of blood, the sour smell of fear, the particular staleness that accumulates in spaces where hope has been systematically extinguished and replaced with the dull acceptance of permanent confinement.

At night, when the official business of treatment and observation gives way to the raw honesty of darkness, the screams begin. They rise from cells throughout the building like a chorus of the damned, each voice contributing its own particular note to a symphony of madness that would drive sane listeners to distraction if any sane listeners remained within these walls.

I recognize some of the voices now, after months of nocturnal serenades that have taught me to distinguish between different varieties of mental anguish. There is the girl in the east wing who hums lullabies in reverse, her sweet soprano voice transformed into something unsettling and wrong by the simple act of inversion, as if she were trying to undo the comfort that such songs were meant to provide.

The man two doors down from my own cell claps his hands in rhythmic patterns that would be cheerful if not for the fact that his palms are perpetually bloodied from the violence of his applause, the flesh worn raw by repetitive motion that serves some purpose known only to the twisted pathways of his damaged mind.

And sometimes, woven through these familiar sounds of institutional madness, I hear my own voice joining the midnight chorus— though I have no memory of screaming, no conscious awareness of contributing to the cacophony that marks the hours between sunset and dawn.

But I don't scream anymore. Not consciously, not deliberately. That phase of my adjustment to life at Broadmoor has passed, replaced by something that the staff finds far more manageable and therefore more disturbing in its implications.

They say I am quiet now. Obedient. Compliant with the routines and regulations that govern daily existence in this place where individual will be seen as a symptom of illness rather than a sign of human dignity. They prefer patients who accept their diagnoses without question, who submit to treatments without resistance, who acknowledge the authority of medical science to determine the fundamental nature of their inner lives.

They like to write notes about me, these doctors and attendants who believe that documenting abnormal behavior somehow grants them power over it, as if putting their observations on paper might trap me in the neat categories, they have constructed to make sense of minds that refuse to conform to their expectations of how human consciousness should operate.

"Patient maintains persistent delusions of identity displacement," I have read in files left carelessly within my view, written in the precise handwriting of Dr. Blackwood, the chief alienist who considers my case particularly fascinating because it combines elements of criminal behavior with sophisticated psychological complexity.

"Presents as articulate and highly intelligent, demonstrating no apparent cognitive deficits, but exhibits profound emotional flattening that suggests fundamental disconnection from normal human empathy and moral reasoning."

"Patient refers to herself alternately as Clara, Eleanor, and 'Mother,' suggesting complete fragmentation of personal identity and inability to maintain consistent sense of self."

Mother. That word still clings to my ribs like a physical presence, like something alive that has taken up residence in the hollow spaces beneath my heart and refuses to be dislodged despite all evidence that I have no right to claim such a title, no legitimate connection to the children whose faces still visit me in dreams that feel more real than the waking hours I spend in this cell.

The label follows me through my days like a shadow, whispered by attendants who think I cannot hear, written in reports that will outlive any memory of who I actually was before my transformation into a case study in the criminal pathology textbooks that future generations of alienists will study to better understand the darker possibilities of human nature.

Sometimes, as part of what they optimistically call treatment, they bring me a mirror—a small, unbreakable piece of polished metal that reflects distorted images with the wavering quality of water disturbed by wind. They believe that confronting one's own reflection promotes psychological integration, that seeing oneself clearly is the first step toward accepting the reality of one's circumstances and beginning the long process of rehabilitation.

"It helps patients remember who they are," Nurse Whitmore explained during one of our sessions, her voice carrying the particular gentleness that medical professionals use when speaking to those they consider fundamentally broken. "Visual confirmation of physical identity can serve as an anchor for minds that have become untethered from objective reality."

But when I look into that warped reflection, the face that stares back at me is not the one I wore during my years as Eleanor Ashcombe, struggling to survive in the margins of respectable society, nor is it the careful construction I built during my months as Mrs. Westmere, the devoted governess who had earned her place in the Harroway household through competence and dedication.

Instead, I see her. Clara's face, wearing Clara's expression of gentle melancholy, framed by hair that has grown out to match the length and color she preferred, shaped by the accumulated weight of experiences that have somehow transformed my features into something that resembles her far more than it does the woman I was born to be.

The similarity is not perfect—the asylum diet and the stress of confinement have left their marks, creating hollows beneath my eyes and sharpening my cheekbones in ways that speak of hardship rather than the comfortable life Clara had known. But the essential structure remains eerily familiar, as if my face has been slowly sculpted by months of inhabiting her identity until the external reality finally matches the internal truth I have never been able to abandon.

They let me keep one personal possession, a small mercy that reflects the institution's recognition that complete deprivation of individual identity serves no therapeutic purpose. It is a ribbon, silk of the finest quality, colored the deep wine-dark shade that Clara had favored for evening wear, rich and lustrous despite the months it has spent in my possession.

I cannot remember whether it was originally mine or hers—the boundaries between our belongings became so blurred during my months in her house that ownership became a meaningless concept, replaced by the more primal recognition of what belonged to the life I was creating rather than the life I was abandoning.

I twist it between my fingers during the long hours when there is nothing else to occupy my hands, nothing else to anchor me to the physical world beyond the smooth silk texture that carries memories of better times, of moments when I had been surrounded by beauty and comfort and the illusion that I had finally found my rightful place in the world.

The repetitive motion has become a form of meditation, a way of maintaining connection to the woman I became rather than the woman I was born to be. Sometimes I catch myself speaking to the ribbon as if it were a confidant, sharing thoughts and observations that I would never trust to the ears of my keepers, who listen with the particular attention of people trained to identify symptoms rather than understand experiences.

One of the nurses—Esther, I believe her name is, though the staff changes frequently enough that maintaining relationships becomes an exercise in futility—has taken a special interest in what she calls my rehabilitation. She reads to me during the quiet afternoon hours when the asylum settles into the drowsy routine that passes for therapeutic activity, sharing passages from books of poetry and collections of psalms that are meant to provide spiritual comfort to minds that have lost their way in the darker regions of human possibility.

"Literature has tremendous healing power," she explains, her young face bright with the kind of idealism that has not yet been worn away by prolonged exposure to the realities of institutional psychiatry. "It reminds us of our shared humanity, of the universal experiences that connect us all despite our individual struggles and failures."

Her readings are indeed little scraps of mercy in this cathedral of rot, moments of beauty that pierce through the perpetual gloom like sunlight filtering through stained glass windows. But I find myself less interested in the officially sanctioned literature she shares than in the words that emerge from my own consciousness, the private poetry that writes itself in the margins of my awareness when I am not paying close enough attention to censor or edit my thoughts.

I compose verses in the hairline cracks that spider across the plaster walls of my cell, my fingernail tracing patterns that might be letters or might be simple decoration, depending on the angle of observation and the willingness of the observer to believe that meaning can be found in the most unlikely places.

I write lines in the condensation that forms on the small window when my breath fogs the glass during the cold months, temporary words that disappear as quickly as they appear but leave behind the satisfaction of having expressed something true, something authentic, something that belongs entirely to me rather than to the medical establishment that has claimed ownership of my mind and future.

Most importantly, I compose entire stanzas in the silence between the questions that punctuate my weekly interviews with Dr. Blackwood, filling the pauses with observations and insights that he is not equipped to hear, reflections on the nature of identity and desire and the terrible prices we pay for refusing to accept the limitations that society attempts to impose on our capacity for self-determination.

They say I killed a woman. The accusation follows me through every conversation, every evaluation, every moment of apparent normalcy that might otherwise allow me to forget the circumstances that brought me to this place. It is written in my file, repeated in medical conferences, whispered by attendants who believe that understanding my crimes will help them maintain appropriate professional distance from someone whose capacity for violence has been established beyond question.

They say I stole a life, appropriated an identity that was never mine to claim, destroyed a family through systematic deception and calculated manipulation that demonstrated a level of moral corruption that requires permanent removal from civilized society.

But what they never say—what they never dare acknowledge because it would complicate their neat diagnostic categories and challenge their comfortable assumptions about the nature of good and evil—is this fundamental truth that has sustained me through months of confinement and will continue to sustain me through whatever years of imprisonment lie ahead:

She had already left.

Clara Harroway, the real Clara, the wife and mother and shining lady in silk who occupied the center of a domestic paradise that I had observed from the shadows of exclusion and envy, had abandoned her life long before I arrived to claim it for my own.

She had grown tired of the constant performance required to maintain her image as the perfect wife, the devoted mother, the gracious hostess who made everything appear effortless while struggling with the growing recognition that her carefully constructed happiness was built on foundations that could not support the weight of her authentic self.

I watched her drift through her daily routines like someone walking in her sleep, going through the motions of domestic contentment without any genuine engagement or appreciation for the precious gifts she had been given through no effort or merit of her own.

She had walked out into the storm of her own discontent without the protective covering of gratitude or recognition that would have sheltered her from the winds of change that were already reshaping her inner landscape. When I found her—or when circumstances finally brought us together in the way that fate had always intended—she was already half-gone, already lost to the family that depended on her for stability and care.

I only picked up what she had lost, what she had allowed to slip through fingers that had never learned to properly value what they held. Is that madness? Is it criminal to claim abandoned treasures, to restore purpose and meaning to lives that were being wasted through inattention and ingratitude?

The doctors say yes, their certainty as unshakeable as their ignorance of the complex moral calculations that drove me to actions, they can categorize but never truly comprehend. The newspapers said yes, their headlines reducing years of careful observation and patient preparation to simple sensationalism that sold papers but ignored the deeper truths about human nature and the distribution of happiness in a world that grants its greatest gifts to those least capable of appreciating them.

Edward, of course, says nothing at all now. Our paths will never cross again, our stories will never intersect in ways that might allow for explanation or understanding or even the basic human acknowledgment that we once shared something that resembled intimacy, however briefly and however founded on deceptions that seemed necessary at the time.

He has remarried, I learned from a newspaper clipping that someone—perhaps Nurse Esther, in a moment of misguided kindness—left where I would be certain to discover it. The announcement was brief and dignified, mentioning his new wife's impressive family connections and substantial dowry, her accomplishments in charitable work and her reputation for the kind of steady temperament that makes for successful partnerships in the upper reaches of society.

The accompanying photograph showed the children at the wedding ceremony, older now, their faces bearing the particular solemnity that comes to young people who have learned too early that the adults responsible for their care are not immune to the kind of devastating mistakes that can destroy everything they had assumed was permanent and secure.

Margaret wore lilac, a color that Clara had always said brought out the green in her eyes, and I found myself wondering whether the choice had been deliberate or accidental, whether someone had remembered Clara's preferences or whether the similarity was simply coincidence. Henry stood beside his father with his hands clasped behind his back, his expression holding the same suspicious wariness that had marked his interactions with me during those final weeks when my performance had begun to deteriorate under the pressure of accumulated lies and mounting evidence.

I think sometimes that they remember me, not as the monster that the newspapers have made me into, but as the woman who had genuinely cared for them during months when their real mother was absent and their father was too consumed with grief and business concerns to provide the consistent attention that children require to feel secure in an uncertain world.

I had loved them with a devotion that was perhaps more intense than what their natural mother had been able to provide, unburdened as I was by the complicated emotions that biological relationships carry, free to focus entirely on their immediate needs and simple pleasures without the exhausting weight of long-term responsibility that had worn Clara down and contributed to her retreat from active engagement in family life.

I think sometimes that I remember them as well, though the distinction between authentic memory and wishful reconstruction becomes increasingly difficult to maintain when the mind has been subjected to the kind of systematic questioning and pharmaceutical intervention that constitutes modern psychiatric treatment.

Did Margaret really prefer her bedtime stories to be told with different voices for each character, or have I invented that detail to fill the gaps in recollection that medications and confinement have created? Did Henry actually confide his worries about his father's health during our walks in the garden, or is that conversation a fiction constructed by a mind desperate to preserve evidence of connection, of purpose, of having mattered to someone during the brief period when I was allowed to participate in the kind of family life I had always craved?

The uncertainty is perhaps the cruelest aspect of my current existence—not knowing whether the memories that sustain me through the long days and longer nights of institutional life represent actual experiences or elaborate fantasies created by a consciousness that has finally severed its connections to objective reality.

And still, despite all doubt and medication and official declarations of my mental incompetence, the mirror waits.


It sits on the small wooden table beneath my cell's single window, reflecting whatever light manages to penetrate the mesh wire and thick glass that separate me from the outside world. The attendants place it there during their morning rounds and remove it before evening lockdown, part of the therapeutic routine that is meant to gradually restore my sense of personal identity and individual responsibility.

But tonight—I think it is night, though the distinction between day and evening becomes meaningless when you live according to institutional schedules rather than natural rhythms—I find myself drawn not to the mirror's carefully controlled reflection, but to the window itself.

I rise from my narrow bed, moving with the careful quietness that has become second nature during months of living in close proximity to people whose mental stability is too fragile to withstand sudden noises or unexpected movements. The floor is cold against my bare feet, the chill rising through the soles and spreading upward through my body like the touch of something that has never been warmed by human contact.

The window offers no real view of the outside world, just wire mesh and frosted glass that blur everything beyond into abstract shapes and shadows that might represent trees or buildings or the dreams of freedom that tantalize patients who have forgotten what liberty feels like. There is no clear glass here, nothing that might be broken and fashioned into weapons or tools for self-destruction, only these distorted surfaces that show reality filtered through the particular lens of institutional caution.

Still, I lean close to the barrier that separates me from the world I once inhabited, pressing my face against the metal mesh until the cold bites into my cheek and forehead with sharp insistence. The wire leaves geometric impressions on my skin, a pattern of small squares that will fade within minutes but provides momentary evidence of contact with something solid and unchanging in a world where everything else seems subject to the fluid interpretations of medical authority.

And I smile.

The expression feels foreign on my face after months of careful neutrality, months of presenting the kind of bland compliance that reassures my keepers that whatever dangerous impulses once drove me to violence have been successfully medicated into submission. But in this moment of privacy, in this space between observation and evaluation, I allow myself the luxury of authentic emotion.

Because in that reflection—blurred by wire and distorted by frosted glass, crooked and dim and bearing only the most approximate resemblance to photographic accuracy—I see her.

Not Eleanor Ashcombe, the failed governess whose desperation had led to choices that society could neither understand nor forgive. Not the criminal defendant whose actions had been dissected in courtrooms and newspaper columns until they became symbols rather than human experiences.

I see Clara Harroway, the woman whose life I had claimed and whose identity I had made more real than she had ever managed to make it herself. I see the mother who had loved those children with perfect devotion, the wife who had appreciated her husband's care and attention, the mistress of a household who had created beauty and order and contentment for everyone fortunate enough to enter her sphere of influence.

I see the woman I had always been meant to be, if circumstances had been different, if opportunities had been more fairly distributed, if the world had recognized my capacity for love and care and dedication to the kind of domestic happiness that had been granted to others through accident of birth rather than merit or effort.

The reflection shows me not what I have lost, but what I have gained—the knowledge that for a brief, shining period, I had been exactly who I was meant to be, I had filled a role that suited my deepest nature, I had experienced the kind of complete fulfillment that most people never achieve regardless of how many advantages they are born with or how many opportunities they are offered.

And in the silence of my cell, with the silk ribbon twisted through my fingers like a rosary, like a talisman, like a prayer made tangible, I whisper the words that summarize everything I have learned through my journey from the margins of society to the center of a family that had needed me more than they had ever needed its original mistress:

"I won."

The statement hangs in the still air of my confinement, neither defiant nor boastful, simply truthful in the way that only private acknowledgments can be. I had achieved something that no amount of legal punishment or psychiatric intervention could undo—I had proven that identity is not fixed, that roles can be claimed by those willing to fight for them, that love, and care and devoted attention are more important than biological connections or social legitimacy.

They can confine my body, medicate my thoughts, declare me mad and dangerous and unfit for civilized society. But they cannot erase the months when I had been Clara Harroway in every way that mattered, when I had inhabited her life with more purpose and passion than she had ever brought to its daily demands.

I had won because I had experienced perfect happiness, however briefly. I had won because I had loved and been loved, however artificially those connections had been established. I had won because I had proven that the boundaries between self and other, between authentic and performed identity, between rightful ownership and determined appropriation, are far more fluid than society wishes to acknowledge.

In the darkness of Broadmoor, surrounded by the detritus of minds that have failed to navigate the complexities of modern existence, I carry within me the knowledge that I had once been exactly where I belonged, exactly who I was meant to be, exactly as happy as any human being has a right to expect.

That knowledge will sustain me through whatever years of confinement lie ahead, will protect me from the daily indignities of institutional life, will remind me that I had achieved something extraordinary even if the world lacks the vision to recognize it as such.

I am Eleanor Ashcombe, and I am Clara Harroway, and I am Mother, and I am all the women I have been and might yet become if circumstances align in my favor once again.

The woman in the glass knows who she is.

And she is smiling because she remembers what it felt like to win.

# Epilogue

## Years Later

The house on Grosvenor Street still stands, though it bears little resemblance to the place where Clara Harroway once tended her roses and Eleanor Ashcombe first glimpsed the life she would kill to possess.

Successive owners have transformed it according to their own visions of domestic perfection, each generation adding layers of renovation that bury the past beneath fresh paint and fashionable furnishings. The façade has been painted in cheerful cream and gold, colors chosen to suggest prosperity and optimism rather than the shadow-haunted gray stone that once reflected the complex moral ambiguities of the lives lived within its walls.

The gardens have been re-tamed according to modern sensibilities, the wild profusion of Clara's beloved roses replaced by geometric flower beds that demonstrate mastery over nature rather than partnership with it. The ivy that once climbed the eastern wall with romantic abandon has been clipped into polite obedience; its tendrils no longer permitted to obscure the windows or create the kind of mysterious shadows that might harbor secrets or encourage the imagination to wander into darker territories.

Children's laughter rings across the manicured lawn on summer afternoons, bright and innocent as birdsong, though these are not the same children who once played here under Eleanor's watchful care, who once called her "Aunt Eleanor" with the trusting affection that she had treasured more than any jewel. These new children know nothing of the woman who had loved their predecessors with such desperate intensity, who had transformed herself into their devoted caretaker through methods that society had deemed too terrible to contemplate.

The Harroways themselves moved away years ago, selling the estate with the quiet efficiency of people eager to distance themselves from memories too painful to preserve. The transaction was handled through intermediaries and legal representatives, Edward's signature appearing on documents he never saw, authorizing the transfer of a property he could no longer bear to inhabit.

His second marriage had ended in scandal within three years—whispers of infidelity and financial impropriety that followed him through the social circles where he had once been welcomed as a tragic but respectable widower. Whether the rumors were true mattered less than the fact that his association with Eleanor's crimes had marked him as someone whose judgment could not be trusted, whose household had been penetrated by evil in ways that suggested either complicity or a dangerous naivety that made him unsuitable for polite society.

Clara, too, had found it impossible to remain in London after the trial. The constant attention from newspapers and curious strangers, the way conversations stopped when she entered rooms, the pitying looks that followed her wherever she went—all of it had proven unbearable for someone who had already endured months of imprisonment and systematic gaslighting that had nearly destroyed her sanity permanently.

They had departed for the Continent with their children, seeking anonymity in places where their names carried no history, where Clara's scars could heal without constant reminder of how she had acquired them, where Henry and Margaret could grow to adulthood without the burden of being known as the children who had been cared for by a woman whose love had been expressed through violence and deception.

The new owners of the Grosvenor Street house know little of what transpired there during those crucial months when Eleanor Ashcombe had worn Clara Harroway's life like borrowed clothes, when the boundaries between identity and performance had blurred beyond recognition. The estate agents had been discreet in their presentation of the property, emphasizing its architectural features and prime location while allowing the darker aspects of its recent history to fade into the kind of vague unpleasantness that might deter some buyers but would not prevent a determined purchaser from making a successful bid.

Or perhaps the new inhabitants know just enough to explain why certain rooms feel perpetually cold despite adequate heating, why the east wing seems to attract shadows even on the brightest days, why sensitive guests report feeling watched by invisible eyes when they venture into spaces that had once been Clara's private sanctuary and later became Eleanor's domain of carefully orchestrated deception.

Perhaps they know enough to avoid the east wing entirely after sunset, when the floorboards creak with footsteps that belong to no current resident, when the curtains stir without benefit of breeze, when the very air seems thick with the presence of someone who refuses to acknowledge that her tenancy has been terminated by forces beyond her control.

No one speaks of Eleanor Ashcombe anymore, at least not in the circles where such conversations matter, where reputations are made and destroyed through careful attention to what is said and what remains diplomatically unmentioned.

Not in the drawing rooms of Mayfair, where hostesses have learned to redirect discussions that threaten to venture into territories too dark for civilized entertainment. The case has been absorbed into the larger category of unpleasant things that well-bred people acknowledge existed but prefer not to examine too closely, filed away with other examples of human behavior that challenge comfortable assumptions about the reliability of social bonds and the safety of domestic arrangements.

Not in the courts of law, where Eleanor's name appears only in dusty precedent books consulted by barristers researching similar cases of identity theft and domestic infiltration. Her trial has become a footnote in legal history, cited when establishing procedures for handling defendants whose crimes blur the boundaries between criminal behavior and psychiatric pathology, but no longer discussed as a living case requiring active attention or ongoing investigation.

Not even in Broadmoor, where Eleanor herself has become just another long-term resident whose initial notoriety has faded into the routine management of chronic mental illness that requires permanent institutionalization. The staff who once found her case fascinating have moved on to other positions or retired entirely, replaced by younger professionals who know her only as Patient #4847, a woman whose files contain references to crimes they have never bothered to research in detail.

Her case was absorbed by newer horrors, fresher scandals that captured public attention with the same intensity that her story had once commanded. The newspapers that had made her name synonymous with feminine evil found other monsters to display on their front pages, other examples of moral corruption that served their readers' appetite for stories that confirmed their worst suspicions about human nature while allowing them to feel safely superior to the criminals whose actions they consumed as entertainment.

Her personal effects were archived according to standard procedures; her diaries and correspondence sealed in evidence boxes and filed away in some vast government warehouse where they gather dust alongside thousands of other relics from cases that once seemed monumentally important but have now been relegated to historical curiosity. The careful documentation of her transformation from Eleanor Ashcombe into Mrs. Westmere, the meticulous record of her study of Clara's habits and preferences, the desperate poetry of her final reflections—all of it has been reduced to inventory numbers and storage locations that grow more obscure with each passing year.

The silk ribbon that had been her final comfort, the last tangible connection to the life she had claimed and lost, remains sealed in its evidence envelope, untouched and unclaimed by anyone who might recognize its significance or understand what it represented during the long months when it had served as both talisman and reminder of everything she had achieved and ultimately sacrificed.

Untouched, perhaps, but not entirely forgotten.

And yet—

Every so often, visitors to the National Portrait Gallery pause before a particular canvas in the collection of family portraits that document the domestic arrangements of England's more prominent households during the latter half of the nineteenth century. The painting in question is not among the museum's most celebrated works, nor does it represent the hand of any artist whose name appears in standard reference works on Victorian portraiture.

It shows the Harroway family in what appears to be their drawing room, rendered in the muted oils and careful composition that marked competent but uninspired professional work of the period. Edward stands behind Clara's chair with the formal posture that convention required of husbands in such compositions, his hand resting on her shoulder in a gesture meant to convey both protection and possession. Clara herself sits with perfect deportment, her hands folded in her lap, her expression carrying the particular serenity that portrait subjects were expected to maintain regardless of their actual emotional state.

The children flank their parents with the practiced stillness of young people who have been coached in the requirements of formal portraiture, their faces bearing smiles that seem strained by the effort of maintaining appropriate expressions for whatever length of time the sitting required.

All perfectly conventional, exactly what one would expect from a family portrait commissioned to document domestic happiness and social respectability.

But some visitors find their attention drawn to a figure in the background of the composition, a woman whose presence in the family grouping is never explicitly explained by the museum's documentation. She stands slightly apart from the central figures, positioned near the tall windows that dominate the room's eastern wall, her dark dress and composed expression marking her as someone whose role in the household occupied the ambiguous territory between family member and employee.

Some observers note that this background figure doesn't quite match the others in terms of artistic execution, that her features seem more sharply defined, more individually characterized than the somewhat generic faces of the official family members. There is something in her eyes—an intensity, a directness of gaze—that seems to pierce through the canvas and engage directly with viewers in ways that the other figures do not.

Others remark that she appears misaligned with the rest of the composition, as if she had been added to the painting after the original work was completed, painted over someone else whose presence had been deemed inappropriate for permanent commemoration but whose ghostly outline can still be detected beneath layers of pigment that have grown transparent with age.

The museum's official position, when inquiries are made, is that the portrait shows the family with their governess, a perfectly common arrangement for households of their social standing. The woman's name, according to their records, was Mrs. Eleanor Westmere, a widow who had served the family faithfully until her death from influenza during the winter of 1872.

No mention is made of trials or accusations, of crimes that had shocked London society, of imprisonment in criminal lunatic asylums or the systematic identity theft that had nearly destroyed one of England's most respectable families. The museum's version of history is clean and simple, edited to remove elements that might disturb visitors or complicate the narrative of domestic tranquility that such portraits are meant to preserve.

But sometimes, when the gallery is quiet and the afternoon light slants through the tall windows in ways that create unexpected shadows and reflections, visitors report feeling an unusual chill when they stand before the Harroway portrait. Some describe the sensation of being watched, of invisible eyes following their movements as they examine other works in the collection.

Others claim that the background figure's expression changes depending on the angle of observation, that her slight smile becomes more pronounced when viewed from certain positions, as if she were reacting to some private joke that only she could appreciate.

The more fanciful suggest that her eyes seem to follow viewers as they move through the gallery, maintaining eye contact in ways that painted eyes should not be able to achieve, demonstrating an awareness that transcends the normal limitations of artistic representation.

Museum staff, when pressed for explanations, dismiss such reports as products of overactive imagination, tricks of light and shadow that can make any painting seem more animate than it actually is. They point out that the human brain is naturally inclined to perceive faces and expressions in patterns that may not actually exist, that visitors often project their own expectations and emotions onto artworks in ways that create experiences more psychological than visual.

But they cannot explain why the portrait was donated to the museum anonymously, delivered without provenance or documentation that might establish its authenticity or historical significance. They cannot account for the fact that no other examples of the artist's work have ever been identified, despite extensive research into the painting's origins and technique.

Most puzzling of all, they cannot explain why conservation efforts have revealed multiple layers of paint in the area where the background figure stands, as if her image had been repeatedly altered, painted over and restored, modified and corrected by hands that were determined to achieve some particular effect that earlier attempts had failed to capture.

The records show only that the painting arrived at the museum on a fog-shrouded morning in November 1875, accompanied by a brief note stating that it represented "a family that no longer exists" and should be displayed "so that their story might not be entirely forgotten."

The note was unsigned, written in a hand that none of the museum staff could identify, though some remarked that the penmanship displayed the particular elegance that marked the education of women from respectable families, the careful script that had been drilled into young ladies as part of their preparation for lives that would require extensive correspondence and social documentation.

Others said it reminded them of handwriting they had seen in legal documents, in court records and police reports, though they could not specify exactly where or when such resemblance had been noticed.

The truth, if there is such a thing in cases where reality and perception have become so thoroughly entangled, may be that Eleanor Ashcombe achieved in death what she had failed to accomplish in life—permanent residence in the family she had loved with such desperate intensity, eternal presence in the domestic arrangement she had tried to claim through violence and deception but had ultimately been forced to abandon.

Perhaps her image in the portrait serves as a kind of memorial, not to the crimes that had made her notorious, but to the love that had motivated those crimes, the fierce maternal devotion that had driven her to actions society could condemn but never fully understand.

Or perhaps it is simply imagination, the tendency of human consciousness to find patterns and meaning in coincidences that actually signify nothing beyond the random convergence of unrelated events.

A trick of the light that makes painted eyes seem alive.

A shadow on silk that suggests presence where none exists.

The whisper of a name that no one speaks anymore, echoing through galleries where the past is preserved in forms that may bear only passing resemblance to the truth of what actually occurred in the houses and lives that inspired such careful documentation.

But sometimes, late at night when the museum is closed and the galleries stand empty except for the watching eyes of painted figures from centuries past, security guards report hearing sounds that cannot be explained by the normal settling of old buildings or the expansion and contraction of materials subjected to London's perpetual damp.

Footsteps that move through rooms where no living person walks.

The whisper of silk against silk, as if invisible skirts were rustling past the cases and frames that hold fragments of other people's lives.

And occasionally, very occasionally, the sound of a woman's voice humming lullabies in the darkness, melodies that seem to drift from the direction of the Harroway portrait, songs that children might once have heard at bedtime, when loving hands tucked them into beds in houses that no longer exist, in lives that ended long ago but somehow refuse to remain entirely in the past.

The house on Grosvenor Street still stands.

But Eleanor Ashcombe lives on in other places, in other forms, in the shadows between what was recorded and what was experienced, in the spaces where memory and desire intersect with the permanent record of human behavior and its consequences.

She had won, in the end, though not in ways that anyone could have predicted or that society would ever acknowledge.

She had achieved immortality of a sort, her story woven so completely into the fabric of the family she had claimed that no amount of official forgetting could entirely erase her presence from the places where love and loss and the terrible prices of desperate choices continue to echo through the lives of people who have no idea why certain rooms feel cold, why certain portraits seem to watch, why certain houses carry shadows that belong to stories no one remembers well enough to tell.

In the end, she had become exactly what she had always claimed to be—not Eleanor Ashcombe, the failed governess whose desperation had led to unforgivable crimes, but something more permanent and essential.

A mother.

A wife.

A woman whose love had been so fierce and so unwilling to accept the limitations that circumstance had imposed that it had transcended death itself, finding ways to persist in forms that defied rational explanation but could not be entirely dismissed by those sensitive enough to perceive the persistence of human emotion beyond the boundaries that normally separate the living from the dead.

The shadow on silk had found its way home.

And it was smiling.

Printed in Dunstable, United Kingdom